DEAD MAN'S MONEY

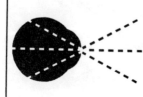

This Large Print Book carries the
Seal of Approval of N.A.V.H.

DEAD MAN'S MONEY

KEN HODGSON

WHEELER PUBLISHING
An imprint of Thomson Gale, a part of The Thomson Corporation

THOMSON

GALE

Detroit • New York • San Francisco • New Haven, Conn. • Waterville, Maine • London

LIBRARY OF CONGRESS CATALOGING-IN-PUBLICATION DATA

Hodgson, Ken.
    Dead man's money / by Ken Hodgson.
      p. cm. — (Wheeler Publishing large print western)
      ISBN 1-59722-382-4 (softcover : alk. paper) 1. Serial murders — Fiction.
    2. Frontier and pioneer life — Fiction. 3. Bounty hunters — Fiction.
    4. Oklahoma — Fiction. 5. Large type books. I. Title.
    PS3558.O34346D43 2006
    813'.6—dc22
                                  2006029343

U.S. Softcover:
ISBN 13: 978-1-59722-382-9
ISBN 10: 1-59722-382-4

Published in 2006 by arrangement with Pinnacle Books,
an imprint of Kensington Publishing Corp.

Printed in the United States of America on permanent paper
10 9 8 7 6 5 4 3 2 1

This book is for Mike Thompson,
a.k.a. Teddy Roosevelt

**Based on
a True
Incident**

If you can keep your head when all about you
   Are losing theirs and blaming it on you;
If you can trust yourself when all men doubt you,
   But make allowance for their doubting too:

    .   .   .   .   .

Yours is the Earth and everything that's in it,
   And — which is more — you'll be a Man,
     my son!
                  — *Rudyard Kipling*

Death comes with a crawl, or comes with a
   pounce,
   And whether he's slow or spry,
It isn't the fact that you're dead that counts,
   But only, how did you die?
             — *Edmund Vance Cooke*

Nature has always had more force than
   education.
                     — *Voltaire*

ONE

"Well, get to looking!" the sheriff roared. "Her head's got to be around here some-place."

Sheriff Emil Quackenbush chewed wor-riedly on the dead stub of a long nine cigar as he stared down at the bloody, headless corpse of a young woman. Incidents such as this would definitely not bode well for him come election time.

"These killings have gone from plain bad to *real* bad." Blue Hand, his deputy, gave a head shake toward the posse. "Which direc-tion do you think we oughtta go?"

"I wouldn't bother looking too hard for her head," Dr. Sedgemiller said, wheezing as he forced his bulk up the small hill to where the dead girl lay. "We sure never found any of those other people's heads. And those two men down by the creek have theirs missing too. Add in the five other bodies that have turned up without their heads, and it's no surprise that this fiend has finally gotten around to killing a woman. We're not dealing with an outlaw here, or even a human being. Only a monster would kill like this."

Emil flashed the doctor an angry look. "Now don't go scaring folks more than necessary. There's got to be a reasonable explanation for absconding with their heads. There *has* to be."

The petulant doctor bent over and examined the headless woman's body. "Ripped right off her shoulders by brute force, or possibly chopped off with a dull ax. It's the same method that was used on the men. Whatever is removing their heads doesn't bother to employ finesse — or a sharp knife."

"This feller down here's Jake Armbruster, the stage driver," Sim Eby hollered leaning over one of the two bodies that lay alongside the rippling waters of Boggy Creek. "He's been in my saloon a bunch of times wearing this same pair of dirty Levi's that has the seat patched with wagon canvas. Even without his noggin attached, I'm sure it's him."

"Then the other man is most likely the shotgun guard," Emil snorted. "I'd reckon he should've been a tad better at his job.

Guards change more often than a whore takes a bath. Root around in his pockets and see if you can find something with his name on it. I'd like to put more on his headboard than just the date he got killed in my jurisdiction."

Blue Hand spoke up. "Cyrus is gonna be plenty mad about the stage being attacked like this. When the thing came creaking into town without nobody on board, blood all over it, an' a door ripped off, I'd say that was reason enough to send someone out to tell him what happened."

"Yeah," the sheriff acknowledged with a sigh. "And I'm sure he'll be mad as a peeled rattler. You can bet Cyrus'll be in my office when I get back to remind me that Henrietta is *his* town and folks getting killed hereabouts is bad for business."

"*How* they're getting dead is a concern," Dr. Sedgemiller added. "Most places are plagued with normal outlaws that just rob stages, not rip the stage *and* the people apart, then go away and leave the money behind."

"There's still money in these men's pockets," Sim Eby said. "Just like the others. This beats all I've ever seen."

Blue Hand rubbed a finger along his thin mustache. He had been raised by the Osage, but his father was of Spanish origin. The deputy was inordinately proud of being capable of growing even a small amount of hair on his face. "I do not know which to fear more, this killer who takes heads, or Cyrus Warwick. I would think Mr. Warwick. He pays my wages."

Sheriff Quackenbush sighed. Both Blue Hand and he had reason for concern about Cyrus Orman Warwick. The man had somehow made a huge fortune after the war. There were rumblings that he had been a carpetbagger and had become wealthy by loaning money at exorbitant interest rates. No matter how he had come by this wealth, Warwick was the sole reason for the existence of Henrietta, Kansas, and the driving force that was causing it to boom.

Within a year or two, by 1878 at the latest, the denizens of Henrietta were certain their town on the edge of Indian Territory would outstrip Abilene, Wichita, and Dodge City as the cattle-shipping headquarters of the West. It was perfectly situated closer to Texas, where most cattle drives originated. With the railroad that Cyrus had worked so hard for already being built to Kansas City, growth was assured.

Sim Eby's two saloons, the Purple Sage and Drover's Rest, were busy twenty-four

14

hours a day. Mattie Rose, madam of the town's only whorehouse, had the best opportunity to count people, as nearly all residents were men. Mattie claimed the population of Henrietta was up to twelve hundred souls with new arrivals showing up daily. All arrived safely, with their heads and money intact. That is, unless they ventured across Indian Territory to the south.

The sheriff spit out the stub of his cigar as his anger grew. He wasn't about to lose a hundred-dollar-a-month job without putting up a good fight. "Boys, I'm going to kill whoever's doing this. I'll hang 'em right in the middle of town so folks can see it ain't no monster. This whole thing's likely been set up to scare folks away. My guess is some grouches from Dodge City or maybe Abilene's behind this to keep our town from growing."

"You could be right," Dr. Sedgemiller said. "But I sure as hell wish you'd explain to me how it was made to look like these folks' heads were ripped off their bodies."

"Well, all I can think of —"

Emil's reply was cut off by Sim Eby, who came from behind a thicket of bushes carrying a blood-soaked reticule. "Dang if we're not in for it now. This is the dead lady's purse. I took a peek inside and it sure looks like that might be Cyrus's only daughter, the one he named the town after. There's a passel of letters and stuff addressed to Henrietta Warwick."

"She's back in Chicago attending college," Dr. Sedgemiller said with a hint of uncertainty. "It can't be her."

The sheriff grabbed the reticule and pored over its contents. Every member of the posse waited in stone silence for the outcome.

"Damn it!" Emil swore. "Her diary's in here. She wrote how much she was looking forward to surprising her father, Cyrus, by making this trip. That girl's Henrietta Warwick. There's no doubt about it."

"I'm glad I'm only the deputy," Blue Hand said to the sheriff. "I wouldn't want to be the one to give Warwick *this* news."

Emil Quackenbush flipped a lock of red hair from his forehead. "A cyclone's fixin' to hit the outhouse, that's for certain. But it's my job and I'm heading to do it." He fixed his gaze on the doctor. "Try to get her cleaned up and in a coffin before Cyrus gets a look at her. I'd appreciate it."

"I'll do what I can," Sedgemiller said. "And I don't envy your task."

"Nope," Emil said walking to his horse. "All I'm certain of is that Henrietta was correct when she wrote that her pappy would be surprised to have her show up."

The sheriff's office and all government buildings, including an imposing two-story courthouse, post office, ten-cell jail, and a gallows designed to hang six at once, were assembled in a square at the center of town. All had been constructed of the finest white oak lumber available. As was its founder, the town of Henrietta, Kansas, had been formed of stern material.

Cyrus Warwick had refused Emil's offer of a chair, and stood as straight as the thick wood wall behind him when the sheriff told of finding his only daughter's body. The sheriff was not at all surprised when the lean, white-haired ranch owner showed no outward emotion. No one in Henrietta had ever seen other than a perpetual scowl on his leathery face.

"Are you certain the body is that of Henrietta?" Cyrus asked coldly.

Emil nodded. "As sure as anyone can be without having a head to look at." He slid the bloody reticule across the top of his desk. "Her diary and several letters from you are in there. That's what I'm basing my identification on."

Warwick reached out, grabbed the reticule,

and thumbed through its contents with all the sentiment of a banker counting money. "Considering the fact that this is my daughter's purse and that she occasionally acted impetuously, I believe the dead girl you found is likely to be Henrietta."

"I'm sorry."

Cyrus Warwick's eyes drew down to mere slits. "Not nearly so sorry as you will be if you fail to bring her killer to justice. I have been increasingly concerned about your lack of ability to do your job. Having a murderer loose in the area is bad for the town and bad for business. I will take measures, Quackenbush, of this you may be assured."

"Whoever's been killing those folks and now your sweet daughter, I plan to hang them on that new gallows you built. I am going to do that right soon after we figure out whose neck needs snapping."

"That, Sheriff, is something I intend to give you a *lot* of help with. Money is the only god people worship. I learned this many years ago. With Henrietta joining my wife in death, all I have left is *my* town. It will be Henrietta's legacy and I damn well will not sit idly by and let it be destroyed. Be it a monster, as some believe, outlaws, a madman, or those out to cause me ruin who killed my only child, I will be the instru-

18

ment of their death. They have unleashed a wind. Now let them reap a whirlwind."

Emil took a cigar from his drawer, thought better of it, and laid it on his desk unlit. "Blue Hand and I won't rest until this fiend is captured."

"If you had been a competent lawman, Sheriff Quackenbush, my daughter would still be alive. I will not impose on the city charter, but if I were you, I would not bother to seek reelection. In the meanwhile, I am going to have posters printed — several thousand of them — offering a twenty-thousand-dollar reward for the killer of my daughter. I will make it payable dead or alive. This should be sufficient inducement for justice to prevail."

"Don't do that, sir." Emil's reply came so quick and sharp it surprised even him. "It would be a terrible decision."

Cyrus Warwick's only show of feeling was a small cold cackle. "You do not understand what drives men. *I* do. This is why you work for a mere pittance while I am wealthy. The posters will be out and broadcast for hundreds of miles distant by this time tomorrow."

The sheriff shrugged, grabbed up the cigar, and lit it. He felt as if he were carrying on a conversation with a chunk of granite.

"Henrietta's body," Warwick said, spinning to leave. "I assume Dr. Sedgemiller has been entrusted with it?"

"Yes, sir," Emil replied. Seconds later, he was staring at a closed door.

The sheriff sighed with relief to have Warwick gone. It came as no surprise that his job would be over come fall. The problem was, Emil Quakenbush was a man of pride. And he had no more idea now who was killing people south of town than when the first headless body had been found on Christmas Day of last year.

That was over five months ago. The number of dead found in the vicinity of Boggy Creek, including Henrietta Warwick, stood at eight. This figure did not include the dozen or so inquiries he had received about missing travelers. Emil held little doubt many of those would eventually be found quite dead.

What puzzled the sheriff most of all was that none of the victims had been robbed. All of their horses had eventually turned up, either still saddled or hooked to a stagecoach. The posses he'd sent out had even brought back a good half-dozen horses that didn't belong to anyone in town or any of the victims. This added to his concern for those still missing.

And there was that terrible stench where the bodies had been found. It was best described as a cross between rotting meat and a skunk. Some people claimed to have seen a huge, hairy beast moving through the shadowy trees, like a ghost. Many more had heard bloodcurdling screams on a moonlit night.

Emil Quackenbush dismissed these stories as springing from an overactive imagination. Yet nothing about these murders fit anything he had learned about the dark side of human behavior during his ten years of being a lawman in various Western towns.

Travelers getting themselves killed and robbed wasn't uncommon. Most always the criminals quickly spent their ill-gotten gains in the nearest saloon or whorehouse making them easy to track down. Being a sheriff was a lot easier when crooks had the decency to act like crooks.

A twenty-thousand-dollar reward would bring a ramshackle parade of bounty hunters that would be far worse than what people had begun calling "the Monster of the Osage."

Emil knew that soon bodies would begin to be brought in by men claiming they had killed the man or men responsible for the crimes and demanding the reward. Most of these deceased would be innocent of everything except for looking like they might be worth twenty thousand dollars dead.

Emil grabbed a writing pad, took a stub of pencil from his shirt pocket, and began composing a squib to telegraph. If bounty hunters were coming to the Osage country, they might as well include the bloodiest one on the frontier. A man who supposedly had killed over two hundred men along with his own bank-robbing mother for bounty money.

The very name of Asa Cain had a tendency to strike fear into the hearts of the vilest criminals. It was a real plus that Emil knew Asa. With any decent luck, he might even get a nice slice of Warwick's reward money. That would make being out of work a lot more palatable.

Feeling happier now that he had a goal, the burly sheriff smiled. He stroked his red beard with one hand as he polished off the telegram. Hopefully in a week or so, Asa Cain would be here. Then some *real* killing could commence.

TWO

"Dag-nab it, Cemetery John," Wilburn Deevers fumed. "I'm here to tell you that you're gonna have to bury that whore. My wife, Mildred, and a passel of churchwomen are claiming she's beginning to scare the kids."

The silver-haired, muscular ex-buffalo soldier folded over the corner of a page in a dime novel he had been reading and regarded the sheriff across the expanse of his walnut desk. "I've just got her laid out in the front window to show how good that new embalming equipment I got from Germany works. Shucks, she's been there for nearly two weeks and ain't even drawing flies."

Wilburn shot a glance at the pretty, rail-thin blond girl inside an ornate coffin. Cemetery John had propped the head of the coffin on a pair of chairs giving anyone who passed the undertaker's parlor a grand view of the deceased. "Mildred says it ain't normal, not burying dead people. And you changing her eyes from one color to another would likely scare hell outta most folks, let alone kids."

"Real eyeballs shrivel up in a hurry." Cemetery John lit a cigar and blew a cloud of smoke toward the ceiling. "If I hadn't put those glass peepers in, she'd *really* look spooky. Maybe I oughtta have changed them around after dark, but I was just trying to make her look better. I've got a whole box of glass eyes. You want to see 'em?"

"No," Wilburn answered quickly. "What I want you to do is plant her."

"Poor li'l gal. It's a shame she had to take an overdose of laudanum just because some cowboy didn't come back like he'd promised. I reckon being a whore's a tad rougher work than most of us think."

"I suppose you're right there. I'd say she's not quite twenty years old."

"Anybody find out her real name yet? There's reasons other than not getting paid for the embalming that I'm using her for advertising. Putting her working name on a headboard wouldn't be a great idea. Polly Goodpoke would give those churchwomen a real bee in their bonnet."

"Baptists and Methodists can go on the

warpath quicker than the Comanche and be meaner to boot. Just carve the name Polly on the board and put her in the ground. I'll get Sam Livermore to pay you fifty dollars, same as for anyone who winds up dead and broke in Wolf Springs, Texas."

"I'll get on it," Cemetery John said with a sigh of resignation. "Here I go and buy me an undertaking parlor, stock a supply of good-quality buryin' boxes, order in the latest embalming supplies to make my customers look good for the Second Coming, and how do the good citizens thank me? By not dying. I reckon it might've been a good idea to have gone around and ask folks how they were feeling before I went and spent all that money."

"You're still a deputy. I'll admit it ain't much, but we both make a living."

"I'd rather be subjected to handling money. It wouldn't be right for me to get married until I can afford to do it."

"You're sure determined to marry up with that new blacksmith, ain't you? Once you get set on a course, you hold on like a bulldog with lockjaw. I'll give you that much."

"Bessie's a sweet lady. I can't have her pounding iron and shoeing horses after we tie the knot. Folks would talk. All my business needs is more people dying and then we would have a good living without her having to work."

Wilburn Deevers took a deep breath. Cemetery John could be exasperating, but he was reliable as sunrise. Deevers couldn't understand what his deputy saw in Bessie Coggins, a woman fifty pounds heavier than he was who spent the day beating iron with a hammer while spitting tobacco juice. Someone had once said love was blind. Whoever had said that knew their elbow from a hole in the ground.

Then Wilburn remembered the main reason he had come to the undertaking parlor. Mildred's harping about the dead whore had made him lose focus.

"A telegram came in for Asa Cain. Tate Webster dropped the message by the office instead of delivering it to the Rara Avis. He's still skittish about going around a man who'd kill his own mother. The telegraph's from a sheriff by the name of Emil Quackenbush up in Kansas. Seems I recollect that name from somewhere."

Cemetery John cocked an eyebrow and took a drag on his long nine cigar. "You should. He was with me when we brought Asa's ma in to collect Governor Davis's reward money."

"Yeah." Deevers twisted his boot on the plank floor. "Now I remember. The fellow was short, wide, redheaded, and didn't stay around long. That was a bad time for me and I'm glad it's over. I reckon I'd have quit my job before I'd hung that lady. Terrible how things worked out for Asa."

"He's sure been working hard at drinking Soak Malone's saloon plumb dry ever since he got back to town." Cemetery John shook his head sadly. "I reckon him having to plug his ma must've upset him more than a tad."

Deevers snorted. "It's a fact that he ain't acting normal. My guess is our bounty hunter friend will be dead before the end of the year if he don't sober up. Fridley Newlin tells me Asa drinks a full quart of Old Crow before the sun's full up. After that, he gets right serious about his drinking."

"I'll go with you back to your office and take that telegram over to Asa. He's generally amenable to my visiting. Tate is right about him being rather surly these days. Leastwise, he generally just sets by himself, sips his whiskey, and ain't no bother. As long as no one gets loony enough to provoke him, I'd venture he won't kill nobody."

"We all hope that don't happen. Asa Cain's been a good friend for a lot of years. I just hope like everything that he whips whatever demons he's fighting before he drinks himself to death, or I have to hang him."

Cemetery John sighed. He knew the demons that Sheriff Deevers spoke of were all too real. "Let's go see what Quackenbush wants. You can tell the churchwomen I'll bury the soiled dove right soon."

Wilburn Deevers nodded as he spun and went outside into the bright afternoon sun. Cemetery John lingered while he locked the door to admire his handiwork. Polly looked as if she would last for years. Aside from being in a coffin, she didn't even look dead. The problem was he had never figured on the denizens of Wolf Springs being so blame healthy. There was always a chance of an Indian raid or possibly an epidemic striking. He could not give up hope. Bessie Coggins would be well provided for if she just showed a little patience. The undertaker clucked his tongue, a habit he'd picked up from Asa, and followed the sheriff down the hot and dusty street.

"Twenty thousand dollars!" Cemetery yelled loud enough to rouse a drunk in the far cell. "Hell's bells and tarnation. Show me an elephant and I'll have seen it all. I never in all my born days heard of such a big bounty.

Why, half of that boodle would set li'l Bessie and me up for life in grand style."

Wilburn Deevers picked up the telegram from the floor where it had fallen when the deputy had been hit with his fit of jubilation. He knew the lust for riches that had struck Cemetery John would soon infect the whole town. Tate Webster couldn't keep a secret any longer than his first beer of the afternoon. Deevers moved the message into a shaft of light from an open window.

ASA CAIN, COME QUICK. HENRIETTA, KANSAS. TWENTY THOUSAND REWARD FOR KILLER OF EIGHT. NEED HELP. WATCH YOUR HEAD.
Emil Quackenbush, Sheriff

"Wonder what he means about watchin' your head." Wilburn folded the note and tucked it into his pocket. "That's one passel of reward money to offer. I'd reckon whoever's killed those eight people must be a real tough character. With a bounty that big, he won't keep running about for long, that's for sure."

"You're right." Cemetery John was so excited he had difficulty speaking. "Asa and me are gonna collect that money. We're gonna leave in the morning. I reckon I'll be taking a few days off from my deputy work."

"Take all the time you need. Not paying you a wage for a spell will make the mayor happier than a politician in a whorehouse. But I think you're forgetting that Asa's the town drunk these days. He ain't killed no one since his mom. I wouldn't put a lot of hope into him counting for much. I'd go by myself if'n I was you."

"When folks find out Asa Cain's about, they'll step easy. I plan on leaving with him in the morning."

The sheriff snorted. "The only way you're gonna get Asa out of that saloon and away from a bottle is to whack him over the head and hog-tie him."

"Yep," Cemetery John agreed. "That's the way I've got it figgered too." Then he turned and was gone.

"Are you sure he's supposed to be blowin' snot bubbles outta his nose an' breathin' funny like he is?" Fridley Newlin asked with concern.

Cemetery John grabbed a flickering coal-oil lamp and studied the blond-haired bounty hunter that lay on the floor of the Rara Avis Saloon. "Yeah," he replied, sincerely hoping he was correct. "That stuff you gave him causes folks to do that."

Fridley Newlin said, "I ain't never give no one a dose of knockout drops before. If anyone but you'd asked by tellin' me it'll sober up ol' Asa, I'd never done it." The skinny bartender held out his hand. "But I do feel obliged to take that silver dollar you offered to pay for the service."

Cemetery John set the lamp on the long plank bar, fished the coin from his pocket, and handed it to Fridley. He looked around to assure himself the four customers in the saloon were still passed out drunk, then said, "If you'll grab his legs, I'll haul the rest of him to my hearse. It's parked just out front. I took the glass from the top window off a coffin so Asa can breath good. When we get him inside, I'm gonna nail the lid shut and leave him there until he's plumb sober."

"He's plenty pickled. That might take a couple of days."

"It's at least a week's trip to Kansas."

"I knowed it. I figgered you were goin' after that reward everybody's talking about. That's a terrible big bounty they're offerin'. Asa's the man to do the job, if he's sober." Fridley grimaced when by the wan light he saw Asa begin foaming at the mouth. "Well, let's get him into that buryin' box. From the looks of things, he may be more in need

31

of it than you planned."

Cemetery John forced a thin smile as he grabbed onto Asa's shoulders. "Don't worry none. I'll take good care of him."

"Reckon Asa's the one that oughtta be worryin'." Fridley bent over slowly and hoisted Asa's boots off the floor. "Well, get to haulin'. Just remember I've only got one leg with meat on it, so go slow."

Dawn was building an orange pyre on the eastern horizon when the ornate black and silver hearse pulled by a matched pair of red geldings rolled swiftly alongside the Concho River.

Sitting in the driver's seat atop the funeral coach, dressed in buckskin and slouch hat with the familiar ten-gauge shotgun by his side, Cemetery John went over his hasty departure in his mind. He had brought along Asa's Henry rifle, his Whitney Eagle pistol, a change of clothes, plenty of grub, ammunition, and — in case it was needed — a bottle of Old Orchard Whiskey. If he'd missed anything, there were always stage stops.

The undertaker shot an impatient glare at the rear ends of his horses, then flicked the reins to hasten their gait. Kansas was a long ways away and he was in a hurry. His main concern at the moment was that he might have inadvertently misjudged the dose of chloral hydrate. That could create a depressing situation.

Then a thin grin crossed his face. Even if worse came to worst, he could always truthfully tell people that he was with Asa Cain. That would definitely garner him some respect. This was one bounty he meant to collect.

THREE

"There goes a pair of reprobates that'll come to ňo good." Emil Quackenbush stared at the open doorway, whacked off a slice of plug tobacco, leaned back in his chair, and continued grumbling to Blue Hand. "That Wyatt Earp fellow made a failure outta being a lawman in Wichita. Now he's over in Dodge City, likely running crooked faro games while pretending to be a square deputy like you are."

Blue Hand rolled a jaundiced eye at the sheriff. The only time he received a compliment was when he was about to be asked to do something without getting paid for it. It was not as if he had room to complain. Both Indians and Mexicans were considered less valuable than horses or mules. Him being half of each, he had been harassed all his life. The badge and gun that came with his job of deputy had the salubrious effect of keeping most people's mouths shut, and gave him the right to crack those over the head who were not smart enough to remain silent about his heritage. Emil had endured a lot of chafe over hiring him. Also, there were not many other jobs available for a half-breed. He tongued his upper lip in thought and decided whatever the sheriff wanted done, he would do without complaint.

"That dentist Doc Holliday, who was with Earp, sure was an odd duck," Blue Hand said. "He had enough whiskey on his breath to kill a canary, but his gun hand didn't seem to notice he was drunk."

Emil poked the slice of tobacco into his mouth. "The problem is, those two hard cases are just the first to show up to collect Warwick's reward money. And they're likely to be the best of the lot. They at least had the courtesy to drop by and let me know they're heading into the hills to kill someone. Most bounty hunters will just go out and start shooting."

"I've heard that Asa Cain fellow you sent for has killed over two hundred men." Blue Hand was anxious to keep talking. It postponed Emil asking for the favor he knew was coming. "That's an awful big number to believe. Him shooting his own mother for bounty money can't be true."

The sheriff grinned evilly. "I can't vouch for exactly how many men Asa's brought in dead, but I was there in Hackberry, Texas, when he went charging in the back door of that saloon and killed his ma along with the whole blasted Dolven gang. I'm plain look-ing forward to him showing up. Whatever's in those Osage Hills that's chopping off people's heads is plenty mean. I'd reckon on Asa Cain to be a fair match for 'em."

After a long moment, a sober-faced Blue Hand said, "I'd venture he just might be at that."

Emil wiped a speck of tobacco juice from his beard with the back of his hand. "The trouble is, there's gonna be an army of nitwits hit here before Asa comes. Cyrus might feel more kindly toward the two of us if we were to be the ones to find that killer first, but I can't figure out anything more intelligent to do than study on the situation for a spell until Asa shows up. He's got a natural eye for manhunting and we can work with him, maybe even get a little cut of the bounty money for ourselves."

"Once the monster's killed."

"Yep," Emil agreed with a twitch of his cheek. "That's when we'll all start looking a lot smarter. And I want you to stop calling it a monster. There ain't no such thing."

Blue Hand could not think of anyone he had ever heard of who had gone around chopping off people's heads, but decided it prudent to humor his boss. "Yes, sir, I agree that it's some lunatic."

The heavy thud of boots coming through the open door brought an end to their conversation. It was Cyrus Warwick accompanied by Thomas Terry Rimsdale. The paunchy, bald-headed lawyer who was the mayor of Henrietta, district judge, owner of the local newspaper — the unimaginatively named *Henrietta Herald* — gubernatorial hopeful, and — to Emil's chagrin — Warwick's best friend.

"It's gratifying to see you are hard at work finding the killer of Miss Warwick," Rimsdale said to Emil as if he was describing the weather. "If I may say so, most criminals require that the local constable actually pursue them, or possibly I am mistaken on this matter."

"We were just working on a plan when you came in," Blue Hand suddenly said, surprising everyone. "Sheriff Quackenbush is of the opinion that it would be prudent to enlist the help of the Osage. As you are aware, I was raised by them and know their ways. The country where these killings have occurred has been hunting grounds for the

Osage Tribe since the time the Great Spirit walked this earth. No people know it better."

Quackenbush coughed to clear a wad of tobacco that had gotten snagged in his throat. Blue Hand's plan was so brilliant, it had caught him off guard.

"We'd just decided the best Indian to go ask for help was that one fellow. . . ." The sheriff cocked his head at Blue Hand. "What was his name anyway? Those Osage have got some mighty strange names."

"Going Snake," Blue Hand said. "He is the shaman of the tribe. Kills Eagles is the chief, but it is the shaman who listens to the wind and hears what it says. This fiend we seek lives in their land. The wind blows where he is, and it will tell Going Snake."

"This is preposterous," Warwick said with a sneer. "Now our duly elected sheriff is relying on heathen mumbo jumbo to find my darling daughter's killer. I would suppose the reading of tea leaves or studying the entrails of a chicken will also be employed to waste time while the murderer runs free."

"Tut, tut, Cyrus," the lawyer said patting him on the shoulder. "Occasionally even idiots get lucky. In the meanwhile, I would place my faith in that generous reward you have posted."

Emil said through clenched teeth, "If you're just here to berate me, please leave."

"No, Sheriff, we're not," Rimsdale said. "We do sincerely hope you solve these unfortunate and quite gruesome killings that have come to plague our peaceful citizenry. It is simply that Mr. Warwick and myself believe this may be beyond your abilities. That is why you will be receiving much assistance in this foul matter from other, hopefully more skilled, enforcers of the law."

"Two of your so-called skilled enforcers left here a bit ago. They were a policeman that got fired from his job in Wichita for running a whorehouse and cheating at cards and a drunken dentist with a surly attitude." Emil forced a grin. "With that pair on the job, I'm sure our problems will be over before it gets dark."

Cyrus Warwick said, "Large amounts of money attract riffraff along with the professional. I have been informed that you have wired for the assistance of the well-known bounty hunter Asa Cain, who has cut a bloody swath throughout Texas. Perhaps he will be successful where you have failed."

"The matter that brought us here," Rimsdale said, "is the recent and strange disappearance of Flavius Skillicorn that has been brought to the attention of my newspaper, the *Henrietta Herald.* While this incident occurred well into Indian Territory, we feel that it should be investigated by our sheriff."

Emil lowered his eyebrows. "I can see where that would cause concern. Old Flavius bought all of his supplies here in Henrietta. But to tell you a fact, Blue Hand and I was gonna visit the stage stop when we go see the Osage shaman. We're leaving just as soon as we saddle our horses and grab a few supplies."

"Then Mr. Rimsdale and I shall be on our way," Warwick said curtly. "Impeding your departure is not our intention."

"You know anything more about Ole Skillicorn?" Emil asked. "This is the first I've heard of his turning up missing."

Rimsdale nodded. "Only that he went into the wooded hills east of his residence in pursuit of a shoat pig that had escaped a pen. The pig came back on its own, but neither his wife nor anyone else have set eyes on Flavius Skillicorn since. This happened five days ago."

Blue Hand said, "By my count this makes thirteen men who have come up missing in that area."

The sheriff fought to contain a grimace.

His deputy had a disgusting tendency to cut to the heart of the matter and speak out whenever keeping his mouth shut would be preferable.

Warwick said, "I and Mr. Rimsdale wish you the best and I do believe that if you check with Judge Isaac Parker in Fort Smith, you will find that one of his deputies also has come up missing in the same vicinity. This adds, if I am not mistaken, one more victim to your long list of unsolved crimes."

The lawyer returned a hand to Warwick's shoulder and guided him away. "We bid you good day," he said. The two were out the door before Quackenbush could reply.

"If a federal deputy's missing," Blue Hand said, "then we've got fourteen missing and eight dead."

"You're so blame good at cipherin'," Emil boomed. "Go count up two horses and get 'em saddled. Then add up how many bullets we're gonna shoot and stow 'em where they'll do the most good."

Blue Hand noticed the sheriff's neck was as crimson as his hair, and thought it prudent to quietly do what he was told.

Quackenbush had a hair-trigger temper, that was for sure. The problem Blue Hand had was determining what had upset the

41

sheriff this time. No matter, there would be plenty of time to think on it while they were in the Indian Territory.

Blue Hand was so happy to be able to visit his people in the Osage Village that he began whistling as he headed for the door. From Emil's scowl he saw reflected in the door glass, it appeared his boss was growing increasingly agitated.

This was why white men were always complaining of stomach maladies, he decided. They simply did not know how to relax.

Blue Hand kept whistling all the way to the livery stable. There was no reason for him to get worked up over matters he could not control. When they came face-to-face with the Monster of the Osage, then he would worry.

FOUR

"I knew I was in too blame big of a hurry to get to Kansas." Cemetery John kept his eyes on the road as he complained to Asa Cain, who sat humped up by his side on the driver's seat. "I should have reckoned on you having that pocket revolver tucked away in your boot. I thought I was a goner when, out the goodness of my heart, I went back to see to your comfort and you started shooting at me through the lid of that spanking-new coffin like you did."

"Waking up inside of a casket, with a headache the size of Texas, not knowing where a person's at, can cause things like that to happen. I didn't hit you, so stop your bellyaching."

Cemetery John pointed to a bullet hole in the brim of his slouch hat. "I'd say you came mighty close to ending our friendship. Come to think on the matter, I got my other hat plugged when we went after the Dolven gang. Being around you is mighty rough on headgear, that's a fact."

"I'd like to know what Fridley Newlin put in my whiskey. Whatever it was would've flattened a buffalo. You two idiots could have killed me."

"Ah, Asa." Cemetery John lit a long nine with a sulphur match and stuck it into his companion's mouth. "We were just thinking of your welfare and trying to keep you from drinking yourself to death. You can't deny you were sure working at doing that. Everyone knows you're in the doldrums over what happened to your poor ma, but drinking like you were wasn't the way out of your problems. Now here we are out in God's fresh, clean air, on our way to kill a fellow that's worth ten thousand dollars to each of us. I would expect you to be plumb happy instead of acting perturbed with me."

Asa puffed on the cigar and surveyed the countryside with a look of resignation. "Tell me again why we're going to Kansas and just who's in need of killing — aside from a certain undertaker and a one-legged bartender that come to mind."

"That's the spirit old friend, focus on the future. Why, there's so blame much money to be picked up on this bounty that you'll keep Old Fridley in drinks for a year just to show your appreciation."

Cemetery John took the sheriff's telegram from his shirt pocket, unfolded it, and held it up for Asa to read.

"Emil Quackenbush is a competent and nervy lawman. If he's asking for our help, he's up against it," Asa said curtly.

"I mean to collect this bounty." Cemetery John's voice was firm with determination. "There's a lady blacksmith by the name of Bessie Coggins that's come to town and I've been courting her. This money will allow me to ask for her hand in marriage."

"There was talk of that in the Rara Avis. I thought that your undertaking business would do well. You used the reward money from the Dolvens to buy a building, a stock of coffins, and the like. What went wrong?"

"Nobody had the courtesy to croak. At least not enough with money. Shucks, I got fifty dollars a planting from the town before I went and bought all that expensive stuff to keep dead folks from spoiling. With the money from *this* bounty, I'm gonna open a new saloon right next door to my undertaking parlor. I already own the lot and it'll be a thrifty location. If someone gets on a tear and winds up dead, it won't be a far piece to drag 'em."

"Soak Malone won't take kindly to the

competition. He'll likely have an attack of apoplexy over another saloon opening."

Cemetery John grinned and said, "Yep, I'd expect he might at that. Then I'll get paid to bury him. Folks tend to forget that eventually us undertakers will get their business."

Asa shook his head to clear away the cobwebs. He knew that he had likely been given a large dose of chloral hydrate and was lucky to be alive. "Let me get this straight. You kidnapped me and now we're going to Kansas to collect a bounty on someone we know nothing about. You plan on marrying a blacksmith that you haven't even asked if she wants to be married to you. And to top off this mess, I'm supposed to do what's necessary to earn all this money. Then give you half. Am I missing anything?"

"Nope," Cemetery John said. "I'd say your head is clearing up just fine. And I'll have you know that when your attitude improves, I'll take off those handcuffs."

"You're a true friend, Cemetery John."

"Yep, I reckon you've good reason to be proud of me."

Asa sighed, leaned back, and watched a circling of buzzards in the distance. He was wondering how to escape from his dilemma when the drug once again overtook him and he dropped into a deep sleep.

FIVE

Skillicorn's way station consisted of four log cabins and a swayback barn set into the side of a hill along the Osage Mission road. Pens containing several horses and a motley assortment of pigs, goats, and turkeys were directly across from the cabins. The wood buildings had weathered to blend perfectly with the grayness of limestone cliffs that stretched as far as the eye could see along both directions of the shallow canyon.

A few tattered Rhode Island Red chickens that were listlessly pecking about the buildings for an occasional insect in the stifling afternoon heat scurried for cover at the approach of the two horsemen. Aside from a whisper of smoke from a single chimney of the first cabin, no other sign of life presented itself.

"Prosperous-looking little place," Emil Quackenbush said wryly. "Just where I'd like to spend the rest of my days."

"Those days would be longer here than in most places," Blue Hand agreed.

"Yep, there ain't no doubt about that." The sheriff reined his horse to a halt at a hitching post, looked about, and dismounted. "I can't say I blame Ole Flavius for skedaddling like he done. He likely just woke up one day, saw where he was, and headed off for someplace else."

"I'm surprised that pig came back," Blue Hand said. "They're generally smart animals."

"Being raised hereabout, I'd reckon that pig ain't the smartest shoat to ever root after an acorn." Emil stood surveying the cabins until Blue Hand was by his side. "Well, let's go rattle a door and see if anyone's home."

The plank door swung open before they got to it. A coarse-looking woman wearing a bun of gray hair on top of her head, a scowl on her face, and a stained apron wrapped around a feed-sack dress stood in the doorway.

"It's about time you got here." The woman glared at the men's badges. "My poor husband's off missin' for nigh onto a week and the law just now shows up."

"Sorry to take so long, ma'am," Emil said. "But we've been busy. There were three people on the stage murdered the other day."

"Hell, I knowed that. The driver was a good customer, shame to lose him. I sent word to the newspaper up in Henrietta that Bertha Skillicorn is not about to be ignored. It's a passel of work for two, runnin' this place. With Flavius being gone, I'm forced to do all the chores by myself. I gotta chop wood, slop the hogs, cook and clean, then tend those darn horses —"

"Yes, ma'am," the sheriff interrupted. "I'm sure that running this stage stop is a mighty big task, but from the looks of the place, you're doing an admirable job of it."

Blue Hand clenched his teeth to force his mouth to remain shut. He knew that the office of sheriff was an elected position, yet it was a discomfort to watch Emil having to kowtow to the likes of this woman in an attempt to stay in good graces with the citizenry.

Bertha Skillicorn's scowl remained, causing Emil to wonder if her face had been fixed in that position so long that it had gotten permanently stuck.

"It would be a comfort to have my husband back." Bertha's tone had softened somewhat. "But I've a terrible feelin' that monster's went and killed him. Flavius ain't never took off like this before and left me with all this work to do."

"Why do you think this so-called monster had anything to do with your husband's disappearance?" Blue Hand asked. "Have you seen it?"

"Hear it on occasion is all." Bertha kept her focus on Emil. "Sometimes on a night when there's a good moon to see by, that beast climbs on top of those cliffs yonder and screams like a demon. It don't sound nothing like a panther; this howling will chill your soul. Scares hell outta the horses to boot."

Bertha rolled her head to stare at the jagged limestone cliffs. "Flavius said he seen it once. This was a couple of months ago when we had a full moon. Around midnight it started yowling. He went off after the thing. All he saw was a glimpse of a big hairy beast outlined agin the sky. Never did get a shot at it. He said the monster took off a-runnin' on all fours, leavin' behind a smell worse'n a skunk."

The sheriff said, "Ma'am, when Flavius went after that pig, did he take a gun with him?"

"Hell, yes, he did!" she bellowed. "Only a fool would go about in these parts without one. Took the twelve-gauge scattergun, he did. I sure wisht I had it back; all I got to defend myself with now is a twenty-gauge revolving shotgun. That ain't much agin some monster."

Emil nodded toward his deputy. "Blue Hand and me will keep our eyes peeled for him. Likely enough your husband just twisted an ankle or busted a leg. I don't put any stock in these monster stories."

"Then how do you explain all those folks with their heads missin'?" Bertha pointed to Blue Hand. "And Sheriff, when you come back, don't bring the half-breed. The likes of him ain't welcome here."

"He's my deputy, Missus Skillicorn, and a good —"

Emil's reply was cut short by a distinct sobbing coming from an open window on the farthermost cabin.

"It sounds like someone's hurt," Blue Hand said, heading toward the source of the crying.

"That ain't none of your affair, Injun," Bertha yelled. "You two git and find my husband."

"I'm *making* it my business," Emil said curtly. "And you're coming along to explain what we find."

"Oh, my God!" Blue Hand exclaimed when he peeked in the window. The deputy ran to the door only to find it locked. Two swift kicks from his boot, then wood gave way from iron hinges allowing the door to fall inside the cabin with a crash.

The sheriff dashed inside to find Blue Hand staring in astonishment at a dark-skinned young girl sitting on the side of a bed wrapped in a filthy white blanket. A heavy steel chain fastened to an eyebolt in the wall snaked across the floor, where it was wrapped tightly around one of the girl's trim ankles and held fast by a brass padlock.

"Please don't hurt me anymore." The girl's ebony eyes were wide with fear. She made a pitiful attempt to move away, only to be halted by the chain.

"Why, that little gal can't be much older than sixteen." Emil's voice was strained as he grabbed onto Bertha's arm and squeezed. "Who is she and what has she done to deserve to be shackled like this?"

"Ain't like it's a person," Bertha said with a shrug. "She's *just* an Injun we traded a good Henry rifle for. Flavius and me rents her out to men that come by. We get two dollars for an hour, and the Injun gets fed. Ain't nothin' wrong with that."

Blue Hand moved slowly to the frightened girl and held out his hand. "No one here is going to hurt you, miss. We're both lawmen from Kansas. Can you tell us your name?"

"Leave me alone!" The chain rattled as the girl drew back against the wall. "I'm hurt too bad to do it."

"Sweetheart, you don't have to do anything you don't want to ever again." Emil turned and gave a twist to Bertha's arm. "The key, damn you, give it up!"

The gray-haired woman yelped, but quickly fished a key from inside her apron. "This ain't right. That's just an Injun. I can't see why you're makin' a fuss over some heathen savage."

When Blue Hand stepped close to get the key, he noticed Emil's neck was growing redder than his hair. That did not bode well. "Boss," he said softly, "perhaps it might not frighten the little lady so much if you hauled the old woman outside and do not kill her until after the trial."

"That'll be tough," the sheriff hissed through clenched teeth. "But I'll manage somehow." He motioned to the girl. "Check out how bad she's hurt. If it's bad, I'm gonna go ahead and hang the old bat here and now."

The sheriff ushered Bertha outside, keeping her in an armlock. He considered turning her loose in hopes that she would go for a gun and give him a splendid excuse to blow Bertha Skillicorn into a warmer climate. Then, as his temper slowly subsided, he reconsidered. This was still a woman, even though a thoroughly mean and despicable one. Folks in general frowned on lawmen hanging any woman without a judge's approval. He took a deep breath and awaited what Blue Hand would say.

Moving slowly as if he were approaching a spooked horse, the deputy bent down and unlocked the chain. It surprised him when the girl did not attempt to run away.

"My name is Sunflower," the maiden said meekly. "I am an Osage, one of The People. Comancheros captured me many months ago. Are you truly a man of the law?"

"Yes, ma'am." He kept a respectful distance and pointed to his badge. "Please call me Blue Hand. My people are also of the Osage, except for a Mexican who was my father. I must say your English is remarkably good."

"I attended the Indian school in Fort Gibson. My family lived a short distance from there where we farmed along the Arkansas River. I was returning home from school when the Comancheros captured me."

"When did this happen?"

"I am not certain. Many men have had their way with me and forced me to drink much whiskey. I do remember that the edges of the river were iced over."

That's a solid six months of hell. Blue Hand shuddered at the thought.

"How badly are you hurt?" he asked as softly as he could.

"I became with child." The raven-haired maiden spoke as if all emotion had been strained out of her being. "The woman who is outside came to me and told me a big belly would make me undesirable for men."

Blue Hand gasped when Sunflower opened the blanket and turned toward him. The girl was nude, but it was the patchwork of angry red and purple bruises spreading across her lower abdomen and thighs that drew his gasp. "My God!"

"The woman told me she was going to beat my baby out of me. That way I would heal faster and make her more money than if she did nothing. I still bleed, but the child is surely dead. That woman used a very big piece of wood to beat me with."

Blue Hand felt weak in his knees and his hands trembled with fury. He looked to the doorway and saw the sheriff standing there with his neck showing very red.

"I heard," Emil said, his voice hard as iron. "We need to get her to a doc real soon." He shook Bertha's arm. "Do you have a buggy?"

"There's a spring delivery wagon in the barn. You can rent it for five dollars."

"I'll see to it you get everything you got coming," Emil said giving her a fiery glare. "That's a promise." He looked at Sunflower, who had wrapped the blanket about her again. "Miss, if you'll just stay on that bed and rest, my deputy and me will hitch up that wagon. I reckon if we put a mattress or two in the back for you to lay on, moving won't hurt you so much."

"Leaving this place will be good." Sunflower daubed at a teary eye. "I wish there was a shaman to help me. I am afraid of the white doctors. Many of my people have died from seeing doctors. A medicine man of The People will know how to stop the bleeding."

That was when Emil Quackenbush noticed the spread of crimson on the mattress where the girl sat. "Darlin'," he said forcing himself to speak softly. "We're closer to the Osage Village than the town of Henrietta. If that's where you'd rather be taken, we'll go there now."

"The tribal shaman is called Going Snake." Blue Hand forced his gaze from the girl's hauntingly beautiful face. "He is a good healer."

Sunflower looked at Emil. "You are the

first white man who has not beaten me or — worse. For this I thank you."

"Get some rest," he said through a burning lump in his throat. Then he turned and headed for the barn dragging a cursing Bertha Skillicorn in his wake.

"I'm glad I took to carrying a little bottle of laudanum in my saddlebags." Emil shot a brief glance over his shoulder at the sleeping girl in the jouncing wagon bed. "Asa Cain told me it was a good idea. His advice is sparing that poor little gal a lot of pain."

Blue Hand said, "She's had more than her share of suffering, that's for certain. If Sunflower's skin was white, she would have been taken back to her family long ago, instead of getting chained to a bed and being abused worse than some animal."

"It was just a few years ago that we had a terrible bloody war to settle the fact that a person's color didn't make them any better or worse than anyone else. I reckon it'll be a long spell before that sentiment takes."

Blue Hand looked at the sheriff and cocked his head. "I'm surprised you let that woman take a horse and leave. As mad as you were, I expected you to shoot her."

Emil spit a wad of tobacco on the hinder of one of the horses pulling the creaking wagon. "Bullets are worth more than that old biddy. It was too much paperwork to arrest her like I should have done. Besides that, we needed to get moving. When I explained that Isaac Parker over in Fort Smith would be her judge if I did haul her in, Bertha got the first good idea that's likely struck for years and decided to head south for her health. Kidnapping and attempted murder of a young girl might have got her even hung. Ole Parker's noted for being somewhat stern."

"I'd say that's the biggest understatement since Lincoln said he didn't think he'd enjoy going to Ford's Theatre. Last September that hangman of Parker's, George Maledon, dropped six men at once. Lately, the sound of necks snapping in Fort Smith is common as crickets chirping. I'd venture Missus Skillicorn figgered her luck would be better elsewhere, for sure."

An evil grin spread across Emil's face. "And with her bumping into all those coal-oil lamps and *accidentally* setting every single building there on fire, there weren't no reason for her to stay around. That husband of hers has likely lost his head anyway."

"It will be near dark before we get to the Osage village," Blue Hand said to change the subject. "I really hope Sunflower gets well. She's suffered more than anyone ever should."

Emil reined the horses to miss a rock that had rolled into the road. "I'm right certain she will. The Osage have got their gods to pray to and I'm fixing to send up a prayer to mine. All that religion in one spot ought to do the job."

Blue Hand sighed and slumped into the wagon seat. He felt desperately tired. He ventured a quick look over his shoulder to a column of black smoke that was swirling upward against the crimson remains of a dying sun. He had once heard a stump preacher ranting about "cleansing fires." It would be a good thing if the evil that happened there would be consumed.

Perhaps if that were to occur, Sunflower might recover. He turned and gazed ahead at the purple hills and hoped that at least this time, the gods would be merciful.

Six

Dr. John Henry Holliday was using a long green willow branch he had chopped off with his bowie knife to hold a rattlesnake over the campfire for roasting. The snake was not a large one, especially as far as rattlers came in the Territories. He had seen some that were over six feet long and big around as his leg. This one, however, would be sufficient to make supper for the two of them. Dying men seldom had much of an appetite.

"That is a mighty puny snake for the two of us to make a meal of," Wyatt Earp said sitting on a large rock across the campfire from his friend. "And the more cooked it gets, the smaller it looks. When a person isn't looking for rattlesnakes, they're all over the place. When your belly's rubbing on your backbone and there is nothing else to eat, the things are scare as hen's teeth."

"Don't fret it, Wyatt. You can have the

whole thing. That's one benefit of having consumption. A person's food bill drops to near nothing."

"You're going to eat some of it?" Wyatt knew the argument would be a futile one, but he felt obligated to his friend. "Whiskey needs some food to land on or it'll burn a hole in your gut."

Holliday chuckled, an act that brought on a fit of coughing that nearly put the roasting snake into the fire. After a long while, he recovered sufficiently to pick up the bottle that was beside the log he sat on with his free hand, and swallowed down a good two fingers worth of Jackson's Sour Mash. "That's an old wives' tale, Wyatt. More people die of too much food than too much whiskey. If I were to cut down my drinking, I'd be dead in a week."

Wyatt Earp made no comment. Doc could drink more whiskey and show it less than any man he had ever known. How anyone could put away two to three quarts of hard liquor every day and keep going was hard to fathom, but for Holliday it seemed to present no problem. Earp was glad to have the dentist along for what he expected to be an easy bounty and a quick pile of money for the two of them. Doc had need of some funds. He had just killed a soldier in Texas defending the honor of a redheaded faro dealer named Lottie Deno. Holliday was heading for Denver to keep the cavalryman's friends from taking revenge for his gutting their friend with a sharp knife, after the soldier had had the temerity to voice complaint about the pretty lady's cheating at cards. Even as sick as he was, the dentist loved being around women. His genteel Southern manners simply demanded that all women's honor be defended, card cheats and soiled doves included. Wyatt opined that a fracas over some lady would likely kill Doc Holliday long before the consumption took him.

"It was a good thing I decided to lay over a spell in Dodge City," Holliday remarked. "I'd expected you were still in Wichita upholding the law and running a stable of whores. But I suppose a ten-thousand-dollar stake in your pocket will be worth chancing losing your new job over."

Wyatt nodded to the rising full moon that was sending wavering shafts of wan light through the towering trees. "This is a strange case. When you arrived in Dodge, I'd just gotten the poster. I agree the money's too good to pass up, but the more I learn about these murders, the more puzzling it becomes."

"I have never heard tell of anyone who just went around chopping off people's heads for fun. But, Wyatt, this seems to be the case here. There hasn't been a dollar stolen from the victims by any account."

"That cock-and-bull story of a monster is a hoot. It'll likely keep a lot of idiots out of our way until we can kill whoever's probably been doing the murdering. My guess is it's just some lunatic."

"If it takes more than two days, I'm out." Doc pulled the snake from the fire and studied it for a brief moment before deciding it needed more cooking. "I'll be out of whiskey by then. I can't allow that to happen."

"Marshal Deger won't abide my being gone from Dodge much longer than that either." Wyatt glared at the snake. "And from the grub available, we need to bring in a body right soon. I'm not up to digesting many rattlesnakes."

Doc Holliday froze. Moving only his free arm, he grabbed onto the double-barrel shotgun next to the whiskey bottle.

"What is it?" Earp asked, his hand steady over his holstered Colt. "I don't hear anything."

"That's the problem." Doc laid the snake on a rock, his rheumy gray eyes darting to and fro at the shadowy woods. "There *is* no sound. Even the crickets have stopped chirping. There's something out there!"

"If that killer's coming for us, so much the better." Wyatt pulled his pistol. "This forty-four will handle him."

Both men stiffened when a bloodcurdling scream built like a thunderclap from a mound of rocks a few hundred feet from their camp began echoing through the trees. The sound was like that of a huge banshee. Neither of the gunmen had ever heard anything like it before. It was as if the gates of Hell had opened and some very fierce and bloodthirsty demon escaped.

"What in creation do you think is out there?" Wyatt asked after a hard swallow. "I never in all my born days heard anything howl like that. Whatever it is, it sure sounds big and mad."

"I don't know," Doc Holliday said, fingering the hammers on his shotgun. "But my stock in monster stories just went up a peg. And one thing's for certain."

"What's that?"

"We should have brought along bigger guns."

Seven

Kills Eagles came out through the low open flap of the shaman's tepee, stood, and glared at Emil Quackenbush and Blue Hand. Rays of yellow moonlight danced on the Osage chieftain's stern features as he spoke. "The young maiden you have brought into our care is gravely injured. If the flow of life-blood cannot be stopped, she will pass into the spirit world. Going Snake is using his strongest medicine. I hope it will be sufficient. The Great Spirit may answer our prayers to be merciful and spare her life."

The sheriff nodded. "I'd reckon we're all sending up the same message. Let's just hope it takes." He turned and spit a wad of tobacco juice into the campfire. "The old woman that beat her so blame bad has gone from the territory. I don't expect her to be coming back. Flavius, her husband, who ran the stage stop, has been missing for quite a spell. Most folks believe what they're calling the Monster of the Osage got him."

The chief turned to the sheriff. "Yes, I have heard much talk of this creature." He glanced around at the tepee he had just left. "I have been among the white man long enough that I now believe monsters walk this earth."

Blue Hand said, "My Chief, Sheriff Quackenbush and I came to your village to ask for your help in stopping these killings. We happened upon the injured girl only by chance."

Kills Eagles fixed the young deputy in a critical gaze. "You have lived too many seasons among the white man. You attended their schools and now even your language is no longer that of The People. I do not know what we can do to help such an educated person as you have become." He faced Emil. "Besides, this monster has yet to harm any of our tribe. It kills only the pale of skin. I do not see a very big problem here."

"I can understand," Emil said, "that the Osage Indians might have a complaint or two about being forced onto a reservation, but all of this happened some time ago and I, along with those folks that got killed, had as much to do with placing any tribe on a reservation as one of those trees over yonder."

Blue Hand said, "I am certain my chief is wise and realizes the cavalry will be summoned to kill this beast, should these slaughters be allowed to continue. Many bluecoats will come. They could even decide to build a fort here to keep watch over the Osage lands."

Kills Eagles stood in stone silence for a long while staring into the sparkling heavens. He looked at no one as he strode off. "Follow me to my tepee. We will smoke and speak of this matter. I shall send for Going Snake to join us when he can. I now believe our clansman, Blue Hand, has become wise. This is good. The People will consider your counsel."

The deputy stepped close to Emil, grinned, and gave him a surreptitious wink as the pair followed Kills Eagles beneath the starry canopy of night.

Going Snake bent over, took a flaming faggot from the small fire that burned in the center of the tepee, lit his pipe, and regarded the sheriff while puffing away.

The shaman was much younger than Emil had expected, likely not much over thirty. Going Snake was also taller than most Indians, stocky with rippling muscles. He wore his raven hair in two long braids, clasped at the ends with silver rings that held the fang of some animal, possibly a bear.

Emil took a quick dislike to the shaman for some reason he could not put a definite finger on. An Indian who claimed to be in league with the Spirit World, he decided, was not a lot different than a white man with a traveling medicine show or a stump preacher. All were varieties that required a sharp eye to be kept on them.

"There is a legend of He Who Kills." Going Snake's voice crackled like the fire. "This story has been passed from father to son since The People began counting time. The Great Waukan, in his wisdom, found to his sorrow and disgust that men sometimes spoke what was not the truth. This was a terrible offense to the spirits, who never speak but what is pure.

"To stop the mortals from speaking lies, the Waukan took an eagle and a panther. From these two he fashioned a beast that flies. It has the strong hooked beak of an eagle for a mouth. On nights when the moon is bright, the spirits cause He Who Kills to soar in the blackness of the above and search out those who have told untruths. Then, the beast dives down and bites off their heads, which it swallows."

Emil took a puff from the long nine cigar he had fired to be sociable. "I'd reckon if that critter ever went to Washington, it'd get so fat it couldn't fly."

Going Snake remained stoic. "Yes, there are many that escape He Who Kills. The story is but that; a tale made up to frighten unruly children into telling the truth."

Kills Eagles blew out a mouthful of smoke that formed a ring. He watched with great interest until it reached the hole at the top of the tepee and escaped into the blackness. "Sheriff, the Osage do not know what is killing those people. He Who Kills is only a story, as the shaman has said. But it is the *only* legend we know of about anything that takes away people's heads."

"It is a puzzle," Blue Hand said, "and that is why we are here. We also do not know why this is happening."

Going Snake sent a trickle of icy fear down Emil's spine when he said, "Then the Indians and white men agree on one thing. Nothing human kills like that."

"Whatever it is," Emil said, "I intend to see it dead."

"Yes," Kills Eagles said. "I am in agreement that this must happen. I will send out some scouts to see what can be found. The sooner this Monster of the Osage is gone, the better it will be for us all."

"Amen to that." Emil nodded to Going Snake. "How's the girl doing?"

The shaman stared upward to where the ring of smoke had gone. "She lives. I shall go to my medicine tent now and pray." He hesitated as if his tongue had snagged. "This night there are many prayers to be said. *Many* prayers."

The shaman turned, slid through the opening, and left the tepee with the silence of smoke.

"Cheerful fellow," Emil said.

"He will do as you ask to help find this beast," Kills Eagles said. "That is what we shall all do. The white man's army will not be needed in the Osage land."

The chief puffed on his pipe. "Sheriff, you and Blue Hand must remain in the village as our guests until the sun is up. The moon is bright tonight, as it is, I believe, every night when the beast kills."

Emil noticed relief cross his deputy's face when he nodded in agreement. "Thank you, Chief. We'll take you up on your hospitality. The Monster of the Osage will be dealt with in good time." He grinned. "I can't see losing our heads over the matter."

"There's one thing that's always set me to

wondering," Emil said lazily. He had decided to let Blue Hand do the driving while he leaned back in the seat with his fingers laced behind his head and enjoyed the beautiful morning.

The deputy looked over his shoulder to assure himself their saddled horses were being led behind the wagon with no problems, which they were. "I know you're going to tell me anyway, but I'll go ahead and ask what it is that has set you to thinking."

"It's that shaman, Going Snake. I've noticed that nigh onto everyone, be they preachers or soothsayers, who claim to visit with spooks are plenty weird. I was wondering if a person has to be a budding lunatic before they go into that trade or become one after they join."

"I believe they commune with spirits, not spooks. But I do agree with you that Going Snake seems more somber than most medicine men."

"Well, I reckon if he can heal up that pretty Sunflower, he's an okay character."

"Yes, what happened to her was a terrible thing. At least when we left the village the bleeding had stopped and she was resting."

The sheriff nodded, then unlaced his fingers and sat up straight. He fished his last long nine cigar from his shirt pocket, bit off the end, and stuck it in his mouth. Normally, he would wait until later in the day for a smoke, but this clear, warm, cloudless morning was one that God was likely bragging about to Gabriel. This was a morning that demanded a man smoke a cigar. He lit it with a lucifer match, taking his time to assure he had a good fire going, then looked over at Blue Hand.

"That was a wise observation," Emil said. "About the Army coming out here to take care of that monster. I hadn't thought of it myself, but with a federal marshal out of Fort Smith turning up missing, that might be enough to make it happen."

"The Osage are no different than the rest of the tribes. The very thought of the government poking into their affairs is enough to scare them into doing nearly anything to keep the white man's army away."

"That's just good sense. I want to let you know that you're a right good deputy and before I'm out of the job of sheriff I'll write you a high-grade letter of recommendation. That's about all I can do, however. I plan on starting to look for another lawman job myself when we get back. Cyrus Warwick's already told me not to make any plans past this fall's election."

"Mr. Warwick is a hard man. With his daughter being killed, he will become ever more harsh. I could not work for him if you were not the sheriff. Not many will hire a half-breed to be a lawman. I may have to go where you do to keep being a deputy."

Emil snorted. "There ain't no reason to go threatening me like that. Here as I was in a plumb good mood when —"

The sheriff's cigar fell from his mouth when the deputy abruptly reined the spring wagon hard to the right to avoid colliding with a somber black hearse drawn by a pair of sleek red horses that came speeding from a thicket of scrub trees that masked a merging road.

"Damn idiot, watch where you're going!" Emil shouted while trying to spot where his cigar had fallen.

Blue Hand drew the wagon to a stop and set the brake. "That man you called an idiot has a very big shotgun. I also do not think his companion cared for your statement either."

Sheriff Quackenbush went ahead and grabbed onto his cigar, which was rolling around on the floorboards. If there was going to be a fight, he could jump down off the safe side of the wagon and shoot at them with a cigar in mouth just as well as if he'd left it alone.

"Is that you, Quacky?"

The familiar voice shouted just as Emil turned to face whoever it was that had nearly run them over and wrecked what had been a really nice day. The sheriff hated to be called "Quacky." There was only one person who could get by with it. He looked up into the twin barrels of a ten-gauge shotgun, then nodded and grinned at the silver-haired black man wearing a slouch hat.

"Howdy, Cemetery John," Emil said cheerfully. "I'd say I was glad to see you if you'd learn how to drive. There's plenty of folks hereabouts to bury without you having to run them over to get their business."

Blue Hand breathed a brief sigh of relief when the driver lowered the hammers on his shotgun and leaned it against the seat. That was when he noticed that the slender man with long blond hair sitting opposite the driver held a cocked pistol aimed square at his heart. He could not fathom why the sheriff kept smiling when it appeared they could both be dead in short order.

"Asa Cain," Emil said gleefully to the man with the pistol. "Meet my deputy, Blue Hand. He's a sight better at being a lawman than he is at driving a wagon."

"Cemetery John was the one speeding." Asa holstered his Whitney Eagle, to the deputy's relief. "He's in a real dither to collect that reward you wired me about."

"You are the man they call Asa Cain?" Blue Hand asked in awe. He had not known what the famous bounty hunter who had killed his own mother would look like, but this clean-shaven fellow with yellow hair and pleasant expression was certainly not what he had expected.

"Yes, that's me." Asa motioned toward his companion. "And this here is Cemetery John. He's a deputy back in Texas along with trying his hand at being an undertaker. Right now he's working on learning to drive a hearse."

"I'd say he's got a ways to go," Emil said with a chuckle. "It's mighty good to see you two reprobates again. That bounty I wired you about is a big one all right, but it may be a woolly-booger to collect."

"We heard talk at way stations about some kind of monster." Cemetery John frowned. "They say this is some kind of beast that chops off people's heads and packs them away?"

"Don't fret it none," Emil said. "We'll just set you to running up an' down the road in that fancy black hearse of yours. Eventually, you'll run over whatever it is."

Blue Hand took note of the sun. "It's going to be time for some dinner in a spell. Why don't I get us a fire going and start the coffee. That'll give us a chance to visit."

"Good idea," Emil said. "When we get to town, there may not be much time for pleasantries. That bounty's bringing in some real bad people."

"Trying to stop killings by paying big money to kill more people has that effect." Asa climbed down from the hearse. "That's why the sooner we learn who we're after and get *our* killing done, so much the better."

Blue Hand walked off and began foraging for firewood. The day had been warm, but with Asa Cain's presence he felt a chill. He wondered if Emil had noticed this too, but decided he would not ask.

EIGHT

Cemetery John produced a pan full of fluffy sourdough biscuits along with an entire sorghum-glazed hickory-smoked ham from a chuck box in the hearse. This had the effect of causing both the sheriff and deputy to overlook his bad driving, or at least postpone any more pestering about the matter.

Asa Cain nibbled listlessly at a biscuit, washing each morsel down with a mouthful of hot coffee, causing Emil to wonder if he had been ill. The bounty hunter definitely had a pallor about his face that hadn't been there before. He appeared spry enough, however. The fact that he had drawn his Whitney Eagle pistol with such lightning speed rapidly soothed any immediate concerns.

While Cemetery John and Asa sat on the tailgate of the spring wagon eating their dinner, Emil and Blue Hand told what they knew about the murders. The lawmen gave dates and details of the eight headless bodies that had been found, then went into an account of the travelers and federal marshal from Fort Smith that had gone missing in the area along Boggy Creek. Finally, Emil described Cyrus Warwick's reason for posting the huge reward and the pressures he had brought to bear to find who — or what — was killing all of these people.

"I'd reckon having a pretty young daughter murdered would set most men to using whatever means possible to catch their killer," Cemetery John said through a mouthful of honey-drenched biscuit. "And I've noticed that rich people have lots of means."

"The town of Henrietta was named after her," Emil said solemnly. "She was only seventeen and Ole Cyrus's only child to boot. Folks say his wife died of typhoid fever some years ago. That little gal was his only kin."

Asa Cain's brow furrowed in thought. "You mentioned there was the smell of a skunk where the bodies were found?"

"Yeah," Emil nodded. "Whoever the killer is, he could use some scrubbing."

"Back in sixty-eight," Asa said seriously, "I made my longest manhunt. The fellow I was after had made a living out of marrying and then killing women for what money they had. He was a weasel of a Frenchman by the name of Paige Ferragus. Texas had a two-thousand-dollar bounty on him for poisoning his sixth wife with strychnine over in Austin.

"Ferragus must have gotten wind that I was on his tail, because I had to chase him all the way through Washington Territory. I eventually caught up with him in Seattle, where he was already fixing to marry another woman. That man was a fast worker; he was only three days ahead of me. Paige complained all the way back to Texas about me taking him away from that woman. He kept ranting about her being his only true love. We hung him quick just to cut down on his caterwauling.

"Why I bring this up is the fact that both Indians and the white folks up there tell of a beast called a Sasquatch. This thing, whatever it is, leaves a foul odor like a skunk. Its scream would scare a panther. I heard it one night. This is a legend that I pay attention to."

Blue Hand set his tin dinner plate aside. He no longer had much appetite. "This Sasquatch, it lives very far from here."

"Animals migrate," Asa said. "It would

not be hard to believe some Sasquatch might have wandered from up north to down here in the Territories."

"Dang it all, Asa," Emil grumbled. "Here I've been trying to calm folks down by telling them there ain't no such thing as monsters. Now you come along and start scaring even me. I suppose this sassy-squat also chops off people's heads and packs 'em away."

"Sasquatch," Asa corrected. "No, according to what I know of the legend, they devour the entire person. When travelers come missing in that country, even a lot of sane lawmen blame the Sasquatch for eating them."

"Wonderful, simply wonderful." Emil grabbed the dead stub of his cigar, stuffed it in his mouth, and began chewing on it. "I was planning on some average everyday lunatic that we could simply go out and shoot. Then we could split Cyrus's reward money and go on our way. Now, the most famous bounty hunter in the West has come to help by telling me there's some hairy thousand-pound monster roaming around that'll likely take a passel of killing before we can collect our money."

Asa cocked his eye at the part of Emil's tirade when he mentioned splitting the bounty money. Cemetery John had already staked his claim to half. He decided this discussion would best be put off until there was some money to divide. "Most claim a Sasquatch weighs around six hundred pounds. But all of them leave a smell like a skunk." The bounty hunter eyed the sheriff. "Has anyone checked for tracks?"

"We've never been able to get to where a murder happened until long after the bodies had been laying about for quite a spell. Buzzards, coyotes, and such pretty much mess up evidence."

Blue Hand spoke up. "I have looked. The country along the creek where these crimes occurred is very rocky. I saw no tracks."

"The place where the stage was attacked and the young lady killed." Asa tossed the remains of his soda biscuit into a bush. "Could we visit this site on our way to town?"

"Ain't even out of the way, and only about a mile younder," the sheriff said with a flick of his hand to the north. "Whatever we're after, it's a fact that being around roads don't bother it none."

Cemetery John and Blue Hand began stowing the remains of their meal, preparing to leave.

"There will be some scouts from my

People of the Osage tribe, who are very good trackers, after this killer," Blue Hand said. "If it walks, they will follow it."

"Asa was raised by the Comanche," Cemetery John said as he carefully wrapped muslin around the ham to keep the flies at bay. "He can track where a lizard walked across a flat rock sometime last month. He's not called the best bounty hunter in the business without good reason."

"I should have known that he was a human being." The deputy's voice lowered. "To follow a man and kill him is not an uncommon skill among The People. But I have never heard of an Indian who would harm his own mother."

Cemetery John stopped working and stared long at the young man. "Let's load this stuff up and get on our way."

"The shotgun guard and driver were found right here beside the creek." Emil pointed to a slight rise on the opposite side of the road from the creek. "Up there's where we found the girl's body."

Asa stood straight and studied the green rolling countryside. Trees were thick and lush with spring leaves. The beginnings of jagged limestone cliffs that followed the meandering Boggy Creek for many miles south were here only a few feet high. He occasionally jerked his head to one side, then the other. Blue Hand knew Asa was smelling the air, something only trained warriors did.

"There is a campfire not far from here," Asa said.

"Bounty hunters, most likely." Emil shrugged. "Twenty thousand dollars will bring in a passel of 'em. Even if there is a sassy-squatch out here, it'll eventually get its hide perforated with lead. I just want us to be the ones doing the perforating."

Blue Hand said, "Two men came by the office to let us know they were going after the reward money. One of them is a policeman from Dodge City by the name of Wyatt Earp. He had a skinny dentist with him named Holliday. We do not know how many others have already come to kill the monster."

"Dag-nab it." Emil glared at his deputy. "There you go calling it a monster again. I don't care what Asa and you think it might be. I'm trying to keep folks from panicking and start shooting each other out of fear an' greed. Let's just say we've got a murdering outlaw on the loose and leave it at that."

"The sheriff is correct," Asa said. "I mentioned the Sasquatch because it's often not smart to quickly dismiss what *might* be. As for this Wyatt Earp, I've met him. If I'm any judge of character, he'll likely shoot himself in the leg trying to draw his own gun before he gets lucky enough to bring in any outlaws. Running with a dentist is a clue how smart he really is —"

"What is it?" Cemetery John asked when Asa froze and grew silent.

"I feel a presence. We are being watched by the killer. I can feel his evil, his hatred toward us."

Emil placed a hand on his pistol and strode up the low hill to Asa's side. "I don't see nothing."

"It is far away."

"Should we go after him?" Cemetery John asked, eyeing his shotgun.

"No," Asa said firmly. "Who or whatever is out there is expecting us. It will be long gone by the time we get to where it is."

"This just keeps on getting better all the time," Emil said with a sigh. "Folks are dropping dead like flies in my jurisdiction. I'm forced to deal with a shaman that talks to spooks. Now I'm being infested with a thousand-pound sassy-squatch along with a partner that can feel evil comin' in on the breeze. I knew I should have gone to Chicago and become a shoe salesman."

Asa Cain turned to the sheriff. "I can understand your skepticism, Emil. But knowing your enemy is out there waiting to kill you keeps a person alive. Have you given any thought as to how Indians can often move about unseen in total silence? They have learned that all living things send out messages or an aura, if you wish. Some of which can only be sensed by those who will take the time to listen and feel. The message of pure hatred and bloodlust is what I feel from what is out there. And it is the strongest I have ever encountered."

Emil glared into the dark foreboding canyon where Boggy Creek flowed. "Is that thing out there a sassy-squatch?"

"There is no way I can say. But I know this much; it is filled with hate and it is alive. Whatever lives can be killed."

"Well, if we're not gonna go shoot at it, let's head for Henrietta. I expect there's getting to be a real town full of idiots about, all looking to make twenty thousand dollars. I'll venture most of 'em will start by looking in all of the saloons."

"Yes, Emil, I'm certain you're right there." Asa hesitated, then fixed the sheriff in his gaze. "I never did get to thank you properly for what you did in Hackberry. That was a hard time for me, with what happened to my mother and sister. I've not forgotten how you helped me. I owe you a favor."

The sheriff shrugged. "There ain't no debt, Asa. Let's all of us get to town. It's going to be a long night and on top of that, we've gotta figure out how to kill that sassy-squatch or whatever's raising the ruckus in these hills. I'm just plain glad to have you here."

Asa Cain smiled for the first time in a long while, then turned to follow his friend back to the wagons.

NINE

Asa Cain was the first to take notice of the circling black turkey buzzards centered a few hundred feet east of the road. He blinked against the glaring sunlight, then turned to Cemetery John. "I reckon we ought to stop and go investigate what's died."

Emil, who was driving the lead wagon, pulled over to one side of the road and set the brake, indicating that he too had seen the vultures. Cemetery John reined the hearse to a dusty stop behind the sheriff.

"Maybe it will only be a dead deer or some other animal," Blue Hand said hopefully as he jumped to the ground.

"It's not a long walk to find out," Asa said. He tilted up his head and sniffed the breeze. "Cemetery, check the loads in that ten-gauge of yours and bring it along."

"You smelling that sassy-squatch, are you?" Emil Quackenbush asked. "Be nice if we could just walk over a ways, blow a bunch of holes in it, split up all of that reward money, and head off to nicer country."

Cemetery John winced at the thought of splitting the reward into smaller pieces, but realized it was only fair. He decided that if just a few citizens of Wolf Springs would favor him by having the decency to die, five thousand dollars would be enough of a nest egg to allow him to ask Bessie Coggins for her hand in marriage. He sighed, thumbed the breech of the shotgun open, nodded at the shiny brass cartridges, then slammed it shut with a satisfying click. "These are double-aught buckshot. One of these will dang near blow a man in two. I'll venture two of 'em will handle whatever's out there."

"Well, let's go find out what died." Emil snorted, heading into the shadows of towering trees. "Ain't nothing to be gained by lollygagging."

Blue Hand turned to Cemetery John. "Has he always been this impetuous?"

"I've never noticed patience being one of his stronger points." The undertaker rested the big shotgun in the crook of an arm. "Let's go see if we can keep him from losing his head, even if he doesn't always put the thing to good use."

Sheriff Quackenbush stood with his fists on his hips as he eyed the headless corpse that was wedged nearly twenty feet from the ground between two branches of a huge pecan tree. "Going to be a task gettin' that fellow down from there."

Blue Hand said, "I'm more concerned about how he got *up* there in the first place. That man must weigh a couple hundred pounds."

Asa Cain clucked his tongue as he studied the body. "Looks like there's a badge pinned on his shirt. I can't say for certain until we get him down, but from here I'm betting it's a federal marshal's star." He looked at the sheriff. "You did mention Judge Parker had an officer come up missing in these parts."

"Yep," Emil said, still staring at the corpse. "And I'm betting once we fish him outta that tree, we'll likely find enough to identify him as Bob Talbot. That's what Judge Parker's telegraph said the marshal's name was."

Blue Hand gave a sigh. "Having a federal marshal killed will be like having a nest of yellow jackets in your outhouse; it'll eventually create quite a stir."

"To say the least." Asa wrinkled his nose.

"And this stench is from a skunk. I can't understand it, but I'm certain it's nothing but a skunk." He hesitated. "The smell is fresh. Who or what put that corpse up there, did it not very long ago."

"That's a fact," Cemetery John said. "There ain't a drop of blood to be seen on the ground. Whenever a person gets their head whacked off, it generally creates a considerable mess."

Emil took a moment to light a fresh long nine cigar. "What I can't figure is why he got put in a tree. Blue Hand is right about that man being a load to just tote around, let alone climb a tree with. This is strange, mighty strange."

"No," Asa said, "it isn't at all. That body was placed up there for the sole purpose of frightening us. It's meant as a warning."

"Right now I'm more pissed off than warned." Emil turned to Blue Hand. "Shinny up there and unwedge that body. The fall ain't going to hurt him none, so get to it."

A few moments later, Asa Cain was poring through the dead man's papers. "There's no doubt about him being Marshal Talbot; here are his orders. What amazes me is the sixty dollars in gold still in his pocket."

"That's a puzzle in all of these killings."

91

The sheriff took a puff on his cigar. "All decent outlaws I've ever dealt with took the victims' money. That generally gives a trail to follow."

"There is a reason only the heads are taken," Asa said. "We just don't know what it is yet."

Cemetery John bummed a cigar from Emil, lit it with a lucifer match, then said, "Figuring out crooks and killers is a difficult task for sure, but what has me really vexed is the condition of that body. Didn't this marshal come up missing a few weeks ago? From the looks of him, he sure ain't been lying out here in the heat all that time."

"Not likely," Asa said. He surveyed the low jagged limestone cliffs that bordered this section of Boggy Creek. "I reckon we got ourselves another puzzle to study on. But who or whatever killed the marshal and put his body up in that tree's out there watching us. That's a fact we don't need to waste any time pondering on."

Blue Hand placed a thumb on the hammer of his Winchester; his dark eyes flitted back and forth as he surveyed the shadowy woods. "I do not see anything, but I doubt the marshal did either. Whatever is killing these people is plenty good at it. A lot of armed men who are used to danger are now dead."

"At least nine of 'em now." Emil snorted. "And every dad-blasted one wound up dead in my jurisdiction. I should have listened to my sainted mother's advice and become a shoe salesman. Now there's a job where hardly anybody ever takes a shot at you and it's also indoor work."

Cemetery John worried his cigar between his teeth. "Asa's right about us being watched. I can feel it in my bones."

"I also feel a presence," Blue Hand said. "I think whatever's out there is watching us like a cat does a mouse, waiting to pounce at the first opportunity."

Sheriff Quackenbush pulled his revolver, turned, and fanned the hammer, sending five lead slugs flying through the forest. He immediately reloaded the Colt and returned it to his holster. "That outta make 'em think twice."

Cemetery John said, "Well, Emil, I'd reckon whoever was watching us has done peed down his leg and ran away. Shucks, you might even have come within a mile or two of actually hitting him."

"He made me mad," Quackenbush replied simply.

Asa shrugged. "Let's get the marshal's

body loaded up and head for Henrietta. I could use a bath and a shave and there needs to be a telegraph sent to Fort Smith." Asa hesitated. "Don't mention anything to Judge Parker about me being about. We've had some misunderstandings in the past."

Cemetery John frowned when he noticed the fire was out of his cigar. "The judge wants to hang him, but he can't do it until Asa shows up in his jurisdiction, which *is* mighty close to here, I do believe."

Emil shook his head. "I ain't even gonna ask the details, I need your help so bad. What Parker don't know won't upset him any, but we *are* in the Indian Territories right here; the boundary's just south of town."

Asa glared at Cemetery. "This trip just keeps getting better and better, thanks for inviting me along."

"Ah, you were in dire need of a change of scenery. Don't go being a sorehead."

Emil spoke up. "We can visit after we get to Henrietta. Grab up either an arm or a leg and get this body into the undertaker's before it starts spoilin' on us. Just because he's kept up to now don't mean our luck will hold."

From deep within the shaded recess of a

sheltering finger of rock, cruel dark eyes watched as the men loaded the headless corpse into a wagon and went on their way. After a while, the hulking creature relaxed. He opened a leather pouch and extracted the hind paw of a skunk, then splayed open the claws. Carefully, patiently, he began to scrape the sharp claws up and down along his jagged yellow teeth, cleaning them, a task he found oddly relaxing. There was no hurry, night was hours away. So was the full moon and another hunt to fulfill his quest.

TEN

The sun was sinking into a wavering green sea of trees when Cemetery John reined the black funeral hearse to a stop in front of an impressive oak building with a sign over the door announcing it to be the office of the sheriff of Henrietta, Kansas.

Asa Cain swept his blue eyes up and down the wide main street. "From the looks of it, folks are mighty proud of this place for some reason; every single business building has the name Henrietta painted on it in big letters."

"I believe I mentioned earlier on," Emil Quackenbush said walking over to join them, "that was the name of Cyrus Warwick's darling daughter. The little gal was all the family the man had in this world. When she got her head whacked off, the event pretty much bumped his mental compass off true north. That was when he turned into a grump and put up that big reward money."

"He was a grump before then," Blue Hand added. "The fact is just more noticeable these days."

Asa said, "It appears every building in Henrietta is made from oak and quite well done. But I can't say I understand why the place is even here. There are no major cities anywhere close. The nearest railroad must be Wichita, Kansas, which is nigh onto a hundred miles away. Dodge City's even further to the west. This Warwick fellow must be both rich and a politician to go full chisel on building a town here."

"He is not yet a politician," Blue Hand said. "But he is rich enough to tell the politicians what to do."

"Reckon that's even better, and it also saves having to act decent every few years to get elected." Cemetery John jumped down to the dusty street. "I'd like to be subjected to being rich someday. That way I could find out firsthand if it drives a man nutty or not."

"How could anyone tell." Asa hopped down from the hearse. The time had come to get on with business. He turned to Emil. "Where's the best hotel? I could use a bath and shave. Having to ride halfway here inside of a coffin causes a man to feel gamy."

The sheriff spit a wad of tobacco juice at a passing lizard, and decided not to ask why his bounty hunter friend had spent a few days in a coffin. "There ain't but one. The Henrietta. Cyrus Warwick owns it along with most every business in town. Saves putting up with competition."

"It is a good hotel," Blue Hand added. "Mr. Warwick demands that everyone visiting Henrietta be impressed. He is working to get the railroad to come here."

"That figures," Asa said. "And having people getting murdered hereabouts isn't good for business, which is why we're here. It wasn't just his daughter being killed. His fortune is at stake."

Emil nodded. "Reckon that about covers the situation. I'm going to fetch Carter Dark, the undertaker, to take care of the marshal's body, then send a telegram to Judge Parker, which will open the floodgates for even more hot water to flow this way. Enjoy getting spruced up. Drop by the office in a couple of hours and we'll go to supper. The sheriff's department has some expense money; might as well use it up while I've still got the job."

"Thanks, Emil," Cemetery John said. "Blue Hand and me will be proud to join you, as long as you're paying."

The sheriff took a hard bite on the stub of a dead cigar clenched between his teeth, sending a stream of brown tobacco juice flying into the sultry breeze. "Well, this just got spendy." Then he spun and strode off into the depths of his office.

Asa Cain lay back in the deep copper bathtub and luxuriated in the warm soapy water. He was also quite pleased that his shave had come off without so much as a nick. Calling in a barber late in the day was always chancy; a shaky, drunken tonsorial artist could often cost a man a considerable amount of blood.

Emil had been correct about Henrietta being a friendly town. Not only was the barber sober, the man at the dry goods store had carefully taken his measurements, then sent over a new suit of clothes and added the cost to the hotel bill. A decent meal would complete the picture of an ideal town to live in. Ideal, that is, if whoever was chopping off folks' heads was either caught or killed.

Asa had dismissed the theory of any monster, even a Sasquatch, which he believed might actually exist, as being responsible for the depredations. To his knowledge they had never killed anyone. The bounty hunter knew full well, however, the savage depths to which a human soul could sink. He had known of entire families being tortured and killed for pure entertainment. The people being decapitated here were almost certainly being killed for a monetary reason. Mammon, the biblical root of all evil, had to be the cause. By all accounts, Cyrus Warwick was the driving force behind the entire town. If the beheadings were to destroy him along with Henrietta, there would be a motive. Perhaps tomorrow it would be prudent to have a visit with Mr. Warwick, perhaps find out who his enemies were. Every man who accumulates wealth makes many enemies, of that there was no doubt.

Asa had reached over to take another sip of some of the best coffee he had tasted for a long while when a harsh rapping on the hotel door shook him from his thoughts.

"Yes, what is it?" the bounty hunter yelled. "I'm taking a bath."

"Sorry, sir," a voice answered through the heavy door. "I'm Jack Fry, the manager. Sheriff Quakenbush sent me to ask for you to come to his office right away. He said there's been another murder."

Asa sighed and muttered, "This place is

almost as bad as Texas."

Emil Quackenbush motioned to Asa when he came into the sheriff's office. "You got some soap suds there in your left ear."

"I was of the impression you wanted me to hurry."

"Nah." Emil shrugged dismissively. "Jack has a tendency to get worked up too easy. I just told him to tell you not to lollygag." He nodded to two men who were sitting humped over on a cot in the nearest jail cell. "The matter's under control. Shucks, we'll even have time for that supper I went and promised."

Asa said, "Who got murdered?"

Cemetery John, who was sitting in a rocking chair whittling on a stick of slippery elm, said, "They've got crooks here in Kansas that are a lot easier to catch than the ones we're subjected to in Texas. Those two darlings in the cell there came in the sheriff's office dragging the body of Carter Dark, the undertaker, demanding to be paid the reward money, claiming they'd killed the killer who's been chopping off folks' heads."

Emil snorted. "Now we're short a decent undertaker and I've got two idiots to hang, or at least I will once Judge Rimsdale gives 'em a fair trial."

From the cell one of the prisoners yelled, "That man had a big knife an' was walkin' down by the creek. He also was actin' mighty spooky. We ain't done nothin' but bring in that monster. You men are just cheatin' us outta our just reward."

Sheriff Quackenbush hollered, "Oh, pipe down or I'll hang you without a trial to stop your caterwauling. Carter was out gathering mint to put in coffins to cut down on the smell. And for your information, a pocket-knife ain't much of a weapon, sure no reason to shoot the man a dozen times."

"We want our reward money," the prisoner repeated in a slurred voice, confirming Asa's suspicions that the man was far from sober.

Emil snorted, stood up, went, and slammed shut the heavy oak door leading to the row of stone cells. "There's no rule I have to listen to 'em, just feed 'em and hang 'em." The sheriff's bushy red eyebrows lowered in thought. "I ain't never hung anyone before, but I guess there's nothing too dang complicated about the process."

"There's more to it than most think," Cemetery John said, sending a curl of wood flying. "If you don't give them a long drop and snap their necks good an' hard, they'll gurgle and dance around for a long while. That always upsets the womenfolk. On the other hand, if you drop 'em *too* far, that'll pop their heads right off their shoulders. Now *that* event generally upsets *everyone*."

Emil paled. "Yeah, I can imagine it would." He focused on Cemetery. "Since you're such an expert on neck-snappin', I'll appoint you to be the hangman. The job pays twenty-five dollars per neck."

"I'll stick to dealing with 'em after the fact," Cemetery John said. "I'll get fifty dollars each for burying them no matter what shape they're in or how badly folks are upset. Besides, you're fresh out of undertakers and it'll also do you good to learn a new skill, since you'll soon be out of work."

Emil snorted. "I'd prefer to leave being a hangman to men like George Maledon over in Fort Smith. Now there's someone who's spooky enough to scare a grizzly bear."

Asa spoke up. "How do you know for sure there even will be a hanging? The judge might go soft and just send them to prison for a few years."

"No chance of that," Emil said returning to his desk and taking a cigar from a box. "Carter Dark's married to Judge Rimsdale's youngest daughter. And from the last time I set eyes on her, she's either swallered a watermelon seed or expectn'. Now, due to those two idiots, Rimsdale will have to support both his daughter and a baby."

Asa's gaze turned pensive. "I'll help you knot the ropes."

ELEVEN

Dr. John Henry Holliday was having a most agreeable dream about the copper-haired love of his life, Lottie Deno. He had first encountered the lovely faro dealer in the dusty, squalid West Texas town of Fort Griffin and fallen madly in love with her.

Unfortunately, the comely lass, for some unknown reason, had not seen fit to return his heartfelt love. Lottie was always courteous to him, as she was to all of the men who placed their bets on her table. But Holliday had a plethora of genteel Southern manners along with an education in both the arts and sciences. Few of Lottie's customers could even read or write. Even fewer had bathed in months. He alone deserved more than simple courtesy from the lady.

Holliday had taken Lottie's apathetic attitude toward him as a challenge not to be denied. His goal was nothing less than to have her hand in marriage. A man who did not have long to live deserved to have a lovely wife to mourn his passing. Having her in his bed until that time came also seemed like an excellent idea.

Then some drunken lout of a soldier had ruined his courtship by pulling a knife on him, necessitating a quick killing of the man followed by even quicker departure from Fort Griffin. Many of the dead man's friends were determined to lynch him without delay.

A prostitute he lived with on occasion, Big Nose Kate, had helped Holliday escape the mob and been with him ever since. But it was the image of the lovely Lottie Deno that filled the dentist's mind's eye. Big Nose Kate was faithful and willing, but her looks were bad enough to stampede cattle.

Doc Holliday listened carefully to every rumor of Lottie's travels throughout the West. He often would pull up stakes and head off after his true love, Kate in tow, only to find the most beautiful lady gambler in the world had already departed.

Now, as he lay beneath a twinkling canopy of stars alongside the rippling waters of Boggy Creek in Oklahoma Territory, John Henry Holliday basked in the arms of Morpheus, dreaming only of Lottie Deno.

He could smell the wonderful enticing

aroma of her lilac perfume. In a swirl of white cloud his love came to him, beaming. With the softness of a velvet shadow, she melted into his open arms. Their lips met in an impassioned kiss. No longer wasted by disease, he scooped her into his strong arms and carried her to the waiting brass bed.

Then, suddenly, the aroma of lilacs was replaced by the pungent odor of a skunk.

Holliday felt a hand tugging at his watch pocket. Instantly he awoke, his eyes wide with shock and fear as he stared into the dark, deformed, and grizzled face that could only belong to a monster.

Before the startled dentist could muster even a yell to his friend for help, the hulking creature bolted upright, then quickly raised high a long metal blade that glistened yellow in the light of a full moon. Holliday managed to roll aside only scant seconds before the sharp steel edge slashed into the ground where his neck had been.

Before the monstrosity could make another chop, Holliday pulled the small derringer from his vest pocket and fired both small-caliber shells into the beast's belly.

A guttural scream of pain ripped the still night air followed by a distinct, "Damn it." Then, the huge apparition melted into the night as silently as a snake glides through wet grass.

"What the hell happened, Doc?" Wyatt Earp sat up, blinking sleep from his eyes.

"That monster the reward's out on paid us a visit. The thing's one big ugly sight and it stole my watch."

"But you *did* shoot it."

"A derringer isn't much of a weapon against something the size of whatever that was. I must have hurt it, though. I distinctly heard the thing say, 'Damn it.' "

Wyatt Earp pulled his revolver and stared into the shadowy darkness. "I've never heard tell of any monster that could cuss in English."

"This one sure as heck does. I wouldn't have been around to tell anyone if I'd been a second slower getting away from that sword or whatever it used to try and whack my head off with."

"You say it was mighty big." Earp squinted at a moving shadow and cocked the hammer on his Colt.

"Not huge, maybe no bigger than a good-sized man, but it was all deformed and stunk to high heaven."

"I noticed that part. Wonder why it smells like a skunk."

"I'm not even sure exactly what the thing

is, let alone why it stinks. But I think it's going to take a tolerable lot of killing."

Wyatt Earp relaxed when he realized the movement in the distant trees was only a flock of roosting wild turkeys. "I reckon that's why all that big bounty money's been put on its head."

Doc Holliday wiped a shaky hand across the back of his neck. He snorted, then grabbed up a bottle of Old Orchard and took a healthy drink. "I'd prefer not hearing the word 'head' for a spell."

"I'm going to build up the fire and boil us a pot of coffee. Reckon we've had all the sleep we're gonna get."

"Go right ahead, Wyatt. I'll stick with whiskey. Coffee makes my nerves edgy and I don't need that right now."

"I'd reckon not," Wyatt Earp said as he lowered the hammer on his Colt. "But it's one helluva lot better being nervous than dead."

Bright orange rays from a newborn sun were shooting through towering green trees when Doc Holliday and Wyatt Earp began studying the tracks the creature had let in the soft earth.

"There's no doubt about it," Holliday said. "These are moccasin prints sure as

God made little green apples. I've seen too many to be mistaken. Whatever it was that damn near chopped my head off last night and stole my watch is wearing moccasins."

"Then it looks like we have ourselves a monster that favors footwear along with cussing when it gets shot. I'll tell you, Doc, I'm for quitting this country. All the money in the world don't do you any good when you're pushing up daises."

"I *would* like my watch back. It was inscribed from my parents and given to me when I graduated from dental school."

Wyatt Earp motioned to a few dark spots of dried blood on the grass. "The question is how bad hurt do we think he really is. If you got lucky enough to plug something vital, we might not only get your watch back, but earn us one nice pie of boodle to boot."

Doc Holliday started to answer when, from a jumble of rocks only a few hundred feet upstream, a terrifying scream of rage ripped the sultry air.

"I'd say it sounds rather healthy," Wyatt said.

"There's a nice clock on the wall of that saloon back in Dodge City to tell time by," Doc Holliday said. "Besides, I'm out of whiskey."

Wyatt Earp said, "Then let's saddle up and ride. Being a marshal or a gambler might not pay a lot, but it's a sight safer work than being a bounty hunter."

Doc Holliday grabbed up his saddle and turned to his roan. "And it's indoor work that doesn't involve heavy lifting."

Scant minutes later, they were gone.

The pain deep in his belly was familiar as an old friend. He could never remember when he did not hurt. As a child there had been the beatings. Then had come the fire. All had brought excruciating pain. And he always had recovered. It only took time.

He scooped up a handful of mud from the creek bed and gingerly tapped some into each of the two small holes in his stomach. The lead slugs were deep inside, but his body would heal around them. He *always* healed.

With a grunt he stood, picking up his most prized possession as he did so. The jagged teeth of the ice saw sparkled in the sunlight like a promise. He would go back to his home to rest and heal. Once he had recovered, the beautiful steel saw blade could once again be employed to help him with his quest.

Staying to the shadows and high rocks to

keep from being tracked, he disappeared into the dark canopy of forest that enshrouded the rugged canyons of Boggy Creek.

TWELVE

"I'm here to tell you, this is the best steak I've stuck a fork into for a coon's age," Cemetery John said gleefully. "And the corn on the cob, string beans, mashed potatoes and gravy's not bad either."

Emil gave a snort. "Remember to save room for some dessert. A big slice of peach cobbler all covered with sweet cream will give you the satisfaction of personally bankrupting my expense money."

Cemetery John grinned. "I *do* like to be remembered."

"The steaks are aged in red wine, then slowly fried in butter with many cloves of garlic," Blue Hand said as he cut another bite. "Cyrus Warwick says this is the best way to cook them."

Emil nodded. "The man might be meaner than a peeled rattler and nuttier than an outhouse rat, but I have to admit he knows his grub."

"That comes along with being wealthy," Asa Cain said. "No one wants to go to the trouble of getting rich and not enjoy letting others know they've got more money than you do. Eating fancy's one way to show it off."

Blue Hand said, "The Indian People would say that a full belly is enough." He hesitated. "But this *is* a very good steak."

Asa asked the sheriff, "How close is Warwick to getting the railroad to run tracks up here? Another cattle town closer to Texas might be an idea that will work."

Emil leaned back, his brow furrowed in thought. "The Indian Territory's the problem. That's federal jurisdiction. Washington politicians cost more to pay off than state or local ones. And being so far away, it takes time to bribe 'em. But my guess is Cyrus will get the job done if his money lasts. The man holds on to a plan like a snapping turtle, I'll say that much for him."

"Where do you think he got his money?" Asa asked softly. They were sitting at a distant table and the hotel restaurant was not crowded, but it paid to be cautious. "No man gets wealthy without stepping on a lot of toes."

Emil scanned the room before speaking. Even though he would soon be out of a job, he wanted to stay around as sheriff long enough to claim at least a portion of the reward money. "That's a mystery. Everyone has their own ideas, but no one knows for sure. The most persistent rumor is that he was a carpetbagger after the war, cleaned out a lot of families. Another is that he went to California in the gold rush and made a rich strike. The only real facts are, he's got enough money to buy nearly anything but his way into Heaven."

Cemetery John spread butter over his third ear of sweet corn. "I'd prefer to have all of the rich people go to Heaven. That way they won't be a bother to me an' my friends later on."

Blue Hand cocked his head in thought. "The white men have different ideas what happens to a person's spirit when they die than do The People. When an Indian passes into the Great Beyond, they can fight new battles, take many wives, and never come home from a hunt with no meat for the squaws to cook. I do not care to spend an eternity floating around on a cloud playing a harp or being roasted in an oven while being jabbed with a pitchfork."

Asa said, "There we agree. I was raised for some years by the Comanche after they raided our wagon train. Every religion has their own ideas about what happens to a person's soul. The Indians just may be right."

Emil finished off his last tidbit of steak, then leaned back in his chair. "The problem with all of this philosophy is that a person's gotta die to find out who's right and who's wrong. I reckon we'll all find out soon enough. What's concerning me is the here and now and what we can do to keep the influx of bounty-hunting drunken idiots from killing more folks than the person doing all the head-whacking."

Asa gave the sheriff a thin smile. "Then you agree it's no monster."

"Depends on what your definition of a monster is. I don't think we're dealing with some ten-foot-tall, hairy sassy-squatch. But if it's a man, I'd say as cunning as he is, he's more of an animal than anyone I've ever run across before."

"There are some men who have no soul," Blue Hand said. He thought back on Bertha Skillicorn and how she and her husband had so abused the lovely Sunflower. "And some women too."

"That's a true fact," Cemetery John said. "But we need to get to focusing here on what's really important, like all that reward money we'll get when we bring in the murderer of Mr. Warwick's daughter."

Blue Hand said, "I think Mr. Cemetery is correct. The sheriff and I will be out of a job soon. Five thousand dollars for each of us will be helpful."

Now even the Indians are whittling down my marrying money, Cemetery John thought as his buoyant mood sank along with the dying sun. But he brightened when he realized at least *some* of the citizens of Wolf Springs had to have the decency to eventually croak and allow him to bury them. No town was *that* healthy of a place to live in.

Asa Cain took a sip of iced tea from a sweaty glass. Briefly, he wondered how far Cyrus Warwick had to freight ice from, but he had to admit it helped make Henrietta more desirable no matter the cost. "What Cemetery John means is that we need a plan. Every criminal has their own way of going about business. They also usually aren't smart enough to change either. What we need to do is go over each of these killings, where they happened, the time of day, day of the week, everything we know for a fact and start adding up the information."

The sheriff gave a snort. "I've got all of that over in the office. All I can tell you for certain is, adding in Marshal Talbot, there's a solid nine dead."

"And we have yet to find any of their heads," Blue Hand said.

Asa Cain clucked his tongue, a trait of his whenever he was nervous or perplexed. "Now *there* is a clue, if we can only figure out what it means. No murderers I've dealt with take only the victim's head." He hesitated. "Except bounty hunters whenever it's inconvenient to bring in the entire outlaw."

"That's a fact," Emil said with a nod. "I've known a lot of rewards paid out on just a head. They're generally fairly easy to recognize, especially if you've got a wanted poster to compare it to. You know, that might explain why those folks weren't robbed too."

"Ain't this a fine kettle of fish," Cemetery John said with a snort. "Now we've got bounty hunters after bounty hunters. Things like this don't happen in Texas. Not generally anyway."

Asa said, "If there is a bounty hunter out there collecting money for each head he brings in, somebody's got to be paying him. Once we figure out who that is, we'll be on our way to catching the killer."

"Or killers," Blue Hand said. "Could there not be more than one man who is cutting off people's heads? There are four of us, and we are all now bounty hunters."

"That kettle of fish Cemetery John mentioned just got more rotten," Emil said. "But I'll have to admit this theory makes more sense than anything that's come to mind up to now." He gave a smile. "If there is someone out there who paid a bounty for Henrietta Warwick's head, and we come up with 'em, then I can hang 'em. Shucks, then I might even be able to keep my sheriff's job. I'd like that for some reason."

"The salary is one hundred dollars a month," Blue Hand said. "That is the reason."

Emil Quackenbush started to say something when a gruff voice from the front of the restaurant boomed, "There's an Injun an' a nigger infestin' this place. If they don't slink out of here like scared dogs, my boys an' me is gonna have to clean this mess up."

The sheriff spun around in his chair to see three burly, unkempt men who were armed to the teeth with bandoliers of ammunition crossing their chests. They all wore two pistols each along with packing huge bowie knives. They were also carrying Winchester rifles cradled in the crooks of their arms. From the way they listed from side to side as if they were on a ship in rough water, it was obvious they were drunk out of their minds.

"You boys settle down now," Emil said,

keeping from wincing when he saw Asa's hand slide beneath the table and Cemetery John sidle toward his big ten-gauge shotgun leaning on the wall in back of his chair. "These men are deputies and my friends. Keep your mouths shut and have some supper and there won't be any trouble."

"The only thing worse than niggers an' Injuns are those white trash that associate with 'em." The man in the middle spit. "Brother Wesley, it looks like we'd do this place a favor if'n we plain up and shot the lot."

Asa gave a low groan. His experiences with people named Wesley hadn't turned out well. Diplomacy was, however, worth a try. "You gentlemen have been asked real nice by the sheriff here to set down and behave yourselves. That would be advice worth following."

The man who had been doing all of the talking gave a snort, as he gave a drunken reach for his pistol. "We don't listen to no advice from nigger lovers."

"Ah, shit," Emil said as he spun and drew. He fanned the hammer on his Colt sending five hot slugs of lead to join those fired by Asa and Blue Hand. Cemetery John's big shotgun put a period to the moment when two blasts of the ten-gauge blew two of the men through the front window and onto the boardwalk.

Asa reloaded his .36-caliber Whitney Eagle before standing to check the carnage. He knew all too well a man could soak up a lethal dose of lead and still be able to shoot a gun.

"Is everyone okay?" the sheriff asked, keeping his eyes on the one man who lay sprawled out in front of the broken window.

"No one except the drunk white men were hurt," Blue Hand said. "They were also stupid. They refused to listen to Asa Cain's good advice."

"They were from Arkansas most likely," Cemetery John said, poking two fresh shells into his double-barrel and snapping shut the breech. "Folks from there are not known for being overly smart."

A groan from in front of the restaurant caused Emil to sidle over to the door and carefully peer out. Since they'd taken a full charge of buckshot square in the middle, he didn't expect either of the two ruffians to be in any shape to make noise. He gave a sigh when he found out what had happened.

"What is it?" Asa and Blue Hand asked at the same time.

Emil shook his head sadly and swung the door open wide. "A case of bad timing for sure. Looks like Judge Rimsdale and Cyrus Warwick decided to come to supper just in time to get hit by some of the lead we were forced to fire at those three idiots."

It was Blue Hand's turn to shake his head. "My grandfather told me to stay on the reservation. My grandfather was right."

THIRTEEN

Judge Isaac Charles Parker sat behind his ornate oak desk running a hand through his long, graying beard while silently regarding his ominous assistant, George Maledon.

The judge had never felt comfortable in the man's presence, yet the hangman was a necessity to help clean out the outlaw element in his jurisdiction as Federal Western District Judge for Arkansas. What was most disturbing was the way Maledon relished hanging people. The thin man's eyes actually seemed to glow with satisfaction when the trap would drop and the prisoner's neck snapped with a dull popping sound that put a sick feeling in most people's bellies, including his own.

"You sent for me, sir," the hangman asked, still standing politely.

"Take a seat, Mr. Maledon." Even in private the judge insisted on a show of propriety. "We have business to discuss, bad business I'm afraid."

"I have six new ropes already knotted and stretched that can be used today." George Maledon scooted the chair back and seated himself across from Parker. "I'm using bear grease to see if it makes the noose slide easier than the lard I've used up until now."

"The job is not here." The judge leaned back and tamped tobacco into his dead pipe. He noted Maledon's dark, deep-set eyes seemed to grow dim. "I'm afraid it will entail a bit of travel."

"How many do I have to hang?"

"Two souls need to be sent back to their maker in Henrietta, over near the Oklahoma Territory. It seems they killed the local undertaker in the drunken belief that he was the murderer who has been cutting off people's heads. The local sheriff, a fellow by the name of Emil Quackenbush, has no experience conducting a hanging and sent a telegraph asking for assistance in the matter."

"Only two necks to snap," Maledon muttered sadly, then brightened. "That task should only take me a day, maybe two. Then I can be back in time to drop Bood Crumpton on his date. That man killed a woman. No man who does a thing like that deserves to live any longer than necessary."

Judge Parker wondered when he would be forced to hire a hangman to hang George Maledon. "Mr. Crumpton will wait for your services."

"Thank you, sir. When do you wish me to go to Henrietta?"

"The sheriff said the trial will be held while you are on your way. I'll make arrangements for you to leave the day after tomorrow. That will give me time to find a pair of deputies to accompany you."

George Maledon was puzzled. "The ride is not a long one, I'll be fine by myself."

"No, Mr. Maledon, I will not allow it. There is a bloodthirsty killer at large in the territory south of Henrietta. I have already lost one deputy in the area. I will not make the mistake of sending another lone officer out there again. You will travel with armed guards and that is final."

"Yes, sir." Maledon lowered his dark bushy eyebrows. "Then Bob Talbot's been found."

"His body was twenty feet up in a tree. They have not yet located his head."

The hangman swallowed hard. "Are you sure two deputies will be sufficient?"

FOURTEEN

Dr. Vernon Sedgemiller came out of the treatment room wiping blood from his hands onto a damp white washcloth. He gave a snorting wheeze, then settled his bulk into a chair before saying a word to any of the worried men who were awaiting his findings.

"Come on, Doc," Sheriff Quackenbush growled. "We're sort of anxious to find out how Cyrus Warwick and the judge are, just in case you were wondering why we're all standing here wearing concerned looks."

"Patience, Mr. Quackenbush," Doctor Sedgemiller said after catching his breath. The last time the physician had weighed himself on the scales down at the feed store, he was nearly four hundred pounds. And he had gained quite a bit since then. Any physical exertion, even speaking, was an effort. "I am now ready to render my diagnosis."

"What we *really* want to know is whether

or not they're going to live or die," Emil said biting hard on his cigar. "You can save your breath on all of the details."

Dr. Sedgemiller grunted. "A pragmatic approach *is* necessary to being a lawman, I suppose." He noticed the blank look on the sheriff's face and said, "Both men were hit by at least two pieces of buckshot, neither seriously. Mr. Warwick was struck in the arm and side. The judge caught his in the gluteus maximus. Most of the blood came from the men who were blown through the window and from cuts received from flying glass. I've sutured their wounds and sedated them. Both will recover quite nicely . . . if they don't get an infection and die."

Cemetery John shuffled his feet nervously. "I'm plain sorry it *was* my buckshot that did all the damage, but it was an accident. Shotguns aren't much on precision."

Dr. Sedgemiller leaned back in his chair. "Considering the circumstances, I believe the judge and Mr. Warwick will forgo any *legal* charges. I must say, however, that before the laudanum took effect, they were not inclined to being overly charitable."

Blue Hand cocked his head. "I do not understand. Where did Judge Rimsdale get shot?"

Asa Cain said, "Let's just say he won't be

sitting at the bench for a while; he'll be standing behind it."

"Cemetery John shot him in the ass, for Pete's sake," Emil grumbled. "I don't know why a lot of folks try and talk things into the ground using words big enough to choke a buffalo."

Dr. Sedgemiller tossed the bloody washcloth into a corner, and fished a cigar from his vest pocket. He had been acquainted with Sheriff Quackenbush long enough to know any attempt at diplomacy would be a wasted effort. "Since my patients are going to recover, I believe it's time to focus on other matters."

"We already got those three toughs who pulled guns on us dragged over to Carter Dark's old undertaking parlor," Emil said. "And I've telegraphed Judge Parker to send a hangman for the two idiots who killed Dark. I'd reckon I'm plenty focused."

Asa Cain suppressed a wince at the sheriff's words. "You asked Parker to send George Maledon here to conduct a hanging?"

"That was Cemetery John's idea," Emil said with a satisfied nod. "He convinced me the procedure was more technical than I'd figured on. Besides, the federal government ain't charging for his services, can't see any downside there."

"Gentlemen," Dr. Sedgemiller said after gathering breath from his last speech, "the matter I was referring to was the apprehension of the killer who has been cutting off people's heads. Cyrus Warwick's darling daughter being murdered was the cause of him posting that huge reward. The shootings and such here in town are merely incidental to the main fact that when the killer is caught and the reward paid, Henrietta will return to being the same quiet, peaceful place it used to be."

"Catching the head-whacker would be easier if we didn't have idiots being a distraction by shooting at us and other innocent folks," the sheriff said. "But you can tell Cyrus when he finishes his nap that we are doing our best."

"I'll be sure to do that," the doctor said. "He'll be *very* relieved."

"Now that no one important's been killed," Cemetery John said, "I suggest we return to the hotel and finish our supper. I never did get to that peach cobbler and sweet cream."

Sedgemiller looked up, a rare smile crossed his face. "Is that cobbler one of Dora May's big thick ones with the crispy biscuit crust that's laced with a lot of cinnamon sugar?"

"Sure is," Emil said. "And it came out of the oven not long before the fracas hit."

"Then I'll join you." The doctor actually sprang to his feet. "And since this entire affair was a direct result of lawlessness, I'm going to let Sheriff Quackenbush pay the bill."

"Sure, come along," Emil grumbled. "I've got nearly an entire dollar left in my expense account. You might as well go ahead and finish off that whole full pan of cobbler."

Dr. Sedgemiller brushed past the sheriff on his way out the door. "Thank you for the kind offer. I'll do just that." Then he bolted into the sultry night.

Asa Cain shot a hard glare across the table at Doc Holliday. "You mean to set there and tell us that a monster stole your pocket watch?"

"I gave you the facts of the matter," Holliday replied. "Wyatt and I came by as a courtesy to let you know we are leaving this country and to give you my address in the chance someone gets lucky enough to kill that thing out there and recovers my watch. It has sentimental value as it was presented to me upon my graduation from dental college."

Dr. Sedgemiller looked up from the remains of his peach cobbler. "May I ask where you studied, sir?"

Holliday adjusted his cravat and ran the back of a hand across his flowing brown moustache. "Baltimore, Maryland. I graduated with honors, I might add."

"Ah," Sedgemiller said. "An Eastern education is a most excellent experience, is it not? I also attended both college and medical school there, only my degree came from Harvard."

Doc Holliday hesitated a moment, remembering back to the good times and what might have been. "Those were our salad years, were they not, Doctor?"

Sedgemiller's eyes widened in surprise. "I see you are also a fan of the Bard. Shakespeare was my second love outside of medicine."

Emil Quackenbush tapped his fork hard on the tabletop. When two overeducated people started yammering, they could go on for hours about nothing. Whoever this Bard fellow and Shakespeare were, and no matter what they were good at, it had totally nothing to do with the matters at hand.

"You say you got a good look at this man who stole your watch and tried to chop off your head with some kind of sword," the

131

sheriff said to Holliday. "Obviously, he was better at stealing gold watches than whacking off heads."

Wyatt Earp said, "I'd say the two slugs Doc put into its belly might have put off his aim."

"You *shot* him!" Emil barked. "Now there's a piece of information I'd like to have had right off."

"I don't think I did a lot of damage," Doc Holliday said with a shrug as he displayed a small derringer pistol. "These things are more of a discouragement than a solution. But often that's all it takes to settle down some sorehead who's lost his bundle playing faro."

Asa Cain's eyes widened slightly. The gun in the dentist's hand had appeared as if by magic. Seldom had he seen anyone faster. The thin consumptive was quick as a rattlesnake's strike, and just as deadly, a fact to take note of.

"Doc is a cardsharp," Wyatt Earp said with a wry grin. "He doesn't cheat; he's just mighty good at any card game you can name."

Emil Quackenbush gave a sigh and lowered his red bushy eyebrows. "You put two slugs into twenty thousand dollars worth of outlaw and now you're heading for Dodge

City before knowing if those bullets took or not. I'd reckon you *are* plenty good at cards to go away and leave a chance for money like that."

Doc Holliday replaced the derringer into his vest, leaned back, and took a puff on his long nine cigar. "I got a mighty close look at that man, if it was a man. He is more of an abomination, a monstrosity, than a human being. I can say this for certain; he's big, deformed, and strong as an ox. Why the smell of skunk about him, I can't even guess, but I know for a fact I didn't give him a fatal wound and my leaving here is just good sense. That thing will be back and keep right on killing. I plan on being in a nice cozy saloon playing cards and drinking whiskey when he does."

"I don't envy your job, Sheriff," Wyatt Earp said to Emil. "I've been a marshal long enough to know all the grief that reward money will cause."

Cemetery John nodded to the door. "We've got four bodies at the undertaker's, including the undertaker himself, along with two idiots in the jail waiting to get hung." He forked his cobbler. "And the day ain't even over yet."

Wyatt Earp motioned with a finger to the cobbler. "That looks plenty good. Is it?"

Cemetery John grinned. "I've never tasted finer. The peaches are fresh and there's lot of cinnamon for flavor."

Earp motioned for the waiter. "Then I'll have a piece before we head out. It's a far ride to Dodge."

Dr. Sedgemiller began choking, and had to clear his throat with a swallow of milk. He hated to have the supply of wonderful cobbler being depleted. If he had to witness the disaster, some conversation with an educated man would make the event easier to take. He looked across the table to Doc Holliday. "Why don't you order a piece? The sheriff is buying. Then we can talk about Shakespeare. I think *The Merchant of Venice* to be his best work. I would like to hear your opinion."

"I'd like that. Since becoming stricken with tuberculosis, I seldom have much of an appetite. Being from Georgia, however, I cannot resist a really good peach cobbler. And I relish the chance to talk about the Bard. *A Midsummer Night's Dream* is my personal favorite, but all of his works are simply wonderful."

Sheriff Quackenbush stood. "Well, I'm going to go pay out every dime of my expense money, then I reckon I'll check about town to see if anyone new's been shot or killed. I can understand it when folks are acting up; it's those Bards and Shakespeare people that I can't figure."

"I'll join you," Blue Hand said.

"Count me in too," Cemetery John said.

Asa Cain nodded at Wyatt Earp. "How about we go along with them to keep 'em out of trouble?"

"I can pass on the cobbler," Earp said. "Considering Shakespeare's involved."

A few moments later, the only two men in the town of Henrietta with doctorate degrees were quoting Shakespeare, eating peach cobbler, and sipping Old Orchard Whiskey. They barely noticed they were the only customers left in the restaurant.

FIFTEEN

Going Snake bent low to enter the tepee of the chief of the Osage. He was far taller and more muscular than were most Indians. Once inside, he went and took his proper place beside Kills Eagles. Facing them from across the small fire in the center sat all six members of the tribal council. The matter to be discussed was a grave one.

"First we must smoke," Kills Eagles said. He took a small faggot from the fire and lit the long pipe that was adorned with beads and animal claws. After he had taken a few long puffs, the pipe was passed to Going Snake, who, after a while, passed it to one of the elders. Two hours would pass before the chief deemed the time proper to proceed with business. To the Osage, any subject that affected The People was never to be hurried into. The more serious the problem, the longer they would smoke and ponder their words before speaking.

"There has been a white-eyes lawman killed on our lands," Kills Eagles said gravely. "This is not a good thing."

Swift Horse, the oldest of the counsel of elders, said, "None of The People killed him. He was a white-eyes. I do not see much of a problem here."

Going Snake said, "A few less white men *is* a good thing."

Kills Eagles took a long puff on the pipe. "But the man was not a usual white man. He was a lawman from Arkansas. When one of them is killed, the Army might be called to stop these killings."

"That would not be a good thing," Laughing Coyote said. "The white man's army has killed many of The People for no reason. Having a government man rubbed out on our lands would be a really good reason for them to come out here."

Buffalo Hair spoke. "If the tribe could learn who is killing the white-eyes and turn them in, the Army would not come."

"That would be a good thing," Kills Eagles said.

"But we do not know who or what is cutting off the heads of the white-eyes," Going Snake said. "It might be an evil spirit that has become angered by the white men. An angry spirit must be appeased before it will stop."

Swift Horse said, "I think we should build a sweat lodge. Then we could go there and sweat while smoking some peyote. That is the only way to communicate with spirits, even the evil ones."

Going Snake nodded. "Swift Horse is right. We should ask the spirits who is killing the white-eyes. If we could convince them this is a bad thing for The People, they will stop."

Kills Eagles shook his head. "The white men do not believe in but two spirits, one good, one bad. Neither of their spirits will even leave their tepees and come to this world. I think a dead body would carry more weight with the white men than advice from even some really decent spirits."

Many Dogs, the youngest of the council, spoke. "It would be a good thing if the body we brought in was the person who is actually cutting off heads. If the white-eyes keep being killed, the Army will still come."

"You are wise, Many Dogs," Kills Eagles said. "The People must find who is killing the white men and either rub them out or turn them over to the sheriff."

"The sheriff of Henrietta is a good man," Many Dogs said. "He has hired one of The

People as his deputy. I think we could trust him."

Swift Horse said, "We have no one to turn over to him. Perhaps after we have had our sweat and smoked our peyote, the spirits will guide us to whoever is doing the killings."

Kills Eagles nodded. "We must do what is necessary to keep the Army from coming to our lands. I will order a sweat lodge to be built and we will smoke peyote. I will also have our two best scouts, Running Bear and Little Badger, go to where the lawman was rubbed out. Perhaps they can find some tracks to follow. They are quite good at tracking."

Going Snake quickly added, "If we are dealing with an angry spirit, there will be no tracks to follow. I think Swift Horse is right. We should do nothing until we have had our sweat."

Buffalo Hair said, "What is important is for The People to turn over to the sheriff who is killing the white-eyes. If it turns out to be a bad spirit, they will not believe us. I agree that we should send our trackers. A human person is what it will take to convince the Army not to come to our lands."

Many Dogs passed the pipe to Swift Horse and said, "We must have someone for the sheriff to hang. It will take that to convince the white-eyes."

"Perhaps if an evil spirit is the cause of our trouble," Kills Eagles said, "when we have made our peace with it, and no more heads will be taken, a troublesome white man can be found for the sheriff to hang. That should settle the matter."

"He would need to be dead first," Buffalo Hair said. "All white men talk too much, but if the killings were stopped, I think the Army would not come."

The chief took the pipe, tapped out the ash onto the fire, and laid it against the side of the tepee. This was a signal that the tribal council was over. "Tomorrow we will begin to build a sweat lodge. At first light, Little Badger and Running Bear will go and look for tracks. The killer of the white-eyes lawman and the others must be stopped. It is decided."

"We are agreed," Swift Horse said as the eldest member.

"So it shall be done," Going Snake said. "The council has spoken."

Late that night, when darkness lay heavy and inky over the Osage Nation, a lone Indian slipped silently from his tepee. Moving like a shadow, Going Snake made his way from the village without being noticed by even the most watchful of dogs. When he reached the rippling waters of Boggy Creek, he took a moment to drink and examine the contents of the buffalo-skin bag that was draped over his shoulder. Convinced all was in order, the shaman took a little-used trail that cut across a limestone cliff before leading into a dense copse of trees. Moments later, the Osage medicine man blended into the somber forest and disappeared into the still night.

SIXTEEN

Asa Cain leaned back in a rocking chair across the desk from where Emil Quackenbush sat smoking a cigar. He laced his fingers behind his head and said, "Two whole days without so much as a dogfight breaking out is a nice turn of events. I'm beginning to think that maybe those slugs Doc Holliday put in our head-whacker went and took after all. Blood poisoning doesn't always need much of an excuse to do someone in."

Cemetery John took a blackened pot of coffee from the potbelly stove and poured himself a cup. "It would be a shame to have a twenty-thousand-dollar outlaw just lay around and decompose."

The sheriff said, "There's a passel of bounty hunters out there looking the country over. My problem's knowing when and if they bring in the real killer. Cyrus won't appreciate paying out all that money for a worthless body."

"I expect not," Asa said. "But from the description Holliday gave, the killer shouldn't be *that* difficult to identify."

"The break's been a good one." Cemetery John frowned at the palm of his left hand. "Dang, I've got myself a blister from all of that grave-digging."

Emil took a long puff on his cigar and blew a smoke ring toward the ceiling of his office. "Those bodies were getting too gamy to delay burying them any longer. The last two graves you dug were out of optimism on your part. Judge Rimsdale isn't going to hold their trial until this afternoon. I've learned never to try and guess what the law'll do. He might up an' let 'em go."

"I'm going to bet he'll fill those holes," Cemetery John said. He took a swig of coffee, then turned to the sheriff. "I would appreciate it if you'd ask the judge to pay me for my undertaking services. Since His Honor is taking his meals in a standing position due to a couple of stray buckshot from my shotgun, he might be more favorable disposed toward you than me if I went and asked him for money."

The sheriff gave a chuckle. "The judge is still sore about that matter in more ways than one. I'll get your money before the trial starts." He added seriously, "Cyrus Warwick's up an' about. He's plenty upset that we haven't caught his daughter's killer after all this time."

Asa Cain looked at the coffeepot and grimaced. "I could go for a decent cup. Is this pot any better than what Emil usually boils up?"

Cemetery John eyed his cup. "There's nothing floating around in it that doesn't look natural. Tastes like it's strong enough to grow hair on a rock."

"Then I'll have a cup," Asa said as he stood and went to the stove. "Weak coffee's not worth the bother."

"We have a swamper in the saloon back in Wolf Springs by the name of Fridley Newlin," Cemetery John explained. "That fellow boils up a brew that'll get a body's attention. Reckon Asa's been kinda spoiled when it comes to coffee."

The sheriff gave a sigh and leaned back. "Cyrus Warwick is not a man with a lot of patience. . . ." The stub of cigar dropped from his mouth when he saw who was standing in the open doorway.

"For once, Sheriff Quackenbush," Cyrus Warwick said as he limped inside, "you are absolutely correct. Not only has my daughter been brutally murdered, but many good citizens of Henrietta — my town — have also been killed. I'm not certain that sitting around drinking coffee is the manner in which crimes of this sort are usually solved, or am I mistaken to believe the law must actually go out and pursue the evildoers?"

"Any manhunt requires a direction," Asa Cain said. He studied the tall, slender, silver-haired man with dark deep-set eyes that seemed to continually dart about the room. The mogul of Henrietta, Kansas, had the appearance of a man whose face would crack if he ever smiled. Warwick was nattily dressed, clean-shaven, and sporting manicured fingernails, and Asa guessed him to be around fifty years of age. "We have been studying the situation."

Cyrus Warwick regarded him coldly. "And you, sir, are?"

"I'm Asa Cain. Cemetery John and I came here from Wolf Springs, Texas, at the behest of Sheriff Quackenbush."

"Ah, yes." Warwick's voice came across as a hiss. "The famous bounty hunter who has supposedly killed over a hundred people for money, including his own mother. With a man of your reputation, I am surprised to not be paying the bounty money out instead of wondering why you are standing around drinking coffee in the sheriff's office."

Asa had dealt with enough politicians and wealthy men not to allow himself to become angry with Cyrus Warwick's words. Men like him looked upon the rest of the world as existing only to serve them and their wishes. All they respected were results or force. "There is a map of Henrietta and the surrounding area on the wall." Asa waved a hand toward it. "The pins you see placed south of town indicate where all of the decapitated bodies have been found — the ones we know of anyway. I believe there are some men who simply came up missing with no one being certain of the exact area they disappeared in."

Cyrus Warwick walked stiffly over to the map. Even though he was in pain, he would never allow himself to show it. Any weakness was an invitation for incursion onto his domain, something to avoid at all cost. "I am impressed. All of the killings have occurred within the relatively small area of a couple of square miles."

"And all are along or near Boggy Creek," Emil Quackenbush said.

"Every killer has a home and every animal has its lair," Asa said with a sweep of his hand. "Now that we know about where that is, we can focus on the area. The problem is, all of the murders, for some strange

146

reason, have occurred only on the night of a full moon. The next one of those isn't due for about another month."

"My dear sir," Cyrus Warwick said. "I am not inclined to wait around and do nothing until the Monster of the Osage murders any more citizens. Might I suggest you scour the area until you find the man — or beast? Then simply kill him, collect your money, and return to Texas. That *is* why you are here, is it not?"

Cemetery John spoke up. "A bounty hunter has to be plenty certain just who he goes out and puts holes in. If you shoot the wrong man, generally you get hung. Now there's an incentive to pay attention to your job."

"Ah, yes." Warwick turned to glare at the undertaker. "I am painfully aware of how careful *you* are when it comes to using guns."

"Well, I'm powerful sorry about that, but there were three men shooting at me at the time, and it *was* an accident you got hit."

"Mr. Warwick," Emil Quackenbush said. "I'm sure you are aware there's a couple of idiots going to be tried this afternoon for plugging Carter Dark over a dozen times, then trying to sell his dead body to me for the reward money. What Asa and Cemetery

John are telling you is that we've got to know for sure who's doing all the killings before we go to shooting at him. We don't need any more mistakes along that line."

Cyrus Warwick turned to the map. After a long moment he said, "Gentlemen, the town of Henrietta, Kansas, is destined to become a major center of commerce. It will, once the railroad arrives, outstrip Dodge City, Wichita, and Abilene as cattle-shipping destinations. Under my stewardship, the town will grow to be even larger than St. Louis, Missouri. This is the legacy I owe to the memory of my slain daughter. I cannot and will not allow the actions of a madman or a beast to delay the course of events. As do all men of vision, I must seize the bull by the horns and do what must be done."

Asa Cain lowered an eyebrow. "May I ask what that might be?"

Cyrus Warwick snorted. "I am going to give a brand-new Winchester rifle, a box of ammunition, along with a twenty-dollar gold piece to any and every man who agrees to go into the area of Boggy Creek and kill whatever is hindering development of my town."

"Don't do that, sir," Emil shouted, bolting to his feet. "The idiots you hire will shoot everyone they see along with each other."

"There will be so many killings going on," Cemetery John said, "we might never actually know if the man who whacked off your daughter's head is one of the bodies that'll get hauled in or not. And besides, I've already got a blister from grave-diggin'."

"When the decapitations stop, I will know the problem is over." Cyrus Warwick took a small glass bottle of white powder from his vest pocket. He poured a line in the palm of his right hand and inhaled it, then repeated the process. "I make the rules here. Do not forget that fact."

"No, sir," Emil said. "But what you're planning is a bloody mistake."

Cyrus Warwick sniffed twice, took one last look at the map before turning and limping away. "Henrietta is *my* damn town," he muttered before slamming the door behind him.

"Charming fellow," Cemetery John said taking a drink of his now tepid coffee. "He's the kind of person an undertaker enjoys having run a town; they're always mighty good for business."

Asa Cain clucked his tongue. "When a man gets so hooked on opiates he uses it in public, he's bucking the tiger in a losing game."

"I've observed," the sheriff said, "that when some folks get rich, they set out to kill themselves with bad habits. I reckon being poor ain't so bad after all."

Cemetery John took a cigar from his pocket, bit the end off, and lit it with a lucifer. "I've never developed any bad habits myself. Leastwise, none that I want to give up. But it would be an experience having the money to subject myself to temptation. That was the reason Asa an' I came here in the first place."

"If I recall correctly," Asa said, "visiting Henrietta wasn't my idea."

"Now don't go being a grump," Cemetery John said. "That big reward money's still waiting to be paid. Let's get our heads together and work on a plan to get our hands on it before others less deserving do."

Emil Quackenbush went back to his chair and slumped into it. "Blue Hand is in back watching over our lovelies, who aren't going to get tried for a couple of more hours. Let's fetch him and see if he's got any better ideas to work with than we seem to have."

"I hope he does," Asa said. "Because if we don't get that head-whacker right soon, the country hereabouts is going to be subjected to a bloodbath they'll be reading about in London and Paris."

"I was in Paris once." Emil stood and headed for the jail cells. "Can't say much for the town, but then I've never cared much for that part of Texas."

SEVENTEEN

Judge Thomas Terry Rimsdale stood rigidly behind the bench and whacked his wooden gavel three times. He gave a sharp glare at Cemetery John, who sat behind the handcuffed prisoners with a shotgun in his lap, then went on with the proceedings. The sooner this was over the better.

"The district court for the town of Henrietta, County of Warwick, State of Kansas, is now in session." Rimsdale again rapped his gavel. "Be seated and the prosecution may begin with the people's case against one Mallet Simpson and Orville McCutcheon on the charge of murder in the first degree of our undertaker, Carter Dark."

"Your Honor," Sim Eby said. He was the owner of both of Henrietta's saloons, the Purple Sage and Drover's Rest. During the war, Eby had been assigned as a courier to the adjutant general's office, which, Cyrus Warwick determined, gave him the qualifications to act as a defense lawyer. "I have not yet pled my clients."

Judge Rimsdale grumbled, "They can plead all they want after I sentence 'em. Proceed with the people's case, Mr. Warwick."

Cemetery John whispered in Emil Quackenbush's ear, "See, I told you I knew what I was doing when I went ahead and dug those two extra graves."

"There will be order in this court!" The judge slammed his gavel, then pointed the handle at Cemetery John. "One more peep out of you and I'll . . . I'll . . . Just keep your mouth shut."

"Sorry, Your Honor," Cemetery John said contritely. "It won't happen again."

"Not in *your* lifetime it won't." The judge turned to Cyrus Warwick. "Please continue, Mr. Warwick, and I assure you there will be no more distractions."

The slender, silver-haired man stood and with an obviously pained movement waved the back of his hand at the shackled defendants who sat quietly slumped in their chairs. It was apparent the now-sober pair realized the depths of their drunken folly. "There is no reason to unduly burden the court by recounting all of the details of the defendants' murderous actions against one of our most esteemed citizens, a loving father, a devoted husband, and one of the leading businessmen in our fair and budding community."

One of the handcuffed prisoners gave a low moan of despair, which caused Cyrus Warwick to hesitate a brief moment before continuing his case. "These ruffians of the lowest sort came to our town driven only by greed. As the court knows, my own darling daughter along with other innocent citizens have recently been foully murdered on nearby soil. This caused the town council to authorize a reward in the amount of twenty thousand dollars to be paid for the arrest and conviction of, or for the body of, this cold-blooded killer. Unfortunately, our generosity also attracted some of those base human beings who are motivated only by greed, those driven by not even a shred of altruism, but only by the love of Mammon.

"Two deplorable examples of such individuals sit before this court. They came into our midst and we gave them our trust. In return they murdered our own undertaker, Carter Dark, for no reason but simple greed. There is no doubt, Your Honor, of their guilt. I leave their fate to the court."

With those words, Cyrus Warwick nodded to Sim Eby, then stiffly took his seat.

After thumbing through some papers, more out of show than for any particular reason, the saloon owner stood, nodded gravely at his two clients, then turned to the judge. Jury had been deemed an unnecessary expense along with a waste of time. Since Judge Rimsdale and Cyrus Warwick had both suffered gunshot wounds and were in obvious pain, any delay in the proceedings stood a chance of endangering Eby's relationship with the city fathers. This was not a good situation. Not a good situation at all. Sim Eby knew which side of the bread his butter was on. Also, Carter Dark had been a really good customer at both of his saloons.

Sim Eby cleared his throat. "Judge Rimsdale, Your Honor, I reckon my clients done went an' killed our undertaker. All I can say in their defense is they saw Carter Dark with a paring knife in his hand down by Boggy Creek an' mistakenly assumed him to be the killer ever'one is after. Add in the fact they each had drunk a quart of whiskey, whiskey they'd brought in with 'em, not bought here in Henrietta, I might add. Your Honor, all I can figure to do in their defense is plead 'em both guilty as hell an' ask the court for mercy."

Judge Rimsdale again banged his gavel on

the bench. "That was an eloquent and heartrending defense, Mr. Eby. The court thanks you for your services and accepts your clients' plea of guilty of first-degree murder. But not the plea for leniency. The law must often deal harshly with criminals as an example to children and others to remain moral and God-fearing.

"It is the final and absolute decision of this court that Mallet Simpson and Orville McCutcheon be hung by the neck at the earliest possible time until they are dead, dead, dead. This court is now adjourned." A final whack of the gavel put a period to the moment.

"Jus' like that, they're a-gonna hang us?" Mallet Simpson wailed with a raspy voice. "We didn't get no fair trial a-tall."

"Quit your bellyaching," Emil Quackenbush said, jerking the prisoners to their feet. "You went and killed an unarmed undertaker by shooting him over a dozen times, for Pete's sake. Now you're gonna get hung for it, so stop whining. I'll have you know that I sent for the best dang hangman Judge Isaac Parker's got to give y'all a painless drop-off into the next world. I'd think a little more gratitude would be in order here instead of a lot of whining and complaining."

"I don't wanna get hung," Mallet sobbed repeatedly as the sheriff dragged him and his dumbstruck companion out of the courtroom.

"That was the most economical trial I've ever witnessed," Asa Cain said to Cemetery John. "The fastest too."

"Reckon we can't say it didn't turn out fair. Those two *did* kill Carter Dark."

"I suppose you're right." Asa nodded to the door where everyone was exiting the courthouse. "Since you're the only one making any money from this trip to Kansas, I'm going to let you buy us some more cigars — we're plumb out. Then you can pay for dinner at the hotel tonight; those steaks over there *are* plenty tasty."

"At the high price of an entire forty cents per steak, they dang well oughtta be good. But since you kinda came along with me sort of unintentional like you did, I'll buy the cigars and dinner. Leastwise, I will this once. I got to think of my future wife, you know, can't go shorting poor li'l Bessie on money."

Asa Cain stood. "Cemetery," he said with a lowered brow, "have you actually set a marriage date with this woman?"

"Nope, ain't even asked her yet. But I will have you know that lady's one fine specimen of womankind. And once I get a stake, I'm gonna ask her out to dinner or church — whatever rings her anvil — an' court her proper like."

"You mean to say Bessie Coggins doesn't even have a clue you intend to marry her?"

Cemetery John shrugged, then headed for the door. "It'll work out, all women like surprises."

EIGHTEEN

Blue Hand slammed shut the massive door behind him, slid home the heavy steel bolt, hung the ring of jingling jail keys on a wooden peg on the wall next to the sheriff's desk, then turned to the men who were sitting around drinking coffee.

"We must come up with a plan very soon," Blue Hand said gravely. "Much more of Sheriff Quackenbush's coffee will surely cause us all a sickness."

"Then don't drink any," Emil growled. "We spent two whole hours earlier today coming up with bad ideas that won't work. If you could turn some of that Indian wisdom you're always spouting into a plan for us to nab that reward money before it's too late, none of us would have to drink any more coffee again ever. We could afford whiskey. Good whiskey too."

Asa Cain raised an eyebrow, but remained quiet. He had already consumed a lifetime supply of whiskey. Now that he was sober, the idea of drinking again he found repulsive.

"At least Cyrus Warwick's decision to give away free Winchester rifles and cash for folks to go manhunting along Boggy Creek seems to have backfired," Cemetery John said staring glumly into his coffee cup. "Reckon we all should have seen that coming. At least maybe it'll buy us some time."

Emil Quackenbush grinned evilly. "Frank Martin over at the Henrietta Hardware Store's plumb out of rifles and had to order another shipment. From all I can gather, every mother's son took their brand-new Winchester rifle an' shiny gold piece and skedaddled off either to the north or east. Can't say that I blame 'em any. It's found money and better than going south and losin' your head."

"Warwick's got some learning to do about human nature," Cemetery John said. "That was not hard to see coming. A free rifle, ammo, and money just for the taking isn't easy to come by."

"Cyrus Warwick knows what he's doing," Asa Cain said. "He simply doesn't care if most of those men up and ride away. It's the law of averages he's betting on; a few souls will feel honor-bound to go after the killer. Remember, Warwick has more money than anyone would ever need and he's letting opiates do a lot of his thinking. Add in the fact he doesn't give a damn how many innocent people get killed, and what he's doing makes an odd sort of sense."

"I've never been able to afford to go crazy," Emil said. "Been forced to stay sane all my life an' work for a living."

Blue Hand coughed, then recovered his breath. "The Osage Tribal Council has met and came to a decision."

"And you're just now getting around to telling me this tidbit of information," the sheriff fumed. "I'd like to know what's going on in my jurisdiction before reading it in the newspaper, if that's not too darn much to ask."

"There has been a murder trial and I have been guarding the jail. You have been busy. I have been busy." Blue Hand rubbed the few chin whiskers he was so proud of. "Beside all of that happening, I only saw Many Dogs while the trial was going on. It was then he told me of the meeting."

"Well spit it out, for Pete's sake," Emil said. "If words could be seen, I'd be forced to put chalk marks around yours to see if they were going anyplace."

White men are always in a dither. It is no

161

wonder they are plagued with stomach troubles, Blue Hand thought. "Kills Eagles has ordered a sweat lodge to be built. The elders will have a sweat while smoking some peyote. Then they will communicate with the spirits and ask for their help to stop the murders. The problem may also be an evil spirit. Perhaps they can convince it to stop if that is the case."

"Wonderful, simply wonderful." Emil Quackenbush leaned over and banged his forehead on his desk, then straightened up. "That'll be a *big* help. A bunch of Indians holding a spook convention is just what we need to straighten this mess out."

"Give the Osage a chance," Asa Cain said seriously. "The People have ways we do not understand. Yet they often accomplish miracles."

Blue Hand said, "Chief Kills Eagles has also sent the tribe's two best scouts, Little Badger and Running Bear, to where we found the white lawman's headless body. They are looking for any signs to track. They are good enough to follow where a lizard walked across solid rock sometime last month."

"Now there's the first useful piece of information to come out of this conversation," Emil said. "If some trigger-happy idiot of a bounty hunter doesn't use his brand-new Winchester an' blow those trackers to Kingdom Come, they just might be able to figger out where Marshal Talbot's body had been all those weeks before we found it up in that tree. Be helpful to know why he hadn't really spoiled, hot as the weather's been."

"I've got a theory on that." Cemetery John scratched his curly salt-and-pepper hair. "Being an undertaker for a lot of years, I've had to deal with bodies that've been laying around for quite a spell under unusual conditions."

"I can believe that," Emil said.

Cemetery John continued. "This sounds strange as a four-legged duck, but from the way the marshal's body finally began decomposing, I believe he was kept frozen."

"That is not possible," Blue Hand said with obvious amazement. "It is the hottest time of summer."

Emil gave a deep sigh. "This cinches it, I'm moving back East and become a shoe salesman. There ain't no way that body was kept frozen. Cemetery, you're plain mistaken, you *have* to be."

Cemetery John clucked his tongue, a habit he had picked up from Asa. "Don't you think I don't know just how blamed odd this sounds? That's why I ain't told even Asa. But I do know how a frozen body behaves when it thaws out. You can trust me on this."

Asa Cain turned to stare at the map on the wall with pins stuck in it. "If Cemetery John says Marshal Talbot's body was kept frozen, that's good enough for me. He knows more about things like that than we really want to hear. The question we've got to solve is how it came to happen."

"That is a real puzzle," Blue Hand said. "I am glad I am only a deputy."

Emil rubbed his brow. He had developed a throbbing headache. "Okay, I'll accept the fact that the marshal's body was kept frozen, even if it is impossible. Just don't expect me to explain how it happened, for Pete's sake. When I'm back in Chicago happily selling shoes to pretty women, even then I won't know how a man can freeze in the summertime in Oklahoma."

Blue Hand cocked his head in thought. "There could be an evil spirit involved here someplace. I know the white men do not put stock in such things, but spirits do exist, and they can often be tricky to deal with."

"As if frozen bodies in the summertime wasn't enough to endure," the sheriff said,

164

still massaging his forehead. "Now I'm forced to put up with renegade spooks."

"We are missing the point here." Asa Cain kept his blue eyes on the map. "Someone very real and very deadly is about. It is a man we are dealing with, not a chimera, not a monster, but a flesh-and-blood human being that's worth twenty thousand dollars dead. The last fact is the one we need to concentrate on."

"Now there's some solid thinking," Emil said, brightening. "With that reward money in my pocket, I won't even care how Marshal Talbot got froze, or if the area around Boggy Creek is infested with spooks. I'll be eating steaks and drinking whiskey."

"You do that here," Blue Hand said.

The sheriff ignored his deputy. "Asa, now that your thinker is working, what should we do to collect Warwick's reward and get the hell outta this country?"

Cemetery John wondered anew as to how easily his hoped for bounty money had gotten whittled down like it had, but decided not to complain. So far, there was nothing to split anyway. "I agree with Emil. You're the experienced bounty hunter hereabouts. Tell us how and when to go about the matter."

"I will do as Mr. Cain says," Blue Hand

said looking at Asa.

The bounty hunter clucked his tongue, then stepped close to the map. "There's a pattern to these murders. We have already broached the possibility a bounty is being paid by Warwick's competitors or enemies to wreck his town and businesses. After studying on the situation, I doubt this is the case. Most of the traffic to and from Henrietta comes from the east and north, not through the area of Boggy Creek.

"If anyone was out to ruin Cyrus Warwick, why wouldn't they kill people along the main trade routes? Doc Holliday seems like a reliable sort. He said he got a look at a huge, deformed man packing a metal sword of some sort. I believe him, and I also believe we're dealing with one lone madman who, for some totally unknown reason, is cutting off people's heads and carrying them away."

"Now that's the kind of talk I like to hear," Emil said. "Even if Holliday's slugs went and killed him, we can still haul his dead carcass into Henrietta and get paid. Once we find him, that is."

"Others are looking," Blue Hand stated. "They might get lucky and stumble across him before we do."

"I'm thinking he's alive and killing,"

Cemetery John said. "I agree with Asa. Doc Holliday gave a good account about what happened. If he don't think those slugs did much damage, he's likely right. Whoever's out there might be even more ornery once he's healed up some."

"I'm not for giving him the time to rest up," Asa said poking a finger at the line of pins. "I'm betting we should start from the center here and work our way east. There's where we'll most likely find his hideout."

"Why not to the west?" Emil asked.

"All of the bodies were found east of the creek. For some reason, he might not like to get his feet wet. Outlaws have a tendency to be creatures of habit. That's what gets them caught a lot of times."

"I reckon we got ourselves a manhunt," Emil said with his first smile of the day. "When do we saddle up and ride?"

"George Maledon is to be here by tomorrow morning," Blue Hand said. "I think Mr. Warwick will want us to be at the hanging."

Asa nodded. "You are both officers of the court. I've had some experiences with Maledon. He likes snapping necks too well to dawdle. My guess is he'll be on his way back to Fort Smith less than an hour after he gets here, considering there's light enough to see by."

"Then we'll head out right after George Maledon does," Cemetery John said. "But you just brought up a mighty interesting point that's been of concern."

"What is it?" Asa asked.

"This killer has only struck on nights of the full moon. I can't help but wonder why this is."

"I've got a theory about that. You know, my father was a doctor. He left me a set of medical books and I have studied them throughly. There is a rare disease I've read about that causes a person to grow to huge proportions and often become deformed, possibly even a hunchback. These unfortunates may weigh twice as much as a normal person and also be twice as strong. That would explain how the marshal's body got up into that tree and the stagecoach door was ripped off."

"Do these people also become mean due to this disease?" Emil asked.

"Not at all. Most generally, they are perfectly normal mentally. Many wind up in the circus or as recluses, living their lives harmlessly. I think what we're dealing with here is a person who has, for some reason, gone insane. I also believe he's been in this country for years and knows it well."

Cemetery John said, "Then you're saying

the town of Henrietta simply sprang up in his territory and that pissed him off."

"It's a theory," Asa said. "We'll maybe never know all of the facts."

Blue Hand turned to Asa. "You have not said why he kills only on the nights of a full moon."

"His eyesight is failing; it's one of the symptoms of this disease. More than likely he holes up in daylight to keep out of folks' way. What concerns me is the fact that with a lot of attention being focused on him and the area he calls home, our head-whacker might start being active in the daytime."

Emil Quackenbush sucked in air and blew it out slowly. "We'll head for the Oklahoma Territory and Boggy Creek right after those two idiots get their necks snapped."

NINETEEN

Artemis "Lightning Rod" Wilcox drove his ornate Dearborn wagon along the rough road that followed Boggy Creek north from the Indian Territories to the new boomtown of Henrietta, Kansas. The heat was oppressive, sultry. From a cloudless sky, the sun beat down relentlessly. The shafts of light shooting through the flickering leaves of tall trees wavered in shadows like fey spirits. Flies and mosquitoes, along with any species of insect known to pester man, darted about his eyes and ears, often heading up his nose, which elicited a sneeze. All told, Artemis Wilcox wished he was back in Cleveland.

Safely ensconced in the back of his Dearborn were several wooden cases of his stock in trade, and the reason for his moniker. Artemis Wilcox was a seller of lightning rods. These wonderful devices, when properly attached to the peaks of a roof and wired to earth by shiny copper wire, assured the complete safety of women and children inside their homes during an electrical storm.

Or at least that was the spiel Lightning Rod Wilcox used to sell his product. He had been at the trade since the end of the war and was quite successful. A fit and hardy man at the silver-haired age of fifty-nine, Artemis could scale rooftops and install his devices with the grace and agility of a man half his age.

Women were always so easy to convince, especially whenever he patted their children's heads and mentioned sadly how at the one town he was in not long ago — some distance away, of course — a lady's husband had refused to purchase a set of even his most economical lightning rods. That very evening a storm had struck, with jagged bolts of lightning striking the home of the poor lady, burning it to the ground along with the entire family of seven, all of whom had sadly perished. And the entire tragic situation could have been avoided had the husband not been such a cheapskate.

Actually, Artemis Wilcox had noticed that some of the homes on which he had installed lightning rods, often houses many years old, seemed to be struck during the next storm, even though they had dodged hundreds or thousands of previous lightning storms. This observation gave impetus to not tarry around a town after making a few quick sales. He was driven to save others was his explanation for making a hasty departure; this was far better than having a storm come through and prove what he knew: Lightning rods attract lighting like a cow plop does flies.

Lightning Rod Wilcox held hopes that the town of Henrietta would be filled with trusting women with many children. Rich, trusting women preferably. If this turned out to be the case, putting up with the heat and myriad insects would be worth the misery he was enduring.

Artemis hoped the new paint job and advertising on his wagon he had just spent an exorbitant amount of money on might help. During an unusually long stay in Bartlesville, Oklahoma, a town populated only by apple-knockers and cheapskates, he had not sold a single lightning rod. Feeling comfortable about staying around town long enough for paint to dry, he had engaged a sign painter to advertise his calling. He thought the pleading face of a little blond-haired girl surrounded by threatening jagged orange bolts of lightning with the caption

"Please, Daddy, love me enough to keep me safe" was an exceptionally nice touch. Yes, it definitely paid to advertise. And nothing got people's attention faster than little tykes threatened with harm.

As he drove now, Lightning Rod Wilcox heard an odd sound over the buzzing insects, a sound that caused him to rein the wagon to a stop. For some strange reason, he thought he heard someone crying.

When the squeaking Dearborn wagon grew silent, it was plain there was someone in a nearby clump of wild blackberry bushes sobbing. Even more disturbing, the person doing the crying had a deep voice, like that of a man.

Artemis pulled back the brake and locked it firmly with a leather strap. No matter who it was in trouble, they weren't worth losing a freshly painted wagon over.

Lightning Rod Wilcox sorted through the collection of weapons he kept at the ready beneath the wagon seat. On several occasions, he had had to resort to his formidable arsenal to settle down disgruntled customers, road agents, grouches, or wild Indians. It never paid to wait too long if there was going to be trouble. Artemis always preferred to fire the first shots. It was healthier that way, especially if there were no witnesses about to muddle up his story.

Selecting a razor-sharp bowie knife, which he stuck under his belt, along with a Navy .36 revolver and a trusty sawed-off ten-gauge shotgun, Artemis Wilcox went to investigate the source of the sobbing.

The thorny blackberry bushes were actually shaking from the throes of whoever was hiding inside the high clump. It mystified him why anyone smart enough to pour sand out of their boots would choose to wind up inside a wild berry patch.

"All right," Artemis hollered. "Whoever's in there come on out. I'm sure not going in there to fetch you."

"Are — are you armed?" a voice answered confirming his impression he was dealing with a man.

"I sure am. Now quit lollygagging and come out where I can see you. It can't be comfortable in there."

The voice asked, "Have you got a really *big* gun?"

"A ten-gauge shotgun is about as big as they get."

"Are you by yourself?"

"Now this is becoming plain irritating. Either come out and tell me what the matter is, or I'm going on my way."

174

"*Please,* don't leave me. I know it's out there!"

"If you don't come out of that thicket, I'm heading off for Henrietta."

"*Henrietta!* I was to go there. Then it came at us."

"Good-bye."

"Nooo." There was a rustling of the bushes as a wide-eyed, skinny man with a dark beard, torn clothes, and bloody scrape marks over his body came slowly into view. "I'm here."

"I can see that part. Now why don't you tell me who you are and what's got you so dithered up that you chose to hide in a berry thicket."

"It was simply awful. That monster came running from the shadows and whacked off both of the deputies' heads. I don't know how I escaped or how I wound up in that thicket."

"Two deputies got killed?" Artemis pointed the shotgun at the man's middle. "You got a price on your head?"

"No, sir." The stranger began to compose himself. "I work for Judge Isaac Parker's court over in Fort Smith, Arkansas. I'm a hangman. My name is George Maledon."

175

"That's quite a story you've been telling me." Lightning Rod Wilcox removed his hat and ran a hand across his bare scalp disclosing that the only hair he owned outside of his gray beard was a narrow strip above his ears. "The fact you went and hid in a wild berry thicket is plain evidence that you must've been plenty scared. This monster whacking off heads, however, sounds like a crock."

George Maledon nearly bolted from the wagon seat when a covey of bobwhite quail took flight. He composed himself as best he could, then went back to daubing at his many cuts and scratches with a rag that had been soaked in coal oil. In spite of the heat, the hangman could not stop shivering.

"It was a demon sent from Hell," Maledon said at length. "That's all it could be." He waited until an especially severe shiver had passed. "It was sent to this earth to stop me from hanging those men in Henrietta. Satan is out to protect their souls for some unfathomable reason. There's no doubt about it."

Artemis Wilcox had, in his many years of hawking lightning rods, run across a lot of people whose minds had packed up and left them to fend as best they could on their own, but George Maledon was coming across as a prime candidate for the loony bin. "So, the Devil's out to get you?"

Maledon ignored him and continued. "The marshals were good men. It all happened faster than a lightning strike."

"That's plenty fast," Artemis agreed. He had had plenty of experience along that line. "But how can you explain anyone being able to cut the heads off a couple of experienced lawmen without being shot a few times in the process? To the best of my knowledge, federal marshals are plenty competent at their job."

"It wasn't a man, dammit." Maledon's voice became a sob, then a scream. "I'm trying to tell you it's a demon sent by Satan to stop me on my appointed task of hanging those men in Henrietta."

"Yeah, it was a demon for sure." Lightning Rod Wilcox flicked the reins sending his horse into a faster gait. The sooner he got to town and was relieved of his tattered, scratched, and raving passenger the better. "There's been a lot of those about lately."

"You weren't there. You can't begin to know how evil this thing is, how monstrous the experience." Maledon was sobbing again. "It was awful. I'm *so* scared."

Wilcox looked hopefully ahead for signs of a town. He was relieved to see they were on the outskirts of Henrietta. "I'll take you straight to the sheriff's office. He'll protect you."

"I'm supposed to hang two men Satan wants left alone. Let us pray for a sign that God is on our side."

"This is the State of Kansas we're in now," Artemis Wilcox said soothingly. "I'm sure there's an abundance of Baptist preachers hereabouts that'll be a lot more helpful in the praying department than me. And look yonder, we can see the sheriff's office from here."

"There's been lots of times I've put folks in jail cells, then have to send for a doctor." Emil Quackenbush poured a cup of coffee and set it on the desk in front of Artemis Wilcox. "But this is the first time I've been asked to fetch a preacher."

Asa Cain, who was standing alongside

178

Cemetery John, said, "George Maledon's mind has suffered a severe shock, causing a break from reality and a retreat into theology for comfort."

Lightning Rod Wilcox eyed the coffee suspiciously. "First he hides in a blackberry patch, then actually begs to get locked up in a jail cell for his own protection. It's a certainty something happened down there in the Indian Territory to cause the cheese to slide off his cracker."

"Maybe Preacher Paulson can settle him down a few pegs," Emil said. "Blue Hand is out trying to rustle him up."

"George Maledon has hung a lot of men," Cemetery John said. "I know that for a pure fact. What concerns me is he didn't even recognize Asa. Hanging my friend here was one of Maledon's life's goals. At least it was the last time we run across the man."

Artemis turned to Asa Cain and surveyed him with a lowered brow. "Judge Isaac Parker's out to hang you? From what I've heard about that man, I'd be on my way out of his jurisdiction as fast as I could get someplace else. The sound of necks snapping in Arkansas is a common noise."

Asa shrugged. "The whole affair was a simple misunderstanding. Henrietta's in Kansas, just outside of the judge's jurisdiction, so there's no immediate problem. It'll all blow over; besides, Parker doesn't even know I'm here. And from the shape George Maledon is in, he's not going to say anything."

The sheriff gave a sigh, then slumped into his chair and regarded Artemis Wilcox with a jaundiced eye. "Tell me, Mr. Wilcox, what were you doing when you ran across our frazzled hangman?"

"A lot of folks call me 'Lightning Rod' due to my profession. I sell and install protective lightning rods on people's homes to keep them and their loved ones safe from electrical storms. We all know just how prevalent and deadly they can be, especially in this area."

Emil snorted and lowered an eyebrow. "Some shyster went and sold my mother a set of those things down in Texas. Her house got struck by lightning a few weeks later. If she didn't live across the street from the fire department, her house would've burnt clean down to the ground."

"I've never been to Texas, my good sheriff. It is a shame how some charlatans who know nothing of the profession or good business practices will sink so low as to sell inferior products to people who have put their trust in them. My sincere apologies from all of us who are in the business of selling lightning rods solely to protect the innocent women and little children."

Cemetery John rolled his eyes. He had to admit this man was one of the best horn-swogglers of other people's money he'd ever run across. "To get to the point, I think the sheriff is wanting to know if you actually set eyes on the deputies that got their heads whacked off."

"No," Artemis said quickly, glad to change the subject. "Mr. Maledon was even more distraught when I coaxed him out of that blackberry thicket than he is now. He told me that he couldn't remember how he escaped, or even when or where the attack happened — even if it actually did. I find the very idea of someone going around cutting off people's heads to be rather far-fetched."

"Not around here it ain't," Emil Quackenbush said with a snort. "With those two deputies getting whacked, I count at least eleven with their heads missing that we know of, more that have most likely occurred that we don't have a number on."

Artemis Wilcox bolted upright. He took a cautious sip of coffee, frowned, and said, "That's a mighty high toll. I would suppose there has been a substantial reward posted for the killer's apprehension."

"Being dead counts just as much as being apprehended," the sheriff said. "Actually, better to my way of thinking since our hangman's went an' lost his mind. But to answer your question, the bounty on the head-whacker that's been plaguing us is twenty thousand dollars, cash money."

"Wow!" Lighting Rod Wilcox exclaimed. "That's a fortune. I might forego my calling long enough to become a bounty hunter. With that much money, I could afford to put up my protective lightning rods on the homes of poor widows and orphans without charging for my services." He hesitated. "Well, at least sell them at cost. Tell me, Sheriff. I assume you have a dodger or wanted poster on this cold-blooded killer with his likeness so a man will know who to shoot?"

"Just think back on your worst nightmare," Asa Cain said. "Then double it. That's the best description we've been able to get. The rest of the people who have seen the killer are dead."

"That does make the fiend out to be more of a monster than a man, I must say."

Emil Quackenbush said, "A lot of folks are calling him the Monster of the Osage, but it's only a man, and my friends here and me are going to track him down and kill him."

"I find that quite hard to believe, Sheriff Quackenbush," the familiar voice of Cyrus Warwick hissed from the doorway. "Considering you never seem to leave this comfortable office I have so thoughtfully provided you."

"We were only waiting until after the hangings, sir," Emil said. "Now we seem to have encountered a snag to the proceedings."

"So I have been informed." Warwick motioned to Blue Hand, who came to his side. "Preacher Paulson is out of town to preside over a funeral. Is it true two more federal deputies have been slain?"

"It is, Mr. Warwick," Asa Cain said. "And the hangman, George Maledon, the fellow Judge Parker was kind enough to loan us, is sobbing away back in a cell. He begged us to lock him up for his own protection."

"He saw it," Emil said. "And just like Doc Holliday said, he's more of a monster than a man. He looked bad enough to cause a hangman to lose his mind and hide in a berry patch. It would take quite a stack of both ugly and evil to accomplish something like that in my book."

"I'll telegraph Judge Parker with the

news." Cyrus Warwick looked perplexed, the first time anyone in the room had seen other than an arrogant expression cross his face. "Those two criminals are going to hang."

"We'll see how recovered our hangman gets," the sheriff said. "I had hopes Preacher Paulson might be able to get Maledon's locomotive back on its rails. Surely there's another Bible-banger available to do the job."

"You are missing the point," Warwick said. "We need to set this example for the citizens of Henrietta. They need to see justice is being done. And this cannot be postponed due to an incapacitated hangman. No, Sheriff Quackenbush, *you* must do this and I *order* it performed at noon tomorrow."

"But I never have hung anyone," Emil said.

Cyrus Warwick's confident expression returned. "By this time tomorrow, my good sheriff, you will not be able to make that claim." He turned to Artemis Wilcox. "And who might you be, sir? I don't believe I have seen you about before."

"Artemis Lightning Rod Wilcox at your service, sir. I am a purveyor of quality and dependable lightning rods that are absolutely guaranteed to protect any and all dwellings, both residential and commercial, from even the most severe of electrical storms."

"He's the fellow who coaxed the hangman from out of the berry thicket and gave him a ride to town," Emil said.

Cyrus Warwick stared at Artemis Wilcox. "Please join me for a drink at the Purple Sage. I would like to hear more of your product. Lightning strikes have always been a particular concern of mine. They are a leading cause of fires, I am told."

"And right you are, sir." Artemis stood with a broad smile and began pumping Warwick's hand. "Why, I must tell you of the unfortunate family I encountered over in Te—" He glanced at the sheriff. "Uh, Tulsa. A terrible tragedy that only a few dollars worth of protection would have prevented."

After Cyrus Warwick and the loquacious lightning rod salesman had left his office, Emil Quackenbush fixed Cemetery John in a hard glare. "You know more about hanging someone than I do. You're appointed to do the task."

Cemetery John shook his head. "I've only dealt with them after the fact. From what I heard, the job's yours. While I'll admit to being present with my hearse at the proceedings on occasion to save time, I've never really paid enough attention to detail to feel comfortable performing the task. Like I said, there's a lot more to it than most think."

"It's almost certain George Maledon's not up to it," Asa said. "I can't say for certain if he'll ever be."

"Ah, shucks," Emil said. "I really don't want to do this."

"The pay for the job of hanging is twenty-five dollars for each," Blue Hand said to everyone's surprise. "If that is the case, I will do it."

Emil shook his head, cleared his throat, and asked, "Why on earth would you want to turn hangman, for Pete's sake?"

"I have need of the money," was all the deputy would say on the matter.

TWENTY-ONE

"I really don't think this will be all that difficult," Blue Hand said to the sheriff late that next morning. "But I am glad I talked with Mr. Maledon while he was still here. The long knotted part of the rope goes under the left ear, not the back of the neck like you thought it did."

"George Maledon's hung enough men I reckon he oughtta know," Emil said. "I'd feel a lot better if he had stayed around and done the job Judge Parker sent him here to do."

Blue Hand shrugged. "I am glad he left on the stage this morning. This way I get paid fifty dollars. If he had stayed in town to hang those men, I would get nothing."

Cemetery John finished the last of a cup of hot chocolate. The undertaker was in a cheerful mood. Not only would he get paid to fill two already dug graves, he had discovered that the restaurant at the hotel served hot chocolate. Excellent hot chocolate, which he relished a lot more than coffee. "I actually figured on George Maledon settling down a mite, but he didn't. Reckon he got spooked worse than I thought."

Emil Quackenbush said, "I'd say his mind has plumb come off its hinges. He cried like a baby until I agreed to leave the lanterns lit all night. From all of his caterwauling about God an' the Devil, he might be more fit to be a stump preacher these days than a hangman."

"Maybe he'll recover and get back to neck-stretching," Asa Cain said, leaning back in a chair peacefully smoking a long nine cigar. "Or maybe not. When a person's mind snaps, it's difficult to know what the outcome will be. One thing is for certain. Whatever happened down there in the Indian Territory was a terrible experience. George Maledon isn't the type of man to frighten easily."

"Well, he's on the eastbound stage bawling his way out of town and I'm stuck with a double hanging," Emil grumbled. He turned to glare at Blue Hand; his bushy red beard seemed to flare. "There's been more than enough folks lose their heads around these parts. If you mess up and pop a couple more off, even if it is legal, I'm going to be mighty unhappy with you."

"Too short of a drop is about as bad," Cemetery John said with a thin grin. He was enjoying his morning; a little badgering of a new hangman seemed like a fine idea. "Maybe even worse. They wiggle around on the end of that rope something awful. Women faint and men lose their breakfasts. It's not a pretty sight when that happens."

Blue Hand remained stoic. "Mr. Maledon told me to drop them six feet. He said the depth of a grave is a good rule of thumb when you do not have access to scales to weigh the customer."

"Customer!" Emil spat. "Where in tarnation and Arkansas did you come up with calling hangees customers, for Pete's sake?"

Asa Cain answered for the deputy. "That's a term George Maledon uses. I suppose one could say he's rather vain about his profession."

"There is no problem," Blue Hand said calmly. "First I tie their arms to their sides and then their legs tightly together. Then I put a bag over their heads after I position the rope under the *left* ear. Then I check everything out, pull the lever, and collect my money once they are good and dead. Mr. Maledon says no one, to his knowledge, has ever lived through a procedure like I

189

described. There is no way they can wiggle much or anything. The bag over their heads keeps any ladies present from becoming faint."

Cemetery John nodded his agreement. "I've never had a problem collecting a customer after a hanging like he just described. It's just that I've heard stories of things going awfully wrong."

"Nothing will go wrong." Blue Hand looked at the hands on the big Regulator clock on the wall of the sheriff's office. "It is about time for me to make my fifty dollars."

The sheriff scooted his chair back and stood with a grunt. "I sure wish I knew why that money is so darn important to you. The deputy's pay is a whole forty-five dollars a month."

"I need the fifty dollars," Blue Hand said simply.

Asa Cain spoke up. "The reward money's what we all need to focus on. Right after this distraction's over with and Cemetery John's got the graves covered, we'll be off to the Indian Territory and a twenty-thousand-dollar bounty."

"Now you're talking," Emil said. "I'm even feeling generous enough to help Blue Hand drag those two idiots to the gallows.

From the way that one fellow's been behaving, I don't think they're going to be happy *customers*."

"I'll pitch in," Cemetery John said, setting his empty cup on Emil's oak desk. "The sooner this is over with the better."

Mallet Simpson lay stretched flat across the trapdoor of the gallows, screaming. His companion, Orville McCutcheon, stood still as a statue, hands tied behind his back, a rope around his neck. He was looking with some degree of interest across the street to the rooftop of the Drover's Rest Saloon to where someone was installing what looked to be lightning rods. He had realized there was no way out of the predicament he had gotten himself into, and decided it was useless to protest the proceedings. His trail friend for the past two years, however, seemed to be having a difficult time accepting his fate.

"We're going to have to hoist him up," Emil Quackenbush puffed. "I could use some help here. This fellow's heavy enough to cause a strain."

"Noooo!" Mallet yelled. "I don't want to hang!"

"Buck up," the sheriff growled. "Carter Dark most likely didn't want you to shoot him full of holes either. Now you're gonna go through this whether you want to or not."

"I'll help," Cemetery John volunteered. He bent down and with Emil's help stood the screaming man beneath the noose, which Blue Hand quickly slipped over Mallet's neck and positioned correctly.

Emil and Cemetery John stepped back, expecting Blue Hand to use some more ropes to advantage, then place the black bags over the men's heads. He did not do this. He hit the lever instead.

With a crash, the trapdoor dropped open. The two men plunged past the opening. Then bounced upward to where the tops of their heads were even with the floor of the gallows. Neither of the two moved so much as a muscle; their necks had broken perfectly. The watching crowd was silent as stone, awestruck at the swiftness with which the hangings had occurred.

"I always thought a preacher was supposed to say some words first," a voice from the crowd opined.

"So did I," a man in the front row wearing a black suit said. "And I'm the preacher."

Emil looked down at the man in black and shrugged. "Reckon it's too late for any preaching now. Blue Hand sure got the job done quick, I must say."

"Things seem to happen mighty fast in Kansas," Cemetery John said shaking his head. "I'd venture we have a tendency to talk more in Texas." He looked down at the swaying bodies. "But I reckon it's no matter to those two."

Cyrus Warwick came bounding up the gallows steps. "Sheriff Quackenbush, this is an outrage, an outrage I say. We needed speeches, a demonstration of how justice is administered in Henrietta. This was a simple cold execution and not acceptable in *my* town. Not acceptable at all."

Emil's red beard folded into a frown. "I would agree they wound up in Hell fast enough to surprise the Devil, even though he *was* expecting 'em to show up."

Blue Hand gave Cyrus Warwick a questioning look. "You wanted them hung. They are hung. You owe me fifty dollars."

Emil gave Warwick an evil grin. "It does appear my deputy has got the job done. Maybe we could hoist 'em back up, let the speeches go on, then drop the trap again. You'll have to admit they ain't gonna make a fuss and distract from the lesson you want taught."

Cyrus Warwick dumbfounded the sheriff and everyone else within hearing distance when he said, "Sheriff Quackenbush, you have an excellent idea there. A most excellent idea. Have your men prop them back up and reset the trapdoor."

Emil looked to Blue Hand, who gave a shrug. Then he turned to Cemetery John and Asa. They also gave a shrug. "Well, get up here and lend a hand. We're going to have to hang these two idiots again and they sure ain't light." He thought back on having to drag the struggling, screaming Mallet Simpson all the way from the jail. "But at least Mallet Simpson's better behaved now."

"I'm not sure what's getting most tired," Cemetery John complained to Blue Hand. "My arms from holding this fellow upright or my ears from having to listen to wind —" He realized Cyrus Warwick was only a few feet away. "Uh . . . speeches."

"You got the heavy one," Blue Hand said. "That is good. I think we should get paid more. It was not agreed that we had to hang them twice."

"I think the politicians are finally winding down," Cemetery John said hopefully. "Then we can collect our money and get on with business."

Judge Thomas Terry Rimsdale swept a hand at the crowd from where he stood at the edge of the gallows. "And in closing, ladies and gentlemen, citizens of Henrietta, Kansas, the future cattle-shipping empire of this great country, I wish to once more say how distressed Mr. Warwick and I are over having to conduct such a terrible event as a hanging in our lovely town.

"But, as we are all aware, evil crept even into God's own paradise of Eden when Satan tempted Eve to break the divine commandment not to partake of the fruit of the apple tree. Yet evil did come to paradise, yea, as it did to our town. As mortal men, all we can do is cleanse this blight from our midst. Citizens of Henrietta, witness the demise of these murderers and know this is the fate of any and all malefactors who dare sully our sacred earth and the good name of our town."

The judge made an obviously painful turn to face the two bodies with ropes around their necks that were being held upright over the trapdoor. "You may now drop the condemned."

Cemetery John and Blue Hand made sure their footing was off the trap. After a long moment, Blue Hand turned to Sheriff Quackenbush. "You need to pull the lever, my hands are full."

"I reckon with 'em being already dead, I

195

can help out." Emil gave the wood handle by his side a yank, sending the two men plunging once again into space.

Cyrus Warwick said to the judge in a low voice, "That was a good crowd we drew. I believe the event will be profitable, quite profitable for the saloons. I've noticed people drink a great deal after witnessing a hanging."

"Let's go join them," Judge Rimsdale said beginning his slow, painful descent from the gallows. "There's potential voters about."

Asa Cain thumbed brass .44 cartridges into his Henry rifle. "In all of my years of bounty hunting, I've never even heard of hanging the same person twice. Leave it to politicians to make the most of any public event."

Emil Quackenbush opened a drawer of his desk, took out a box of shells, and stuffed it into his pocket. "That proceeding sorta teetered on the edge of being gruesome to my way of thinking." He gave a sigh. "But when politicians get involved, I reckon they can mess up even a decent hanging."

"Blue Hand got a little too quick on the lever," Asa said. "Being around you has made him impetuous, an odd trait to find in an Indian."

"He got the job done. I reckon I should've taken more pains to inform him just how much some white folks like to drag out their social gatherings. Anyway, we'll be off on a manhunt right after Cemetery John and Blue Hand get those graves filled and drop by the courthouse to collect their pay. Shouldn't be a long wait, with all that big reward money to look forward to."

Asa looked to the sheriff, his expression one of concern. "I have a bad feeling about this manhunt for some reason I can't put my finger on. A lot of people actually believe that I've killed over two hundred men. The count's actually not much over two dozen or so, but none have caused my skin to crawl like this manhunt's beginning to do. There's going to be a lot of folks get killed before it's over. I can't explain how I know this, but I do."

Emil fired a cigar and grinned through the swirling smoke. "When Ole Cyrus starts counting out all that reward money, you'll find a way out of your blue funk. Let's get ready to ride."

Asa had begun to answer the sheriff when the crack of distant gunfire began to rattle off the windows like hailstones. After possibly ten shots had been fired, silence reigned once again.

"This doesn't bode well for us getting off anytime soon," Emil said, testing the action of the double-barrel shotgun he had grabbed up.

"No, it doesn't," Asa said, heading for the door, his Henry at the ready. "Let's go see how many and who got shot this time."

TWENTY-TWO

The day was dying without a breath of wind to relieve the oppressively humid, almost liquid heat of summer in the Osage hill country that covered a large portion of the northeast part of Oklahoma Territory. Even though darkness had yet to fully claim the land, a few lightning bugs flickered about the lush green bushes that lined Boggy Creek, optimistically awaiting the coming night.

Going Snake missed no movement or sound of nature as he made his way down from the limestone cliffs to return to his village. As a trained shaman, he often stopped to gather various plants, herbs, and mushrooms he encountered. Some had medicinal properties, others held value more in the spirit realm, yet all needed to be gathered and stored. With his buffalo-skin bag now empty, there was ample room to carry the needed tools of his trade as healer and spiritual guide of the Osage tribe.

His heart was heavy now that two more white-eye lawmen had been slain on tribal lands. Going Snake realized the building situation was certain to bring the Army to put a stop to these offenses. This action would bring grief and death to The People. The white-eyes viewed every Indian as the same, innocent or guilty. All could be killed without fear of punishment or reprisal.

Life on a reservation was not intolerable as long as the Army left The People be. They could follow their customs and religion without interference. But not if the killings of the white men continued. And the beheadings certainly *would* continue; of that, there was no question.

The shaman fervently wished for and sought another path to follow, but could find none. As one of The People, he had to do what he must to keep his soul anchored to the earth. Some things had to be left to the Great Spirit to sort out. Yet he would keep beseeching the gods for another path. Perhaps some kindly spirit might intervene and stop the army of the Great White Father from coming to their lands. A man should never give up hope.

In the fading light, Going Snake noticed a patch of sassafras. The aromatic bark along with the roots were wonderfully powerful medicines. He extracted his razor-sharp bowie knife from its sheath, then bent to begin cutting the plants. He froze when a voice spoke from his back.

"We have followed you, Shaman. You left an easy trail."

Going Snake stood and turned to face the scouts, Little Badger and Running Bear. The shaman had hoped this would not happen, but the gods had obviously willed it.

"You are good trackers," Going Snake said to the two scouts after taking a moment to ponder his words. "I knew I could not hide my footprints from your eyes. I did not try very hard."

Little Badger stepped close. "My Shaman, our chief, Kills Eagles, will be displeased."

Running Bear came to his friend's side. "Now that we know of your secret, Shaman, we must inform our chief. But we wish you to know that we do understand why you are here, and why you are doing this."

"Yes," Going Snake said sadly. "I do only what I must."

With those words still on his lips, the shaman slashed out with his bowie knife with the speed of a striking rattlesnake. His first blow sliced across Little Badger's throat, nearly severing his head from his body. With a nimble backslash so fast an eye could not follow, he jabbed the long steel knife downward into the base of Running Bear's neck, then twisted the blade with all of his formidable strength.

In less than a heartbeat, the two Osage scouts lay dead and bloody on the forest floor at the feet of the shaman.

"You should not have been such good trackers," Going Snake said as he studied the bodies in the last fading rays of twilight. "If you had not found me, you would still breathe."

The shaman, however, had thought ahead on such an eventuality. The Osage produced some very competent scouts. The killer that would certainly bring the Army had, so far, rubbed out only white-eyes. When Running Bear and Little Badger's bodies were found with their heads missing, it would be a new pattern. Perhaps now Going Snake could convince the chief and council of elders that an evil spirit was indeed responsible. This might buy him the time he needed to take care of the matter. Going Snake could only hope and pray to all of the spirits there would be sufficient time before the Army came.

Appearances had to be kept. The shaman went to the creek and washed his knife free of blood before gathering the sassafras. It was while he was digging up the wonderful roots that he decided what to do with the scouts' heads after he had cut them off. It was a brilliant idea, one that might help save The People.

Buoyed with hope, Going Snake stowed his sassafras, did what he had to do, then thoroughly washed both himself and the trusty, sharp bowie knife to remove even the smallest droplets of blood. All Indians could not only see but smell the presence of blood.

While lightning bugs played about the bushes and the nighthawks and owls gave their welcoming cries to the night, the muscular shaman, carrying his slight burden, made his way gracefully alongside the rocky shores of Boggy Creek, heading home.

TWENTY-THREE

"I swan," Sheriff Quackenbush grumbled as he strode out the front door of Madam Rose's "rooming house," which had a sign over the door with a large red rose proclaiming it to be THE THORNLESS ROSE. "This town is becoming a real peeve to get away from."

Blue Hand nodded sadly to the batwing doors of the Drover's Rest Saloon. "One of the men will go straight to Cemetery John. After I collect twenty-five dollars for another hanging, he can then bury the one who shot the man in the saloon along with that girl."

Asa Cain came through the batwings, pushing in front of him a handcuffed rough-looking man who was bleeding profusely from a head wound.

"I hate idiots who get blind drunk and start shooting up the place," Asa growled. "Especially when they cause me a delay."

"I — I didn't do nothing wrong," the

bleeding man muttered. "That damn rotten freighter drew down on me first."

"Aw, stow it," Emil boomed. "Fred Durbin never packed a gun in his life, and he sure didn't have one on him this afternoon when you decided to ventilate him along with everything and everyone in his general direction.

"But I — I saw the gun pointed at me," the manacled man whined.

"It was his corncob pipe, you idiot," Emil said with a head shake. "You not only shot an unarmed man, but one of all those bullets you fired — folks said you even took time to reload your pistol — went through a couple of walls an' hit one of Rose's girls."

"Her name is Thelma Pine," the blond, voluptuous woman who owned The Thornless Rose said, as she swished past Cemetery John and Blue Hand to face the sheriff. Mattie Rose left the heady aroma of lilac perfume floating heavy in her wake. "I expect you to make an example out of him, Emil. Thelma is one of my biggest moneymakers."

Cemetery John raised an eyebrow. From the familiar manner in which Mattie Rose was acting toward the sheriff, it was obvious they were more than casual acquaintances, but he decided to keep quiet on the matter and wait until a more opportune time for some needling.

"You can depend on it, Mattie," Emil said with a nod to the bleeding prisoner in front of Asa. "He's already gonna be hung for killing an unarmed freighter. It's hard to get much tougher on 'em than that." He tilted his head down and gave the short blonde a concerned look. "How bad did little Thelma get shot?"

"The bullet must have been slowed considerably going through the two walls first. Doc Sedgemiller's with Thelma now, patching her wound. To answer your question, the slug hit her in the upper thigh. It didn't do a lot of damage, but it'll cause her to have to rest up for a few weeks until she heals."

Emil gave Mattie Rose a grin that caused his red beard to flare. "Staying out of bed for a spell will likely do the trick."

The blonde said, "Since you're going to have him hung, I suppose I'll go see to Thelma's welfare and take care of business. That double hanging has kept all my girls plenty busy." She smiled up at Emil. "Are you coming by later?"

The red from the sheriff's beard seemed to flow outward to his cheeks and forehead. "Uh . . . no, Mattie, I can't tonight. We've got a manhunt going on."

Mattie Rose gave Emil Quackenbush one of those eye-batting come-on smiles that a girl uses to get what she wants. "You drop by and see me just as soon as you have time." With a swirl of her red dress, she was gone, leaving behind the wonderful aroma of lilacs to further tantalize the sheriff.

"There goes a very pretty lady," Cemetery John said. "And from the way she's acting, I'd venture you have at least one voter you can depend on."

The sheriff gave a snort and spun to Asa Cain, ignoring the undertaker. "Well, let's get this latest idiot locked up. With any good luck we might be able to convince Cyrus Warwick to hold off on the fair trial and hanging until we get back from our manhunt."

"I shot that feller in self-defense," the still-unnamed prisoner wailed, struggling against the handcuffs that pinioned his arms behind his back. "You all ain't gonna hang me. I'll kill ever single one of ya first. Once I get outta these things."

"Oh, shut up." Asa Cain whipped out his pistol and cracked it alongside the man's head sending him crashing to the earth in a cloud of dust. "I told you to settle down or I'd whack you again."

"Dang, I wish you hadn't done that," Emil said as he walked over and studied the prone figure. "Now we'll have to pick him up and pack him all the way over to the jail. After suffering with Mallet Simpson like I had to do, all this heavy lifting is going to cause me a backache for sure."

"Once we get that big reward money," Cemetery John said with a grin on his face as he motioned to The Thornless Rose, "you can afford to pay for a lot of really good back rubs."

Without taking time to think, the sheriff spouted, "Oh, I don't have to pay for it." Then he gave a cough and growled, "Well, quit standing around lollygagging, pitch in, and help me transport this idiot to a jail cell."

"I just knew this was going to happen," Emil Quackenbush said to Asa Cain as he looked out the front window of the sheriff's office. "It seems that everything and everyone along with their dogs are conspiring to keep us from going on a decent manhunt and getting our pockets full of money. Dag-nab it all!"

Asa turned to see what had further upset the already cantankerous sheriff, although he had a good guess what the matter was.

When he saw Cyrus Warwick along with Judge Thomas Terry Rimsdale striding toward them, he had to agree with Emil's consternation; with the speed with which things were progressing in Henrietta, he should consider investing in real estate.

"Mr. Cain, Sheriff Quackenbush," Cyrus Warwick said in a cheerful tone of voice. "Judge Rimsdale and I are in receipt of a telegraph from Judge Isaac Parker over in Fort Smith. He is very distressed over the two additional marshals being slain in his jurisdiction. His message said that he is not only forming a posse to leave for the Indian Territory in a few days, but also the cavalry is going to accompany them."

"These murders and terrible depredations that have cast a dark shadow over our fair town are going to finally be stopped," Rimsdale said with a distinct slur. The judge, in his quest for future votes when he would run for Congress, had been quite liberal with both the buying and consuming of whiskey, which everyone knew was a prerequisite for election to public office. "The sheer volume of lawmen and soldiers will scour the Indian Territory like a cleansing, purifying wind. They, in their righteous quest for God's own justice, will leave no stone unturned, no nook nor cranny unin-

209

vestigated, until this scourge upon our land has been removed."

Asa Cain noticed the pupils of Cyrus Warwick's eyes were mere pinpoints. This left no doubt the mogul of Henrietta had indulged in considerable quantities of more than whiskey. He wondered how much longer Warwick could keep the dogs of an opium habit leashed. When the man spoke again, Asa realized the time was short.

"Sheriff Quackenbush," Cyrus Warwick said loudly, waving his arms about nervously. "My good friend. I wish for you and your friends to be the ones to bring this foul killer to justice. Having our own lawmen apprehend the fiend before the federal marshals or the Army does will be wonderful publicity for my town of Henrietta." Warwick turned to smile upon Judge Rimsdale. "I am *so* grateful to you for pointing this out to me."

Thomas Terry Rimsdale beamed from the praise. With the wealth and resources of Cyrus Warwick behind him, his future election as governor was assured. Then, once firmly ensconced in office, he could cast off the arrogant lout and run for president. It would be most pleasant not to have to kowtow any longer to a man who grew more insane on a daily basis. But he had to admit that with the huge quantities of opiates Warwick had been consuming, it was a simple matter to lead him around like a pet.

"Thank you, Mr. Warwick," Judge Rimsdale said fawningly. "I am most gratified you are in agreement that our own competent lawmen bringing the killer to justice will enhance immensely the image of Henrietta, Kansas, as a serene haven where women and children are safe and families secure in their homes."

Emil Quackenbush leaned back in his swivel rocker and eyed the pair with a disbelieving gaze. "You're telling me we can just ride out to the territory on a manhunt without hanging that man who shot the innocent freighter first?"

"Why, yes, of course, Sheriff," Cyrus said, still waving his arms about. He spun and looked around the room. "And the sooner the better. I built a most excellent jail. We can hang him anytime I decide it will be good for business. Where, may I ask, is your deputy and the undertaker?"

"Blue Hand is back in the cell block keeping an eye on the prisoner. Cemetery John went to the hardware store to stock up on ammo for that big shotgun he packs around."

"Excellent, my good man," Cyrus Warwick

said. "I will have someone take over your deputy's task. With Blue Hand being at least half Indian, he might be quite helpful to have along. I can now understand your percipience in hiring him."

Emil rolled his tongue along the inside of his cheek. He didn't know if he had been paid a compliment or not. Big words always were a chore to figure out, but having never seen Warwick in a good mood before, he simply smiled and nodded in agreement. What he had heard so far sounded too good to take a chance on messing up by opening his mouth unnecessarily.

"We'll leave before dark," Asa Cain said. "Whoever has been doing these killings can't hide forever. That's a fact to rely on."

Judge Rimsdale said, "I should add that Mr. Warwick and I are depending on your being efficient; time is of the essence." The lawyer lowered his eyebrows. "Uh, should any — ah — *mistakes* be made by any of you, I want you to know that we will stand by you. Simply put, the incident will be covered up, the dirt swept under the rug, so to speak. Results count more than — well, *you* know."

"We understand," Emil said. "But we'll only plan on doing in just the head-whacker, or bringing him back for a hanging."

Cyrus Warwick sniffed, then said, "That would be an excellent scenario, Sheriff. *Do* accomplish it. The saloon business alone would go a long ways to paying off the reward money I — uh, the town has posted."

"Perhaps, Mr. Warwick," Judge Rimsdale said as he placed a hand on Warwick's shoulder, "an added inducement could be given to our stalwart lawmen as an incentive before we leave and allow them to get about their pressing business."

"Ah yes." Cyrus Warwick had a trickle of spittle running down the corner of his mouth from forming the sibilant, a fact he seemed ignorant of. "An excellent idea. For bringing my daughter's killer back alive, I will double the reward to forty thousand dollars. If you are successful in only bringing back a dead body, I will still, out of the goodness of my heart, add another ten thousand dollars. I want Henrietta's killer! Damn it."

Thomas Terry Rimsdale realized it was time to steer his client home. "Remember, Sheriff, if the Army or federal marshals do the job, you and your men will receive nothing." He gave an urging hand to Cyrus Warwick in the direction of the door. "We now bid you our leave and wish Godspeed to you all." Then the pair were gone.

Emil Quackenbush gave a snort, then fished a long nine cigar from his desk and fired it. "I don't know what it is about becoming educated that prevents the folks it happens to from speaking plain English." He took a long puff and said through the swirling smoke, "But if I read it right, Warwick went nuttier than a peach orchard boar about the same time he decided to act nice. That forty-thousand-dollar reward's the biggest I've ever heard tell of. That'll make the splitting more agreeable too."

Asa Cain came over and fished a cigar from the sheriff's supply. "Cyrus Warwick's likely taken so much opiate I doubt he knows what he's doing. Judge Rimsdale seems to be calling the shots, but if we're successful, I think we'll get paid. There's simply too much at stake. If the killer isn't caught soon, the railroad might not come to Henrietta. The whole thing boils down to business. Warwick wants his daughter's murderer brought to justice, but his motivation with the huge amount of bounty money's strictly to protect his own interests."

Emil grinned. "Let's help him protect them then."

The slamming of the front door caught their attention.

Cemetery John came inside, leaned his

ten-gauge shotgun against the wall, and set a small wooden box of shells beside it. He turned to survey Asa and the sheriff. "Anything happen while I was gone?"

"You could say that," Asa Cain said. "It'll be better and more profitable if we were to explain what-all's happened once we're under way."

Cemetery John smiled. "Then we've got ourselves a manhunt."

The sheriff grabbed a handful of cigars from his desk and began stuffing them into his vest pockets. "Yep, we sure do. Let's rustle up Blue Hand and ride south. That outlaw down there's gotten too valuable for any more dawdling. Let's head out. There's a fortune walking around down there somewhere and I aim to collect on his hide."

Cemetery John collected his shotgun. "Emil," he said stuffing some cartridges into his pocket. "Let's not use the word 'head' any more than necessary."

Twenty-Four

Judge Isaac Parker silently regarded George Maledon from across the expanse of his huge oak desk. The once-efficient hangman seemed to be unable to quit sobbing and whining. This was certainly not a desirable trait for a man in Maledon's line of work. The numerous cuts and scratches over every visible bit of flesh were a further distraction from a man who had built a fearsome reputation by snapping the necks of his fellow human beings.

The ex-Congressman-turned-federal judge had noticed that the tougher, the more of a bully a man acted, the easier they were to break. He had seen the truth of this borne out more times in his court than he cared to remember. One of the meanest men to come before his bench was a scallywag of the worst sort by the name of Matt Music, who was charged with raping a young woman.

Matt Music had strutted about like a dandy in the courtroom, totally disregarding decorum and formality. The man seemed totally unflappable. At least that was the way he acted until Parker had ordered him hung by George Maledon for his despicable crime against the fair sex. There were too few women in the territories to allow any of them to be mistreated. *Far* too few.

The moment the sentence had been pronounced, the formerly granite Matt Music melted into a sad, sobbing, repenting mass of humanity. His pleadings and caterwaulings were heartrending to the extreme. The man cried out for his sainted mother in Heaven to have mercy on his pitiful soul. He begged for a Bible to hold as a comfort against the coming eternal night. All in all, Matt Music seemed a changed man, so much of one that the judge, in a moment of weakness, had reversed himself and commuted the hanging sentence to merely life in prison.

Matt Music had broken out of the wagon while it was transporting him to the penitentiary, killing two guards and the driver in the process. The outlaw was still at large and from the last accounting, still practicing his career as a rapist at every opportunity. *Leopards do not change their spots.*

Yet, Judge Parker reminded himself, George Maledon had, up to this point in time, performed his tasks on the side of the law, and should be given an opportunity to explain why he'd failed to hang those two miscreants in Henrietta, Kansas, and then given a chance to redeem himself. Having two deputies get their heads whacked off while escorting him was most certainly a difficult event to suffer through.

"Mr. Maledon," Judge Parker said evenly after lighting his crooked-stem pipe. "I can understand how the recent sad turn of events down in the Indian Territory could have a disturbing effect on one, but as an officer of this court, I need you to do your best to pull yourself together."

George Maledon was forced to wait until another harsh shiver passed through his lanky body before replying with a meek, "Yes, sir."

"Now take a deep breath and answer me this. Are you able to give an adequate description of the man who attacked and killed the two deputies?"

"It was more of a monster than a man. I remember a scream, like that of a panther; then he was upon us swinging a long, jagged metal object. In the length of time it takes to blink, both deputies' heads were falling from their shoulders."

"How did you escape after the officers fell?"

Maledon stared down at his boots. "My horse spooked and ran off. I would have been killed if it had not. I honestly do not remember much after that. But to answer your question, I can identify the murderer. Judge, I will never be able to get his image *out* of my mind."

Isaac Parker nodded. "Then, Mr. Maledon, some good may yet come from this terrible incident. Your being an eyewitness to the crime will allow a certain conviction."

The hangman suppressed an almost overpowering urge to burst out laughing. The hulking, deformed, scarred man — if it actually was a man — who had lopped off those marshals' heads in a heartbeat would never be taken alive. At least he hoped not. Having to hang something from out of a nightmare was a terrifying scenario. "I can identify him, Your Honor. I can promise you that."

A hint of a smile washed across Isaac Parker's bearded face. "Excellent, Mr. Maledon. See, when a person forces themselves to focus on points of law and removes all emotion from the case, it makes the entire judicial process more palatable."

"I'm feeling better already, sir."

Judge Parker said, "I have ordered a posse of a dozen men to go after the murderer. The Army has agreed to send along another dozen or so cavalry officers to accompany them. Rest assured, Mr. Maledon, the guilty will be brought to justice. They always are." He thought back on Matt Music. "*Almost* always are anyway, given time."

"Yes, sir, I wish them Godspeed."

"As do we all. Bad business when fine lawmen are struck down in their prime. Both marshals were family men. But this is something I am sure you already knew."

George Maledon pondered how to frame his answer. Due to his rather grisly occupation, few would say more than an occasional word to him. The two slain marshals had been no exception. Their desire to be some distance from him was the reason he had been riding a hundred feet behind the men when the attack had happened. "No, sir, they pretty much kept to the business at hand."

Isaac Parker's gray eyes turned misty. "Yes, they would have. Good men, very good men."

"Yes, sir."

"I am going to ask something of you, Mr. Maledon."

"Ask it, sir."

"The jail is becoming dreadfully cramped and smelly, more so than usual in the heat of summer. I believe we could do with another hanging of six men with one drop. This will also make room for other future inmates. Sadly, the supply seems unlimited."

George Maledon brightened. It was as if the dark clouds that had been floating around inside his mind had blown away. "Do you mean it, sir?"

"Absolutely. When you hung those other six at once, it received a great deal of play in the newspapers. Publicity to let people know the stern hand of the law is watching over them is a good thing indeed."

"Ah, yes, I remember how well that hanging turned out. All six of my customers had their necks broken perfectly." Maledon gave a contented sigh. "I did tell you that I am going to try bear grease on my ropes instead of lard? I'm in hopes a better lubricant will give that much-needed hard fast snap that is required to sever the spine."

"I wish you success. You may wish to try it on Bood Crumpton tomorrow at high noon. The hanging of six at once, we will have to schedule for later on. I need to allow time for the reporters and photographers to arrive for the event."

George Maledon's smile was broad, genuine. "I will give them all a quick and painless send-off to the next world, Your Honor."

"Where you can rest assured they will face an even sterner court than mine. You may go now, Mr. Maledon, I have much paperwork to attend to."

The hangman stood straight and tall. "Yes, sir. I'll go to the hardware store and buy some more bear grease and prepare Bood Crumpton's rope for tomorrow's execution." He spun and was gone, a spring to his step.

Judge Isaac Parker felt he had managed to save himself from having to hire another hangman, at least for a while. The brooding little man was the best at that grim task of any he had previously employed. Parker grew immensely proud of himself as he began signing death sentences. Good help was hard to find.

Twenty-Five

Artemis "Lightning Rod" Wilcox jacked the lever on his shiny new Winchester rifle to check the action. He thumbed back the hammer and gave it a dry-fire. The weapon seemed perfect. The fact that it was free made it even more attractive. The rifle had even come with a hundred rounds of ammunition and a glistening twenty-dollar double-eagle gold piece. Deals like this were too sweet to pass up.

The lightning-rod salesman stowed the Winchester and cartridges in the box beneath the seat of his wagon, and longingly studied the batwing doors of the Purple Sage Saloon. From inside, the tinny sounds of a honky-tonk piano played its luring siren song of temptation on his soul. A few drinks to brace himself for his first manhunt seemed a delightful idea, almost a necessity actually.

Henrietta, Kansas, had, so far, been like

finding a gold mine. Once he had shed himself of the sobbing, lunatic hangman, things had gone smashingly well. The man who owned most of the town, Cyrus Warwick, had shown the good sense to have protective lightning rods placed on all of the business buildings he owned along with his palatial, three-story Victorian home.

The wonderful sale had exhausted the salesman's entire supply of fifty Armbruster lightning rods and put over three hundred dollars in his pockets, which, since each rod cost him only a quarter, was a nice windfall in itself. Then Cyrus Warwick had amazed him further by offering him a new Winchester rifle, complete with ammunition, along with twenty dollars in gold, simply to agree to go shoot that lunatic who was lopping off people's heads. The fact that one of those heads had belonged to Warwick's daughter surely explained why the mogul of Henrietta was determined to get the killer. Then Cyrus had astounded him by offering to pay forty thousand dollars bounty, an unbelievable sum of money.

Artemis Wilcox could simply not believe his good fortune. Being only a day or two away from becoming a wealthy man was certainly cause to celebrate. There really shouldn't be much of a problem locating the head-whacker, or at least someone who would pass for being him. From all accounts, the killer was big and ugly. That description fit a lot of people in the Indian Territories, both male and female. That forty thousand dollars was as good as in his pocket. Should he make a slight, quite understandable error and bring in the wrong body, Artemis Wilcox planned on being in New Orleans living the good life before that fact became known. Yes, the town of Henrietta and Cyrus Warwick's seemly unending supply of money were definitely cause to celebrate.

Lightning Rod Wilcox flipped the twenty-dollar gold piece into the air with his thumb. He grinned as he watched it glisten in the sunlight like a yellow promise. "Okay, Mr. Warwick," he said under his breath. "Heads I win, tails you lose." He snatched the twirling coin from out of the air and slapped it onto the back of his hand.

"And we have ourselves a winner, ladies and gentlemen." With those happy words, Artemis strode to the batwing doors of the Purple Sage Saloon and melted into the murky, smoky interior.

The gentle, even rasping of a fine whetstone against steel was the most soothing task he had found to while away the long dark hours between hunts. Try as he might, he could not recall exactly where or even when he had come by the long gray stone he had grown to love. No matter, it was his now.

In the dim cold, gnarled hands kept a razor's sharpness to the multitude of knives kept at the ready. Most of all, he devoted the majority of time to his beloved ice saw. The keen, jagged teeth dulled so easily when he employed it against bone. But the steel always regained its edge when given proper care and a loving touch.

His life, his very reason for existing, had been born that fateful night when he came to own the long shiny beautiful ice saw. For then he held the tools of the hunt.

Pain, more pain than he thought anyone could endure, had also come along with his beloved ice saw. Ever since the fire, pain had followed him constantly, like a faithful dog. Pain, however, caused the mind to focus, allowed him to concentrate on the hunt and his wonderful collection that was nearing completion.

The stinging from the twin holes in his belly from when the sleeping man with the pretty watch had shot him was nothing compared to the always pain. Nothing at all. And he now had the man's watch. It was just too bad he did not also have the man's head. The sleeping man had been far faster than any of the others. He needed to be more careful, employ his ice saw quicker in the future. But he always healed.

He knew many men with guns were coming to kill him. Let the fools try. They would never find his hideaway, his wonderful dark sanctuary. If any got lucky, the ice saw was ready and awaiting their arrival.

Carefully, he tested the keen edge of a sawtooth with the end of his little finger. A droplet of crimson blood glistened in the cold yellow flickering light of the small fire. A semblance of a smile rippled his scarred face as he sucked the blood and swallowed.

The ice saw was ready, it was time to wait. He leaned the long saw on a log by his side and took the skunk paw from the leather pouch he always wore on a belt. He splayed open the paws to expose tiny claws. Then he began to clean his teeth to while away time until the hunt.

TWENTY-SIX

Asa Cain reined his horse to a stop in a rare clearing along Boggy Creek. Huge, towering trees formed a thick green covering over much of this portion of the Indian Territory. To the east and west, the normally hilly terrain gave way to sheer cliffs of limestone, many of which stood as high and stark as a medieval castle of some feudal lord.

"I suppose you're feeling evil coming in on the breeze again." Emil Quackenbush chewed nervously on a stub of cigar. After snorting a particularly annoying insect from out of his left nostril, he added, "But that can't be the case this time, because there ain't no breeze. It's stuffy enough out here to cause anyone with the sense to put their boots on the right feet to want to head for most anyplace else, except maybe Arkansas."

"It's never wise to stop where you could easily get yourself ambushed," Asa said, turning to the sheriff and Cemetery John, who had been riding close behind him. "But to answer your question, I feel nothing. He is not here. However, it always pays to be cautious."

"I've buried lots of folks who weren't nervous when they should have been." Cemetery John took off his slouch hat, mopped sweat from his brow, frowned at the bullet hole through the crown, then eyed the darkening sky. "We might ought to make camp here. All of those delays we've suffered through has made for a short day of manhunting."

"I'm thinking maybe our lovely has plain up and died," Emil said as he squinted into the shadows. "If that's the case, I reckon we'll need to start looking for circling buzzards. We know for sure they can even scout out bodies up in trees, can't figure how they'd miss one lying around on the ground."

Asa Cain clucked his tongue. "Now there a problem presents itself. How do we prove that body, providing we actually do run across one, was the killer? Factor in the heat, buzzards, coyotes, and all kinds of insects, he's liable to be in pretty poor condition for any kind of identification."

Cemetery John quickly lowered his hand to the trigger of his shotgun, then relaxed when a red squirrel scampered nosily across a patch of fallen leaves. "Asa, you're too used to dealing with regular law. Cyrus Warwick ain't going to be real picky about paying out that reward money, anxious as he is to boom the town of Henrietta."

The sheriff spit out the stub of cigar and began fishing a fresh smoke from his vest pocket. "I've known Warwick long enough to say for certain he's the type to get rather peeved if those head-whackings continue after he's handed over all of that reward money."

"If he doesn't quit using opiates like he does," Asa Cain said, "the man won't be around long enough to lodge any objection. It's a common cause of death among addicts when they forget how much of the drug they've used and consume even more, causing a fatal reaction."

"That's a fact," Cemetery John agreed with a nod. "Mostly, however, those customers are a lot more common in the big cities. Down in Texas, I've had to bury more folks who died from lockjaw after stepping on a rusty nail than ones who accidentally killed themselves with too much laudanum or opium."

Emil fired his cigar, slapped at whatever was trying to crawl into his right ear, and said, "Anyone can buy all of the opium they want at most any drug or hardware store. The stuff's even available at way stations and trading posts. It's cheap and about the only thing aside of whiskey that'll stop pain. I can't figure, however, why anyone would choose to use it without cause. Whiskey, now there's a substance that makes life worth living."

"Opiates get in a person's veins and grow roots," Asa said. "The facts are, if Cyrus Warwick doesn't stop, he'll keep using more and more until it kills him."

"I fail to see a problem, if we can manage to get a high-priced outlaw back to Henrietta before that event happens," Emil said swinging off the saddle. "But it's gonna be too dark to follow buzzards here in a bit. And since Asa ain't feeling spooks in the woods, I'm agreeing with Cemetery John that we make ourselves an early camp. I'll bet there's still light enough we can shoot a nice tasty brace of squirrels to fry up for supper. I don't know about the rest of y'all, but my belly's beginning to rub a sore on my backbone."

"Yeah." Asa Cain dismounted and walked over and stood alongside the sheriff. "It's been a long and tiresome day."

Cemetery John swatted with his hat at a

swirling swarm of black bugs that were circling his head. "And from the way things are going, it's gonna be a long night too."

"I always favor the gray squirrels over red ones." Emil Quackenbush sucked the last morsel from a small bone and tossed it over his shoulder. "My guess is they feed on more hickory nuts than acorns, makes 'em taste better."

"Can't tell a whit's worth of difference myself," Cemetery John said. "At least they were both plentiful and didn't resist being shot."

Asa looked through the rustling trees to where a wan moon was rising along with a smattering of black clouds. "There's no full moon, but it's going to be light enough to see to get around if those clouds don't build into a storm."

"Wonderful, simply wonderful," Emil grumbled after a distant flash of light and deep rumbling put a period to the moment. "Not only are we stuck out here in the heat with swarms of biting bugs and woods filled with spooks, now we're going to suffer being rained on. I knew I should have gone for an indoor job."

"Nah," Cemetery John said with a dismissive swing of his hand knocking a June bug off course that was headed for his left eye. "That storm will miss us by a mile. My knees always develop an ache before it rains. They're feeling fine."

"You've spent too much time in Texas," Emil said. "Up here the rain's made up different than it is down there, might be able to sneak up on your joints unsuspecting like."

Asa Cain poked a fresh piece of wood into the campfire sending up a shower of sparks. The time had come for more serious discussion than the weather. "I've been puzzling over the body of Marshal Talbot's we found being frozen like it was. I've had some mighty mysterious clues to decipher being a bounty hunter, but in all my years of man-hunting, I've never been stumped like this."

Cemetery John moved to one side to avoid the new direction the smoke was taking. "Now back home in Wolf Springs, Texas" — he grinned at Emil — "where the rain's normal, Soak Malone, who owns the Rara Avis Saloon, gets all of his ice delivered in big blocks that have been packed in thick straw and sawdust. I wish now I'd asked him where it's shipped from."

Asa Cain leaned easily back against a big oak tree and watched the dance of distant lightning. "Soak, like most every business that requires ice, buys it in big blocks from a dealer up north where it snows and freezes hard in wintertime. Cutting blocks of ice from lakes and rivers with a saw and storing them in buildings covered with piles of straw for later shipment is a booming business."

"Cold beer's come to be a necessity rather than a comfort," Emil opined. "I'm of the opinion folks are getting too soft these days. I'll stick with whiskey straight out of the bottle. Now there's a man's drink."

Blue Hand, who had remained strangely silent and brooding, said, "White men always like their whiskey and beer. When I have ice, I like to drink it with sweet tea. That is a good drink, especially when the weather is hot like it is now."

"Now there's a concoction that'll never catch on," Cemetery John snorted. "Except maybe with womenfolk or big-city Percypants." He turned to Blue Hand. "Reckon I didn't phrase that well, sorry."

"There is no offense taken," Blue Hand said. "The Indian half of me cannot drink, and alcohol is not allowed on the reservation because of this malady. The Mexican part of me feels sad because of this, but I cannot allow myself to go half crazy."

Sheriff Quackenbush lowered an eyebrow

and started to say something, then obviously thought on the subject long enough to decide to keep quiet.

"Whiskey and alcohol in any form," Asa said, still staring at the distant lightning, "is, to some people, the same as opiates. There is a rule I have heard many doctors use when referring to any addiction; you either control your intake of the substance, or the substance will control you."

"Reckon that about covers the situation," Cemetery John said, taking out his pocketknife to carve a whistle from a piece of slippery elm. "But I'd like to have the money to be able to find out if Emil has a drinking problem or not. My whiskey intake is strictly limited to medicinal purposes."

Emil Quackenbush's green eyes sparked in the flickering light of the campfire. "That's the only reason I ever touch the stuff. The problem is, a man's never really able to predict when he'll suffer an injury or come down with the ague. Practicing preventative medicine's what I believe in doing. Heck of a lot cheaper to snort a few drinks of whiskey than pay a high-priced sawbones to cure you after the fact."

Asa Cain had been ignoring his friends' banter. "There's no way anyone could have kept that marshal's body on ice out here in the heat. I'm of the opinion he was taken to a building where they store ice and kept there." He looked away from the distant storm to Blue Hand. "You've been around these parts longer than even the sheriff. Where does the saloons store their ice?"

The deputy said, "Mr. Sim Eby owns both the Purple Sage and Drover's Rest. He also sells ice to Mattie Rose's whor—" Blue Hand noticed the harsh glare the sheriff was giving him. "Uh, ah — rooming house. But all of the ice is stored in the basement of the Drover's Rest. That is the busiest place in town. I do not think anybody could have been put there and kept around for weeks, then taken out again, without a lot of people noticing."

"Blue Hand's right," Emil agreed. "That place is open all day and all night, seven days a week. A headless body being hauled in and out of there would have been a sight that'd be remembered."

"I reckon it would have at that," Asa Cain said, his brow lowered in thought. "But I'm wondering now where the outfit Sim Eby buys his ice from gets and stores theirs. The facts are, it'd have to be fairly close to Henrietta and yet secluded enough to store a body in without anybody seeing it come and go."

Blue Hand gave a slight shrug. "Dink and Joe are the ones who cut and deliver the ice. They are contraries. I do not even know their last names. They stay to themselves most of the time."

Emil snorted. "I never could understand how any fellow could pass up a nice, tender, sweet-smelling female in favor of another sweaty man. Just don't seem possible to me how something like that occurs, gotta come from drinking messed-up rainwater."

Asa gave a wide-eyed look to Blue Hand. "They *cut* and deliver ice. How and where do they do this?"

Blue Hand said simply, "From the big ice caves. They have a cabin not far from one of them, maybe two or three days' ride east of where we are camped."

Emil Quackenbush growled, "Now there's a perfect example of the sort of thing you do that peeves me off. Why didn't you part with this gem of information earlier? That would've been helpful."

The deputy stared off into the shadowing woods to his left. "You did not ask me until only now where the town of Henrietta gets its ice. You are the sheriff. I am only a deputy. You need to remember this, but I think we have other matters to concern us."

"And just what might have come up

237

important enough to change the subject of my chewing a good-sized hole in your hinder?" Emil fumed.

"Someone or something is attempting to sneak up on us."

"Now *that's* a good reason," the sheriff said reaching for his rifle.

TWENTY-SEVEN

Asa Cain cocked the hammer of his Henry rifle and scooted around behind the tree he had been leaning against while keeping an eye toward where Blue Hand was staring. "I don't see or hear any . . ." The sound of a snapping limb and rustling leaves, possibly a couple of hundred feet inside the wavering dark forest, caused him to become silent and hunker down like a badger, rifle at the ready.

"Whatever's out there's doing the worst job of creeping up on a camp I've ever encountered," Cemetery John said, looking down the barrel of his double-barreled ten-gauge shotgun pointed at the approaching rustling leaves and snapping of limbs. "That rules out Indians or skilled outlaws."

"But it *is* big," the sheriff commented.

"Might be only a stray cow or maybe even a wild pig," Asa said quietly.

"Indians are supposed to know about

things like this." Blue Hand shook his head. "But this one has me stumped."

"Maybe we just ought to start shooting," Emil said. "A few dozen hot slugs of lead heading in his general direction should be enough to teach some manners about not sneaking up on folks, especially right after they've just had their dinner. That can cause an upset stomach."

"Hold your fire," Asa whispered. "Wait until we see what is really out there. Then if we have to shoot it, we can economize on ammunition. It's a long ride back to stock up."

"Reckon that is good advice," Emil said. "And from all of the racket that thing's making, it won't be much longer before we get a gander at it."

"I'm not going to wait," Asa said, standing up on the sheltering side of the huge tree. "Just don't get trigger-happy until you can see what you're shooting at. I'm going to go around and come up behind whatever's out there."

The sheriff started to protest, but it was too late. Asa Cain had already melted into the night.

Thin yellow shafts of moonlight wavering through the sheltering trees gave Asa enough light to negotiate silently around sticks and leaves. He kept low, darting from one tree to another, keeping his eyes peeled for any sign of danger. A few scant moments later, he could plainly see his quarry.

A wan beam of moonlight caused the bald head of a man cradling a rifle to glow like a candle in a window. Whoever it was appeared to be alone. And from the way he was leaning on a small tree for support while waving the barrel of his rifle about, it became obvious the man was quite drunk.

Asa had no difficulty making his way behind the gunman unnoticed. From the way the stranger was listing from side to side, the bounty hunter doubted the man would notice a freight wagon coming up from behind him.

"All right, fellow," Asa said, placing the cold steel barrel of his Henry against the back of the man's neck. "Drop it."

"Ah, shucks, thish is a brand-new rifle. I hate to go an' scratch it all up."

The voice sounded familiar. "Then use one hand and lean it against that tree. You make one wrong move and a scratched rifle won't be of any concern. I promise you that."

Without turning around, the man slowly lowered his weapon; wobbling around while attempting to do as Asa had instructed, he missed the tree sending the rifle crashing to the ground. "Well, dang it all anyway."

Asa shook his head sadly. "Okay, now see if you can turn around without falling down."

"Jus' don't shoot me, I'm a bounty hunner. It ain't good business to shoot nobody that ain't worth the effort."

When the man turned and stepped into the light of the moon, Asa couldn't help but smile. "You're that lightning-rod salesman who gave George Maledon a ride into Henrietta."

"Artemis Lightning Rod Wilcox, at your service, shur. Pleash forgive my unorthodox approach, but I saw your campfire an' figgered it might be the head-whacker."

"The four of us are after the same killer. You keep sneaking up on folks like this, you'll have the shortest career of being a bounty hunter on record. Being drunk isn't helpful either."

"I only imbibed moderately to forti . . . forti . . . get ready for goin' manhuntin'."

"That's a crock," Emil Quackenbush grumbled coming out of the shadows, already lowering his pistol into its holster. "You're more pickled than a jar of my grandma's beets. I'm surprised you made it

242

as far as you did without falling off your horse."

Artemis Wilcox's brow lowered in thought. "Now that you mention it, I wonder what became of that horse. It's mostly all brown, I think."

Cemetery John had come to see what was going on. He sized up the wobbly lightning-rod salesman. "I'll put on a fresh pot of coffee. He's gonna have a headache tomorrow worse than if someone had hit him over the noggin with a long-handled shovel."

Lightning Rod Wilcox sat propped up against a stack of rocks the men had built up for that purpose. The drummer had kept rolling around any handy trees and falling over. Several cups of Cemetery John's strong black coffee had made little improvement in his condition.

"We finally had ourselves a fairly decent manhunt under way," Emil Quackenbush fumed after taking a sip of coffee and frowning. "Now we've got a drunk to contend with."

Cemetery John moved the boiling black coffeepot over to the edge of the campfire. "He'll sober up eventually, my good coffee never fails."

Asa Cain said, "In the morning we're going to start working our way east along the cliffs in the direction of those ice caves Blue Hand told us about no matter what shape he's in. I'm thinking we've already done him enough favors by not shooting him. Almost any other camp he'd pulled that stunt on would have put more holes in him than you'll find in a screen door."

Artemis Wilcox rolled bloodshot eyes to Asa. "I'll be in splendid shape to accompany you gents; all I need is a little bit of good sleep. I was just overly tired when I went inside of that den of iniquity, and failed to notice there had been knockout drops placed in my whiskey."

Asa Cain shot Cemetery John a glare that would curdle milk, then turned to the sheriff. "How about it, Emil, does Sim Eby ever roll any customers?"

"Nope, at least not personally, but if our traveling lightning-rod peddler here showed too much money, there's generally someone who'll relieve them of the worry of hanging onto their boodle. Most often card games do the trick, but there's been more than a few either walloped on the noggin or slipped a Mickey Finn to get the job done."

"Do you still have any money on your person?" Asa asked.

"I think I have a horse someplace. There

oughtta be a wagon around somewheres too, now that I'm concentrating on the matter. Had to get all the way out here somehow other than walking."

Cemetery John said, "If he was slipped a dose of chloral hydrate, that would go a long ways toward explaining why my good coffee ain't working."

"Oh, for Pete's sake," Emil grumbled. "All this mollycoddling isn't accomplishing any more than the undertaker's lousy coffee." He went over and started going through the unresisting Artemis Wilcox's pockets. "There's money in every pocket he owns. The idiot just went and got corned, that's the plain and simple of the matter."

"Sir," Lightning Rod mumbled, "I represent that statement — uh, well, anyway, I've lost my horse and wagon. That was a good horse too."

"Put a cork in it and sleep it off," the sheriff said standing up and attempting to work a kink out of his back. "Tomorrow morning, after you've recovered what wits you own, we'll figure out what to do with you. . . ."

Asa Cain held out a hand, palm down, and motioned for quiet. A quick look at his serious expression caused everyone except

Lightning Rod Wilcox to grow silent as a stone.

"Oh, you got a crick in your arm," Artemis said to Asa. "I have some really good liniment in my wagon that'll fix you up good as new." He gave a loud belch. "If you'll help me find my wagon, I'll sell you a bottle at a discount."

From atop a sheer limestone cliff only a short distance from their camp came a loud and long scream, like from a panther in agony.

"Jaysus H. Christ on a crutch!" exclaimed a suddenly sobering Artemis Wilcox. "That hangman I gave the ride to said whatever cut the heads off those marshals screamed like that."

Asa Cain stared out into the night. "I'm sure George Maledon spoke the truth. Whoever's out there is unspeakably evil, and he's making sure we know he's come calling."

TWENTY-EIGHT

Cemetery John cocked his head and looked up at the high cliffs through shafts of wavering moonlight. "Whoever's up there sure sounds pissed off about something."

"I hear both rage and pain," Blue Hand said. "Perhaps the dentist shot him in a bad place."

"*Any* place is a bad one to get shot in," Emil said, thumbing back the hammer on his revolver. "At least now we don't have to go chasing after buzzards or worry about making an identification that'll take."

"He's plenty alive all right," Asa said, joining Cemetery John in attempting to peer through the darkness for any movement to shoot at. "The fact that he's up there screaming his tonsils out brings up a possibility we ought to concern ourselves with."

"I know what you're thinking," Blue Hand said. "And you just might be right."

Emil Quackenbush chewed hard on his

stub of cigar. "Well, fill the rest of us in on the revelation, why don't you. This isn't a grand time to be trying to decipher Indian lore or much of anything else."

Asa said, "If there is a plot afoot to destroy Cyrus Warwick and the town of Henrietta, all of that caterwauling going on up there could simply be a diversion to allow another killer or killers to sneak up from our backside and do us in."

The sheriff bit down so hard he severed his cigar. "I never thought of that! Hell's bells and little green apples, this ain't no fun a-tall." With that comment Emil fanned six slugs of lead through the branches in the general direction of the screaming, then yelled at the top of his lungs, "And there's lots more where those came from!"

All of nature seemed to hold its breath after the sheriff's barrage. Even the buzzing of insects grew silent, as did the screaming from atop the towering cliff.

Cemetery John had turned to keep his huge shotgun pointed to their back. The possibility of someone coming at them from that direction seemed all too plausible. He speculated that this very same diversion might have been used successfully before, which could account for experienced lawmen being killed like they were. He felt a cold chill trickle down his spine when he realized that until Asa had brought up the possibility of a sneak attack from the rear, the thought of something like that occurring had not crossed his mind.

Then, an uneven sputtering sound, like a plugged rain gutter trying to drain, broke the fragile shell of silence that had claimed this portion of the Osage country. All four of the armed men who stood with weapons at the ready spun in the direction of the new noise, which turned out to be a snoring lightning-rod salesman.

"Not everyone can doze off over gunfire," Emil said, poking fresh cartridges into his Colt revolver. "That's a talent."

"At least he's sleeping off the whiskey," Asa said. "Having to watch after a drunk is an added problem we don't need right now."

The sheriff kept his gun out of its holster, held at the ready. "There's a reason to favor decent drinking over opiates. Once a man sobers up, he's pretty much the same as he was before going into the saloon. I'd reckon you can't say that about drugs."

"You're right about that," Cemetery John said still flicking his eyes about the forest. "But getting corned when there's a head-whacker about can make the argument a moot one."

Asa Cain gave a sigh, then cradled the Henry rifle in the crook of his arm. Slowly, the usual sounds of a summer night in the Osage began to fill the lush forests. "I think he's gone, at least for a while."

Blue Hand said, "At least no others have tried to come and cut off our heads. That is good."

"We could have simply had a warning to leave," Asa Cain said eyeing the coffeepot. "Animals do this; warn others to leave their territory. Perhaps he is hurt and only wants to be left alone. Then again, the screaming might have been a ruse to catch us off guard. It's things like this that makes bounty hunting so interesting."

Emil decided to fish another cigar from his vest. "Being a piano player in a whorehouse, now that's interesting. Trying to decipher what-all's going on here to keep from getting killed is downright worrisome. When this is over, I'm getting out of this spook-filled country and either go back to Texas or become a corset salesman in St. Louis."

"I thought you wanted to be a shoe salesman," Blue Hand said.

"Oh, whatever. Let's just try to not only get out of here alive, but with enough money to not have to fret the details."

"Let's have a cup of coffee and relax," Asa said. "We'll take turns doing guard duty, but we'd best catch some sleep. I've a feeling this manhunt's just getting started."

Emil Quackenbush glared at the blackened pot and snorted. "An easy way to put an end to this might be to set out a couple of cups of Cemetery John's coffee and wait. When the bad man comes along and drinks some, we can slap the handcuffs on him while he's trying to recover his breath."

The undertaker said, "After that remark you can take the first watch." With those words, Cemetery John sat down, leaned up against a tree, laid his battered slouch hat in his lap, and immediately engaged Artemis Wilcox in a snoring match.

"He's not really of a nervous disposition, is he?" Emil said while pouring himself a cup. "But I reckon, in his usual line of work, his customers aren't much trouble."

Blue Hand sniffed the air and fingered the handle of his holstered pistol. "There is the odor of skunk on the breeze. This happens everywhere the killer has cut off heads. I think I will be nervous enough for all of us this night."

"That's not a bad idea, Blue Hand," Asa said as he sat and leaned against the most comfortable tree he could find. "We think we are the ones doing the hunting. That might not be the case here at all."

Going Snake finished the last of his gory handiwork under the shooting red rays of a newborn sun. He felt a sadness in his heart for using two of The People as he had, but it was for the good of all Osage. A small sacrifice really. Little Badger and Running Bear were now with the Great Spirit, who would surely explain to them why they had to die, along with telling them of the great good to come from their leaving the world of mortals.

His plan was one of genius. The white-eyes who believe only in one god would, very soon, certainly have to accept the fact that an evil spirit was at work here. Kills Eagles, along with the other tribal elders, had smoked their peyote while sweating for many hours in the lodge. They had not been visited by any spirits. This was not what Going Snake had hoped for. Now his actions would leave neither The People nor the white-eyes any reason to doubt that an enraged evil spirit was the cause of people getting their heads cut off.

Going Snake raised his bloody hands high to greet the coming day. He prayed loud and long for the future of his people and the safety of his family, beseeching many gods, including the lesser ones whose job is to look after the sick, the elderly, and those who have lost their minds.

The shaman hoped also the one god of the white-eyes would take time and listen to his prayers. It could not hurt to do so. His teacher had said that all gods exist only because The People believed in them, and the only way a god could die was when The People lost interest in them and quit believing in their existence. A lot of white-eyes believed in their god and carried his book with them wherever they went. Surely their god was a powerful one. Having him on the side of the Osage would be helpful.

The sun was a blazing ball against an azure sky when Going Snake ceased his praying. Having done all he could, he resigned himself along with The People to whatever fate the gods decreed. Then he went to the rippling waters of Boggy Creek and thoroughly washed every trace of blood from his person.

Lastly, the medicine man surveyed his craftsmanship one final time, satisfied he had done his best. With a grunt, the muscular shaman turned and headed south along the trail that followed a jagged canyon; scant moments later he had blended with the shadows and was gone.

TWENTY-NINE

"They serve a brand of rotgut whiskey in Henrietta that makes pulque or panther piss seem like an improvement," Lightning Rod Wilcox complained as he sipped coffee while blinking into the rising sun. "The place ought to be closed as a menace to the public and the owner tarred and feathered, then run out of town on a rail."

Emil Quackenbush snorted and tossed a saddle on his horse. "I drink there myself and it's not the quality of the product that you're suffering from, it's the quantity. Fifteen drinks a day's my limit. When I tap it light like that, I feel fit as a fiddle the next morning."

Asa Cain remembered back to when his whiskey consumption was measured in bottles, not drinks. He was glad to be sober, especially now with unknown dangers all around. The possibilities surrounding the decapitations were seemingly endless. A plot to destroy the town of Henrietta along with its cornerstone, Cyrus Warwick, seemed the most plausible, but there were many other scenarios, and all of them deadly. What bothered the bounty hunter most of all was the fact that his once-never-failing intuition of lurking danger seemed to be, at best, waning. Last night Blue Hand had caught the scent of skunk — a smell everyone reported when the killer was about — yet *he* had not. This was disturbing, a sign he needed to be extra cautious. There were some good people, good friends, depending on him. He vowed to not let them down.

Cemetery John gave the lightning-rod salesman a glare of pained tolerance. "If you can remember where you left your horse and are feeling up to it, I reckon you're welcome to come along with us. Another gun, even a shaky one, might come in handy."

Artemis Wilcox stood and smiled. "I'm feeling quite peachy, thank you. This excellent coffee was just the palliative I needed to purge my system of that foul whiskey they forced me to imbibe to excess. I stand ready to assist in tracking down this murderer of fair women and men of upstanding character. My gun hand is stable and my eyes are keen."

Sheriff Quackenbush had frowned hard at Artemis ever since he had complimented Cemetery John's coffee. Anything the undertaker brewed up was more suitable for varnishing coffins or patching leaky boats than drinking. "Okay, you've proven you can remember how to use big words, but putting it plainly, where the blazes is your horse?"

"That would be helpful information," Cemetery John said in a kindly tone. Any compliment directed his way always mellowed him out. "It couldn't have been far — you weren't in any condition last night to walk much of a distance."

Artemis Wilcox's expression firmed to one of determination; then his usual mischievous grin returned. "Ah, the scales have fallen and given the eyes of memory the ability to reexamine past events with crystal clarity."

Emil gave a moan and cinched the saddle extra tight.

"My trusty steed," the drummer continued, nodding toward Boggy Creek, "is tied but a short distance upstream where it could water." An eyebrow lowered. "And it *is* brown."

"We'll accompany you," Asa Cain said. "I don't feel this is good country to be alone in."

Blue Hand said, "From Mr. Maledon's experience in these parts, three armed men can also run into trouble."

"Let's go get that dang horse," the sheriff said angrily mouthing a dead cigar. "We've got a manhunt to continue."

"Yeah," Asa Cain said. "Let's get on with it." But as he mounted his horse and reined it into a slow lope, the bounty hunter could not shake the feeling that on *this* manhunt, they might be the hunted instead of the hunter.

"I sure didn't expect this to happen when I left my trusty steed tied to this tree," Artemis Wilcox said with obvious awe.

Cemetery John kept his wide-eyed gaze fixed on the horse's head that dangled from a tree limb, held only by bridle reins. "I'd venture the horse didn't either."

Asa Cain dismounted and went over to study the horse's body, which was already attracting swarms of flies. "From the ragged cutting, it's almost as if the horse had his head sawed off. I can't see a mark on him other than where his head was removed."

"Our lovely went out of his way to leave us a message to quit this country," Sheriff Quackenbush said. "And anyone strong enough to do what we're looking at sure ain't bad hurt. Thinking on the matter, I don't see how one man could accomplish this even if nothing was wrong with him."

Blue Hand's voice was dry as old paper. "It is the work of a monster, an evil spirit. The strongest and most depraved of men would not saw the head off a living horse."

Emil's green eyes flicked nervously back and forth probing the verdant, shadowy forest that surrounded them. "Blue Hand's right about this whole thing being mighty strange. We find a hundred-and-eighty-pound headless federal marshal twenty feet up in a tree who'd been frozen in the summertime; now we run across a decapitated horse. I'd feel a lot more comfortable if we were pursuing normal outlaws who had the decency to take a potshot at you once in a while. Now *that* I can understand."

Asa Cain realized this line of conversation could not be allowed to continue. Frightened men make mistakes, and there were enough strange goings-on in the Osage country to cause the hair on the back of almost anyone's neck to stand up.

"Boys," Asa said with authority, "spirits stay in the spirit world, we all know that. This is the work of a man or men; that's something we can be sure of. It takes muscle to wield an ax or sword or whatever is being used to cut off these heads. And anything with muscle is also flesh and bone; therefore it is a man, a man who can be killed with a single well-placed bullet."

Blue Hand said, "If it is only a man, why has only the dentist seen him and lived? Outlaws are always making mistakes; that is why the sheriff and I can catch them. I have heard stories of spirits, especially evil spirits, coming to earth and walking the land."

"And stories are exactly what they are," Asa said to Blue Hand. "Keep your gun ready and your eyes peeled. We'll not only figure all of this out, but put a pile of money in our pockets for doing it."

Blue Hand brightened. "I have need of money. I will shoot whatever it is, even if it turns out to be an evil spirit. Perhaps, if it has taken human form to walk the earth, a bullet might kill it." He shrugged. "Who can tell when it comes to spirits?"

"That's the spirit," Emil said, then frowned when he realized his choice of words could have been better. "This is a moneymaking venture we're on, not some spook hunt."

"Would someone help me recover my saddle?" Artemis asked. "I hid my wagon in a clump of trees just off the road. It'd be appreciated if you kind gentlemen would be of assistance. I'll owe you a drink in any saloon not in Henrietta for your efforts."

"We'll help you get that saddle off," Sheriff Quackenbush said. "But I'm deputizing you here and now. There's a likelihood we might need every gun we can find before this plays out. Blue Hand's light as a feather, you can ride double with him. Give me any lip and I'll shoot you where you stand for deserting a legal posse in time of need."

"There's no need to become testy, Sheriff," Artemis said quickly. "I want to come along. All I was asking was a little assistance and an escort to my wagon. There's a reason aside from safely storing my saddle to go there."

"Well, spit it out," Emil fumed. "God ain't gonna make more daylight just so you can ramble on."

"In the war I was involved with the making and setting of booby traps along roads and trails. There are a half-dozen kegs of gunpowder and some pull-type detonation triggers under the seat of my wagon. Since whoever's out there stalking us at night likes to circle our camp, I'm thinking we ought to arrange for him to have a bang-up greeting, one that would leave enough intact for a reward."

The sheriff grinned, his red beard flaring like a provoked cat's tail. "I like this better than having to shoot you. Let's roll that dead horse over and get your saddle; the smell's already bad enough to contend with and the flies ain't getting any less."

THIRTY

"Being a seller of protective lightning rods is a somewhat more hazardous occupation than most people suspect," Artemis Wilcox said to Cemetery John.

The undertaker inspected the contents of the wagon with an astonished look. "I'd venture small wars have been fought with less weaponry. What in the heck is this thing that looks like a cannon?"

Artemis gave a thin smile. "That's a punt gun, or a single-shot, six-gauge shotgun. Market hunters fix them to the bow of a boat because no one can take the recoil. They can wipe out an entire flock of ducks or geese with one shell. I keep this one on a pivot where I can swing it back and shoot at anyone coming after me. There's a stunt they'll only try once."

"I'd reckon so," Asa Cain said. "You not only have kegs of gunpowder, but the steel containers to make bombs out of, and even a stock of minié balls. I've visited forts that had less firepower."

The lightning-rod salesman nodded in agreement. "The frontier's a dangerous place for the unprepared. You could say I'm prepared enough to catch most folks off their guard." He squinted in thought, then quickly added, "Only when I'm forced to defend myself, of course."

"Oh, I'm sure of that," Sheriff Quackenbush said. He was mentally going through wanted posters, trying to remember if he'd seen one for a lighting-rod salesman with a nice reward attached. There was no reason to limit his income since he'd most likely be out of work soon. After a few moments, he shrugged and gave up on Artemis Wilcox as being worthless. "Maybe some of this armory will be helpful even if we are dealing with a sassy-squatch monster. There's enough firepower here to blow his furry ass all the way back to Oregon or wherever the heck he's from."

"I sort of cotton to the idea of planting a couple of booby traps around our camp, maybe let whoever's out there blow himself up," Cemetery John said hoisting a five-pound keg of gunpowder. "Should be less hazardous to our health if that would do him in."

Asa Cain clucked his tongue. "Provided there's only one outlaw after us or they're all together at the time. We really don't have any good idea who's involved with the killings, and trip bombs have their drawbacks."

Lightning Rod Wilcox nodded his agreement, then reached over and grabbed the wooden gunpowder keg from Cemetery John. "There's a thin wire attached to this one. If somebody's foolhardy enough to try and steal my powder, when they get about twenty feet away, which is far enough to spare my wagon any damage, this keg will explode and blow 'em to bits."

Cemetery John stepped back and spread his palms open. "You've got me convinced to leave well enough alone."

Artemis grinned his mischievous grin and continued. "Asa's correct about booby traps. The reason they weren't used much during the war is the fact that about as many troops on our side triggered them as did the enemy. A lot of times the person who set the trip wire wouldn't remember the landscape well enough and set the bomb off themselves. Then one has to consider animals such as deer or bears can also trigger the explosion. Oh, my, I can tell you of all sorts of sinister things that can go amiss."

Blue Hand had been watching from a

distance. "White men always have a tendency to complicate matters. I would prefer to simply shoot the bad men and be done with it." He pointed to the open box beneath the wagon seat. "I have never seen a bow-and-arrow rifle before."

Lightning Rod Wilcox grabbed up the object of Blue Hand's attention and held it high with a smile. "This is called a crossbow; it is an ancient weapon used as far back as medieval times. They are silent as sunrise and can put a shaft all the way through a man easy as this." He swung and fired at a nearby tree over a foot thick. The arrow made a dull *whump* as it penetrated deep enough to have a few inches of the iron shaft extend out the opposite side. "And the person getting shot never even hears where it came from."

Asa Cain frowned. "Artemis, you had that thing cocked and ready to fire. Do you keep all of these guns loaded?"

The drummer gave an astonished look. "Why on earth would anyone carry around an unloaded gun? It has been my experience that when there's going to be a fight, the other party or parties aren't prone to giving you a lot of time to prepare. Not only is every one of my weapons fully loaded along with the punt gun, I also keep a cartridge under the firing pin of all my pistols. This can fool folks into thinking you're out of ammo."

Emil snorted. "And if a twig or something causes you to drop it, you can watch your own gun shoot you."

"I don't let that happen," Artemis said simply.

Blue Hand came walking over. "Would you teach me to shoot the crossbow?"

"Sure," Artemis said. "Being an Indian, it should come natural."

"I am only half Osage," Blue Hand corrected. "My father was a Mexican."

Artemis grabbed a handful of arrows. "No matter, it sights just like a rifle. Come on over in the shade and I'll show you how to crank the bow. The tighter you bring it back to a notch, the more power it gives the shaft. I always crank it as far back as it'll go."

"Somehow I thought you would," Blue Hand said as he followed Artemis Wilcox to beneath a sheltering copse of elm trees.

While the lightning-rod salesman was instructing Blue Hand in the operation of a crossbow, the sheriff, Cemetery John, and Asa Cain took the time to sit in the shade of the wagon, smoke a cigar, and discuss their plans to apprehend a forty-thousand-dollar outlaw.

Emil took a couple of long nines from the dwindling supply in his vest, bit the end off one, and mouthed it, then passed the other to Asa. Cemetery John had what he deemed an adequate supply of his own.

"Asa," the sheriff said after lighting his cigar and handing over the match. "You're the experienced bounty hunter here, but I've always been of the mind that some sort of trail to follow was a vital ingredient of any manhunt. Maybe I'm missing something here, but it appears to me that all we're doing is riding around in an area where a lot of people lost their heads. Is there some clue I've missed?"

Asa Cain rolled his cigar in the flame to start the tobacco burning evenly. He passed the stub of match over to Cemetery John, then said, "Actually, Emil, to make a clean breast of it, you're dead right. There's simply no trail *to* follow. I'm hoping the killer or killers will make a mistake and leave us one. It seems a fact we've got the attention we need, considering our little visit last night."

Cemetery John added, "And a decapitated horse that left a puzzle. Whatever they used for the task, along with the person who did it, should have left a blood trail a blind man could follow. All I noticed were some bloody bushes, that's all."

"He used those leafy bushes to clean up on," Asa said. "That shows planning and cunning. I looked for tracks and found none. Of course, if he was wearing moccasins, that would account for it. They're mighty hard to follow, nothing like boots."

"Are you saying our screaming head-whacker is an Indian, for Pete's sake?" Emil asked. "There's a twist I hadn't considered. Generally Indians are plenty obvious, shooting folks full of arrows and then scalping them. I ain't never heard of any tribe that'll bother to take the whole head."

Asa Cain said, "That never happens. The taking of a scalp is a trophy, a way of keeping score. When a warrior removes a scalp, this is not always fatal; there are many accounts of people being knocked unconscious, then walking up with their hair missing. The scalp is honored by being dried and the skin painted; then it is used as decoration. No Indian I've known of would remove an entire head, unless it was to be used for a warning, and to the best of my knowledge, there hasn't been a single head found except for the lightning-rod salesman's horse."

"Then we're coming back to the possibility the whole affair has been staged to ruin

Cyrus Warwick and destroy the town of Henrietta," Cemetery John said, after sucking a finger he had singed when he lit his cigar with the too-short match. "But why take the trouble to make it look like some monster has been killing people? I can't figure the screaming and the heads being taken."

Emil said, "And not a single head's been found. There's another puzzle for you to put in your pipe and smoke."

"Nothing fits any normal outlaw I've dealt with," Asa said. "And I've gone after and brought back a passel of the worst there are. The Schull clan came to West Texas over five years ago from New Mexico Territory. They were about the most horrible I can remember encountering. There were three of them, Old Man Banes Schull and his twin boys, Pete and Joe. They'd rob a store or way station and kill every living soul. Man, woman, or child, it made no difference.

"I followed a trail of carnage they left behind all the way from Wolf Springs to the Mexican border, then west to El Paso, where I managed to catch up with them when they'd made camp after one of their horses went lame. Like a lot of outlaws, they had a streak of yellow down their backbone.

I took them easy, then watched when they cried like babies at their hanging a few days later. No, whatever we're dealing with here, we're going to have to figure out as we go."

Sheriff Quackenbush said, "Let's hope they'll make a mistake and leave a trail, like you're hoping they will."

"All outlaws eventually do," Asa said. "The hardest part of being a lawman or bounty hunter is watching all the bodies keep turning up until they do. Innocent people being killed like they are here is never easy to take."

"What Blue Hand told us about the ice cave further to the east is interesting." Cemetery John puffed on his cigar. "There's no doubt that's about the only place Marshal Talbot's body could have been kept."

Asa Cain looked up at the jagged line of high limestone cliffs. "When you're dealing with caves, and I think you're dead right about an ice cave being used to store that body we found — there's generally more than one cave. I'm betting there's caves scattered all along these cliffs."

Emil scanned his eyes across the rugged landscape and snorted. "And scouting them out could take months. Some of that country's steep enough to scare a mountain goat into a heart seizure."

Cemetery John brightened. "Any ice cave where the marshal's body was stored has to have a good trail to it; he wasn't a small man."

"Well, that'll be a big help," Emil snorted. "Might only take us a few weeks instead of months, following all the game trails in this country."

Asa Cain's eyes narrowed. "Whoever's out there's not the patient type. They know we're here and they'll keep coming for us. I feel that in my bones."

"There's a cheerful notion." The sheriff ran a hand through his bushy red beard. "I thought we were the ones who are supposed to be hunting *them.*"

Cemetery John grinned. "Having the bad men come to us is a new twist. I like it, saves wear and tear. But I think we're going to have to do more than boil up some coffee and set around playing cards until they show up and let us kill 'em."

"All we can do is keep poking about," Asa said with resignation. "This isn't open country like West Texas. Let's work our way along the base of those cliffs; that'll give us a chance to check for caves and signs. No one can move about without bending over weeds, snapping off small limbs, or leaving an occasional track on the muddy bank of a creek."

"Yep," Emil Quackenbush muttered as he rose to his feet. "We'll keep chasing after 'em until they find us. There's a plan to be proud of, being really tough manhunters like we are."

"Results are what counts," Asa said. "All the way up to forty thousand dollars."

Emil's beard flared into a smile. "Then let's round up Blue Hand and a hungover lightning-rod salesman and go rile the bad man."

THIRTY-ONE

Artemis Wilcox was quite uncomfortable riding double behind Blue Hand, but realized it wouldn't be of any use to complain, considering the circumstances. At least he had recovered his saddle and still had his wagon, along with most of the money he'd made selling all of those protective Armbruster lightning rods to Cyrus Warwick. A new horse shouldn't cost over fifty dollars at the most. This would be nothing to concern himself with after splitting a forty-thousand-dollar reward.

It galled him to think of having to cut the money up five ways. Then he cheered up when the realization crossed his mind that he might have to do very little, or possibly nothing, just be there to collect his share. The trigger-happy sheriff would most likely do the shooting, Asa Cain the tracking, and Cemetery John could lug the body around. Blue Hand wasn't a total loss either; the deputy *was* sharing his horse, and had agreed to pay him twenty dollars for the crossbow that now lay across his lap. All in all, if Artemis simply stayed out of the way, he stood to collect eight thousand dollars with little or no effort on his part or threat to his person. To Artemis Lightning Rod Wilcox, dodging both work and peril came as natural as breathing, and every bit as desirable.

"You told me the crossbow was made for shooting nights," Blue Hand said over his shoulder while keeping a watchful eye out for danger. "How is it possible to shoot in darkness?"

Artemis chuckled. "The word is knight, and it is spelled with a K. Hundreds of years ago in a faraway land called Europe, which is a cold country across the ocean, this was what they called warriors who wore armor and rode on valiant quests to protect their king or seek the most worthy of all treasures, the Holy Grail."

"If they were great warriors, why would anyone want to make a crossbow to shoot them with. And while I am asking, what is armor and a grail?"

The lightning-rod salesman had a building pain over his left eye, an aftereffect, no doubt, of being served inferior whiskey. He really wished to ride along in silence while regaining his health, but Blue Hand was kind enough to share his horse. Also, the deputy wasn't likely to check with a book should Artemis take some minor liberties with history.

Artemis Wilcox cleared his throat. "Now back in those days there were lots of different kings, sort of like Indian tribes today. These kings often got in fights with each other over land, or women, or whatever; then they would go to war. The knights' armor was like thick steel shirts and pants; most normal arrows or swords just bounced right off without damage. This wasn't really a good thing because all a war accomplished was to tire out the soldiers without any land being conquered or maidens rescued. Then a really smart man by the name of Sam Cross invented the crossbow that shot steel arrows which went right through the armor and killed the knight. After that they were able to fight successful wars for many years."

"I do not think armor to be honorable. A warrior should face his enemy on an equal basis to find out which one is the bravest. Mr. Sam Cross, who made this fine crossbow, I think would agree. It is a really good weapon, and a quiet one too."

"Armor wouldn't work in this country,

honorable or not. The weather's hot enough in the summertime to cook anyone dumb enough to wear it."

"I would think that to be true. What is a Holy Grail?"

Artemis suppressed a sigh. The pain over his eye was now throbbing. "The Grail was the drinking vessel that the Son of God in the Bible used to drink his wine at the Last Supper. It has been pursued for centuries, and never found."

Blue Hand said, "To have a cup that was held by a god is a worthy quest. I hope they find it someday."

Then, to the lightning-rod salesman's relief, Blue Hand grew silent, content to ride along the burbling creek while keeping his eyes peeled for any sign of danger.

Cemetery John had been riding close enough to Blue Hand and Artemis to catch their conversation. He slowed down and allowed his horse to come alongside Emil and Asa.

"I've always thought lightning-rod peddlers were basically pests," the undertaker said. "The one we're stuck with, however, is not only a professor of humbug, but he's warping that poor deputy's mind with some of the worst balderdash and made-up history I've heard since the last time Congress was in session."

The sheriff kept carefully scanning the shadowy forest that was often thick enough to blot out any trace of sunlight. "I most likely should have shot him instead of deputizing him, but I figured we might could use his help. From the arsenal he travels with, Wilcox might be a lot tougher than most think." Emil shrugged. "Besides, I am the sheriff. I can shoot him nice and legal anytime. And I can't see how a tad of shoddy education's going to damage Blue Hand when he has me to rely on to set him straight later."

Asa Cain sniffed the sultry air and held up a hand to stop. Blue Hand had already noted the scent of skunk and reined his horse to a halt.

"What do you see?" Emil asked, resting his gun hand on the butt of his Colt.

"Nothing, but there's the odor of skunk about," Asa Cain said. "He's out there. I can feel his evil and he is close, very close."

Emil Quackenbush lowered an eyebrow as he scrutinized the gloomy depths of the thick forest. "There ain't nothing moving, not even a leaf. It's quiet enough to hear a bird fart. I do smell skunk, however. Do you reckon whoever's out there's just keeping an eye on us?"

"He's going to attack and kill whenever possible." Asa Cain's blue eyes were mere slits, his face tight with tension. "There's more evil and pure hate directed toward us than anything I've ever felt. He wants to kill us. And he will try to do it just as soon as we give him the opportunity."

"Let's not make it easy for 'em," Artemis Wilcox said, waving about the double-barreled ten-gauge shotgun he had brought along. "We've got a lot of firepower and we're on the lookout for an ambush."

Blue Hand sat tall and straight in the saddle, studying the still woods for any movement. He saw nothing amiss, but he could feel unseen eyes. "We are being watched, of this I have no doubt."

A squirrel chattered a warning from its nest of leaves and twigs, high in a towering hickory tree, then grew silent as stone. The five loaded guns that had swung in the animal's direction lowered.

"Dang, but we're getting jittery," Emil said.

"It's time to be scared," Asa Cain said. "That'll help keep us alive."

Cemetery John said, "Like I told you earlier, I've buried lots of people who weren't nervous when they should've been. When you know someone's out to kill you, that's reason enough in my book to be on edge."

Artemis Wilcox jumped to the ground. "I want to see whoever's out there for just long enough to blast them to Hell. I take offense to being pestered by folks out to get me."

"We'll make our acquaintances soon," Asa said, his voice absolutely emotionless. "But for now I'll be content to thank them for being so obliging."

"Obliging!" The sheriff's outcry was hoarse with frustration. "Have you lost your mind and gone daft on us? If you have, you've picked one heck of a bad time to turn into a lunatic."

Asa Cain's eyes darkened dangerously as he stared into a thick copse of trees. "We were hoping for a trail to follow. Now all we have to do is cut his sign. Then we'll be the ones doing the chasing."

"I'd like that a lot better, be easier on my stomach," Emil said. "Let's get to it. I plumb forgot to bring along my bicarbonate of soda."

"We'd best proceed slow," Blue Hand said. "And stay close together."

"The deputy's right about that." Artemis kept his shotgun cocked and held at the ready. "An ambush is mighty hard to pull off when it's expected."

"Let's go get that head-whacker," Sheriff Quackenbush growled, then turned to Asa. "You're the one who says he's out there. Tell us which direction to go."

"That way," the bounty hunter said with a nod. "Toward those high cliffs and Boggy Creek. I think that's also where he hides out and where we'll find another ice cave." Asa hesitated. In all of his years of being a manhunter, he had never felt such a sense of fear. Even in the building heat of a cloudless afternoon, a cold chill passed through his lean body. "Stay close together, boys. We're expected."

Less than a quarter of an hour later, Asa Cain, with Blue Hand by his side, stood staring down at a muddy patch where Boggy Creek widened in a rare flat part of the steep canyon.

"It is plain," Blue Hand said. "I do not understand."

"Neither do I." Asa bent low to study the obviously fresh footprint. "But there's no doubt he is wearing moccasins. I sure never figured on an Indian to be the killer."

"There are bad Indians, same as bad white-eyes." Blue Hand followed the tracks for several feet to where they disappeared onto a rocky ledge. "The man is big, his moccasins sink deep. One side of his is heavier than the other for some reason."

"He's maybe carrying something heavy," Artemis Wilcox said as he stepped close. "Like a saw big enough to cut off a horse's head. I'm plenty sore at him for doing that."

Asa Cain thumbed his chin. "There's also a possibility he's either crippled or deformed. Doc Holliday thought the man might even be a hunchback he was so misshapen."

Emil Quackenbush had stayed a few feet away keeping an eye out and his Colt at the ready. "No matter how gimpy he is, I've got a cure for his problem, five of 'em, all of the forty-five-caliber variety."

"This country is so blasted rugged, buggy, grown over, and downright nasty to be in." Cemetery John scratched at the back of his hand from where he had brushed against some poison ivy. "I can understand why he became so irritable."

Artemis Wilcox kept looking up and down the rugged cliffs; his eyes were flat and unreadable as the stone walls themselves. "This is some of the meanest country I've set foot in. A person could hide forever in here if they were of a mind to do so. There could be a dozen eyes watching us right now and we'd likely never see who was doing the spying, the brush is so thick. Following any tracks very far isn't possible."

"Nor will it be necessary," Asa Cain said rising to study the few patches of blue sky that were visible through breaks in the trees. "He will continue to hunt us. This is his home, we are the trespassers. All we need to do is wait, he will come to kill us."

"I've always admired that cheerful, never-say-die, the-world-is-my-oyster attitude of yours, Asa," Cemetery John said forcing himself to quit scratching the back of his hand, since he knew it was only making the condition worse. "We'll just relax, play some cards, and have ourselves a gay ol' time until that forty-thousand-dollar outlaw obligingly comes over to whack off our heads, allowing us to shoot him full of holes first."

Emil Quackenbush gave a beaming grin. "A simple plan is always best, less to go wrong." He noticed Asa staring off to the west. "What's got your attention now?"

Asa Cain clucked his tongue. "They're some distance away, downstream maybe a mile or so. A circling of vultures has their attention being drawn by something."

"Let's go see who or what's been killed now," Cemetery John said as the five men gathered to return to their horses. "Another thing folks say about being on a manhunt with Asa Cain. Nobody's who's lived through one has ever complained any about being bored."

THIRTY-TWO

Hate-filled eyes watched from the gloom of a shallow cave as the armed men mounted and rode away. He was angered that two rode on one horse. His object in killing the horse was to cause one of the men to leave his territory. There was never any predicting what the white-eyes would do. The only way to keep his land, his beloved collection safe was to kill all of them.

If only there were not so *many.* And they kept coming like bugs to a fire; you slap and kill a dozen, only to have more take their place. No matter, he would do what he must. Eventually, there would be no more white-eyes to endure.

The two small holes in his belly were now leaking only a small amount of vile-smelling fluid. He was, as always, healing. He felt a wave of bitter hatred for the skinny man with the pretty watch who did this to him. In the future he would employ his wonderful ice saw first, then take whatever prizes he wished at his leisure.

He rose and went outside to stand on a rock ledge. The always pain came sharp to his body, keening his senses. The pursuers would not be returning to this place. What they would soon encounter would definitely hold their attention for a long time. A blackened, scarred finger touched the glistening ice saw, played lovingly along the cold steel. Yes, what the white-eyes were heading for would *definitely* keep their attention. Until he could slip up and kill them, that is.

He realized the white-eyes, at least one or two, needed to live, to tell of what they saw, to warn their people to never come to this country again. It would be difficult, *very* difficult not to kill them all, but he resolved to try his best.

Carrying his beloved ice saw, accompanied by the always pain, he blended into the dense forest, silent as a snake gliding through wet grass, and was gone.

Less than an hour later he was home. The entrance to his wonderful cave had been obscured before he had planted more bushes and trees to hide it even further from prying eyes.

The cold bit against his skin when he entered. It was a miracle, winter in the middle of summer. The stinging cold was so useful for preserving his food along with his wonderful collection. And best of all, here he was alone, safe and secure.

Misshapen fingers with nails that were more like claws reached into a wooden box that was on a ledge nearby. A moment later, he held a lit candle to guide his way into the inner sanctum. The blue green of ice glittered like the stars of the Great Heaven from the light of the flame as he made his way deeper into the grotto to where his collection lay. It was nearly complete. Soon, very soon, it would be.

A sense of well-being, a feeling of serenity overshadowed the always pain when he came into the Chamber of Spirits, his very own altar. A few moments later, he had a small fire burning in the center. It was his good fortune to have a tiny natural opening above to allow the smoke to escape.

The blue ice walls sparkled and danced along with the flickering flames. He was home. Here he could rest until the night, and the hunt. Using a thick green willow stick to hold it over the fire, he roasted the hindquarter of a raccoon he had killed weeks ago. It was marvelous how well his cave preserved meat. He savored the sweet smell, took delight in the sizzles small drops of grease made when they fell into the fire.

Then, The Panther thought of the white-eyes and what they had surely found by now. Laughter seldom came from his mouth, but he could not contain the low chuckle that came across more like a growl. The Panther laughed his eerie laugh, roasted his meat, and awaited with glee the coming night.

And the thrill of the hunt.

THIRTY-THREE

For the second time that afternoon, Asa Cain, who was in the lead, held up a hand to call a halt. The posse had just rounded a sharp bend of Boggy Creek and was nearing a flat, open area where the stage road ran that went from the Oklahoma Indian Territory to the town of Henrietta, Kansas.

Emil Quackenbush, Blue Hand, and Artemis Wilcox rode to his side and reined their horses to a stop.

"Now what?" the sheriff grumbled. "Are you feeling more spooks coming in from out there on the breeze for us to fret?"

"Not this time." Asa waved his hand at a number of Indians that were riding toward them from the opposite direction. "Company has come calling."

Artemis Wilcox first cocked, then started to swing his big ten-gauge shotgun toward the Indians as Blue Hand grabbed the barrel with a surprisingly firm grip.

"Those are my People," the deputy said. "The braves would not like to be shot at. I think it would be wise to lower the hammer on this fine gun of yours and not point it toward someone who might take offense and shoot back."

The lightning-rod salesman quickly did as Blue Hand suggested, urged on by the fact he could count a lot more Indians than he had shells in his gun. "I'm glad to find out they're friendly," Artemis said. "It's just that I'm not prone to taking a lot of chances."

Sheriff Quackenbush rode out a short distance to meet Chief Kills Eagles, who he had quickly recognized. He held up a flat palm in a greeting that also showed he had no weapon. "Greetings, Chief, what brings y'all out on such a fine afternoon?"

Kills Eagles returned the greeting and reined his horse to a stop in front of the sheriff. "We are on a spirit quest." The Osage chief waved a hand to Going Snake as the medicine man approached. "The shaman has had a vision that we must check out."

"If Going Snake is on a spirit hunt," Emil said chewing on a stub of cigar, "he ought to get along famously with Asa Cain who's behind me. He's always feeling the presence of 'em about."

Kills Eagles took a brief note of the many circling buzzards that were concentrating their attention only a few hundred feet downstream. "I wish to meet with this man."

"Asa," Emil hollered over his shoulder while motioning with his hand. "Come on up here and meet a friend of mine." He hesitated. "And bring Cemetery John along too." He hesitated once again. "Ah, shucks, everybody come on up here so we can talk without having to shout at each other, for Pete's sake."

A few moments later, the groups were facing each other, greetings along with introductions having been made.

Blue Hand was obviously surprised to see all of the tribal elders were present. "My Chief," he said with respect. "I know only the most dire of circumstances ever calls for a gathering of all of the elders. May we know the reason for everyone being summoned?"

Kills Eagles' voice was resonant and impressive when he spoke. "I will share what I know. There have been many white men murdered in this part of our Nation. We of The People wish these mutilations to stop. The Army shall surely come and blame us and rub us out for something in which we had no part.

"I and the council of elders have done everything we could to find out why the white men have been killed and their heads stolen away. We built a sweat lodge, smoked many pipes, and asked for the Great Spirit's help in this matter. He must have been too busy elsewhere for he failed to answer our pleas. Then, only last night, our shaman was visited in his sleep by a lesser god that told him of a great evil that has been loosed to ravage this section of our land. This evil spirit has gone crazy, so crazy it was thrown out of the heavens. Now it is here, among us. This vision has been a sign, a warning given to all people, both the Osage and the white men."

Going Snake spoke, his tone oddly gentle and reserved. "It is a terrible thing to be visited upon this earth by an evil entity from the spirit world. Flesh-and-blood beings can be reasoned with, dealt with by force if necessary. This is not so with a spirit. They cannot be reasoned with, only appeased. I have been told in my vision of many terrible things to come if we do not heed the warnings of the gods."

Kills Eagles spoke again. "In the shaman's vision, we were all summoned to this place. The fact that you white men are here is truth that all of us have been summoned.

Let us go together and see what the gods have sent for us to look at and make our decisions from."

Sheriff Quackenbush gave a nod to the circling buzzards. "Whatever the spirits dropped off, it must be plenty ripe."

"I don't have a feeling this is going to be anything pleasant myself," Cemetery John said. The undertaker had had too much experience with what attracted vultures to take any chances. He took a small jar of camphor from his pocket, smeared a healthy amount under his nose, then lit a fresh long nine cigar to help cut down even further on the vile smells that accompany flesh rotting beneath a blazing hot sun.

"You're the one who makes a living from being in touch with the spirit world," Emil Quackenbush said to Going Snake. He could not place a finger on just why he had taken such a dislike to the husky medicine man, but he felt a provoked, coiled-up rattlesnake would be more trustworthy. "Lead the way, Shaman."

Kills Eagles motioned to the circling of black birds against a cloudless sky. "Take us to your vision, Going Snake." Then, with a flick of the reins, they were off.

After the initial wave of shock had passed,

Emil Quackenbush was the first to find his voice. He stared down at the remains of the two figures that had been laid out, side by side on a flat outcropping of white limestone, like grisly carrion for sale in a store found only in nightmares.

"My pappy" — the sheriff's voice was hoarse — "told me there'd be bad days, but he never said there'd be one like this."

Asa Cain clucked his tongue, then dismounted but kept away from the bodies waiting for Kills Eagles to join him, which was a matter of respect for the chief of the Osage.

Cemetery John, Kills Eagles, and Going Snake came together to join Asa in inspecting the macabre scene that was more shocking than anything any of them had ever encountered.

"The badges still on their shirts are U.S. marshals' stars," Asa said, his face a mask of stone. "I reckon we can telegraph Judge Parker the two lawmen who were attacked while escorting George Maledon to Henrietta's been found. The rest of the matter has me stumped."

"Ieeee!" Going Snake screamed at the top of his lungs. "The evil spirit has replaced the white men's heads with those of Little Badger and Running Bear. He has taken away the bodies of our scouts as a warning."

Cemetery John was glad to have the camphor under his nose. He stepped close to the bodies and bent low while swatting away clouds of flies. After a moment he choked out, "Blasted buzzards always go for the eyes first, sorta messes up people's features. But the heads on both bodies have been stitched on with heavy thread. They're sure as hell Indian heads too."

Going Snake shouted, "It is a warning to both whites and The People: An evil spirit claims this land!"

Asa Cain's eyes narrowed when he turned to Kills Eagles. "How does the chief of the Osage explain why a spirit would need a needle and thread to attach heads from The People onto bodies of white men? I believe this to be the handiwork of a man."

"There is much to consider." Kills Eagles kept staring grimly at the bird-pecked, fly-covered remains in front of him. "Spirits have been known to go crazy. If this is the case, we must consult with other gods, pray, smoke peyote, and sweat. To appease any god takes a lot of effort. A crazy one will be more of an undertaking than any of us have encountered up to now."

Going Snake said, "My Chief, the god

who visited me in my sleep and led us here told me more, much more."

Kills Eagles stood erect and said to the shaman, "Then say your vision to all here so we can parley and come to a decision as how to deal with these bad things that have come to our lands."

"The voice of the god in my vision boomed like thunder," Going Snake said, flicking his dark eyes back and forth from Indian to white men while holding out his hands, palms open to the heavens. "There *is* a spirit here who has lost his mind. Even in the Great Beyond of our Ancestors, not all is perfect. Not all is honorable. Not all is good.

"The evil spirit takes and eats the heads of white men. He has no desire for heads of the Osage, but he eats their bodies. This spirit has claimed only a small part of this earth as his hunting grounds. If all people, both white and Indian, avoid the place called Boggy Creek and the cliffs that contain it, the evil spirit will have no one to kill. Then someday he will grow bored and either regain his mind or return to the spirit world. No matter which, he will then be gone without any effort on our part."

"That spook's not only gabby," Sheriff

Quackenbush said, "he's also plenty arrogant."

Asa Cain said, "Chief Kills Eagles, all here who have white skin honor and respect the ways of The People, but we are sworn to also honor the laws of our great chief in Washington. These killings, all of them, both Osage and whites, are by the hand of man. I urge you to consider why any spirit, all of whom can roam free at will, would chose to stay in one small place. There are other reasons for these killings, reasons rooted in *this* world, not the next. We need to work together to find out what they are."

"There is no reasoning with *any* white-eyes," Going Snake growled. "The killings will continue until all people stay away from Boggy Creek. So said my vision."

Buffalo Hair turned to Swift Horse, who was the eldest of the council. "I do not know why any god would need to sew on a head with thread. The white man has a good point."

Swift Horse said, "Even if an evil spirit did do these deeds, the Army will still come. The cavalry won't believe they cannot destroy it. But I think Going Snake's vision is flawed; perhaps he should have smoked more and gone with us to the lodge and had a long sweat. Maybe another spirit guide would have shown him a better, more useful vision."

Kills Eagles stepped close to the bodies. After a moment, he returned to the gathered men. "These are facts. The heads are those of our scouts, the bodies are wearing lawmen badges, the heads are sewed on with thread. The biggest fact The People must consider is, as Swift Horse has counseled us, the Army will still come to our land."

Going Snake's face became a mask of fury. "Do not be a fool, My Chief, I am Shaman, I speak for the gods. Heed this warning and forbid the Osage from visiting this place and the killings will stop. Let the white men make their own decisions. If they choose wrongly, they will die."

Cemetery John said, "Both preachers and medicine men tend to be really gloomy sorts. Always have been for some reason."

Asa Cain turned to Kills Eagles. "There is a man or men doing these killings, not some evil spirit. We know the way of your people is to smoke many pipes and have a long powwow, but the Army is on its way here from Fort Smith as we speak."

Swift Horse said, "I think it is better to fight an evil spirit than the Army. If we win against the spirit, the Army might then return to Arkansas, which will be a good thing."

Kills Eagles glowered at Going Snake. "Do not call me a fool again or I will stab you with my knife. I am Chief, do not forget this."

The shaman's eyes lowered. "I beg your forgiveness, my vision was a strong one."

The Osage chief surveyed the assemblage. "Let us go and make a camp — upwind. This evening and tonight we shall smoke our pipe and parley. Tomorrow at first light we will all ride across this land together to see what we can find. I have spoken."

Asa Cain noticed a flicker of agony and dread in Going Snake's eyes as they mounted to leave and make camp for the coming night. The shaman obviously had his own deep reasons for wanting all people to leave this land alone, reasons more powerful than those found in a dream. Somehow, someway, the hulking medicine man fit into the puzzle of the killer or killers who took their victims' heads. Asa decided to keep an extra-close eye on the shaman, then reined his horse around to follow the group into the shadowy depths of Boggy Creek.

THIRTY-FOUR

The Panther had begun the hunt early. A lowering sun was still clinging to the day with fiery fingers that were the delightful color of fresh blood. Inside his cold and comfortable cave, it was always pleasantly dark, peaceful. He relished the night, felt safety in the shadows.

Yes, the night belonged to him. It had ever since the bad thing happened that gave him not only the always pain, but his mission. He squinted into the setting sun while running gnarled fingers through his long, greasy black hair. A full moon, a hunter's moon, was when he preferred to do his hunts, but now with all of the many enemies on his territory, he had to be more flexible.

Killing was what mattered, not the time in which he did the act. And kill he must to protect his nearly complete collection, his mission in life. All that mattered to him was to protect what he had accomplished. A few more heads was what he required. Just a few more.

Going Snake had insisted the white men and the Osage would leave him alone after they found the warning he had left. The Panther doubted that would be the case. All were out to stop him from finishing his collection. He did hope Going Snake might be right, or at least the warning might buy him some much-needed time. If they were to leave him alone, he could collect his heads from distant farms and the outskirts of towns and bring them home to his ice cave. To be allowed a season of peace in which to fulfil his mission would be a wonderful thing indeed.

The Panther nervously tapped a long black fingernail on his wonderfully sharp ice saw as he surveyed the tree-covered lowlands of Boggy Creek from the vantage point of an eagle, high on the white cliffs of limestone. In the red glow of the dying sun he could not help but see them. Many men, both white and Indian, on horses milling about, obviously setting up a camp for the night.

Bitter hatred boiled upward through every fiber of his being, enveloping him like a robe. *Going Snake has been wrong.*

At that moment he knew why the gods

had sent him from his cave to go on his hunt early. Now it was up to him to kill all of them, drive the hated ones from *his* territory, his sanctuary.

But he must be careful, very careful. They would be watching for him, waiting. No matter, he always killed his prey when he was on a hunt. Tonight, he simply had to plan his attack well, catch them totally by surprise. First he had to wait until blessed darkness claimed the land.

Seething with the fires of hate, driven by the always pain, the misshapen, scarred hulking brute named The Panther leaned his precious ice saw against an outcropping of rock. He then extracted a fresh skunk paw from his leather carrying case. After splaying open the pads to expose the sharp claws, he sat in the shadows and cleaned his teeth while awaiting the night. And the time of much killing.

THIRTY-FIVE

After wood had been gathered and the campfire built with a pot of coffee set out to boil, Artemis Wilcox endeared himself to the Osage by producing a pouch of fragrant Turkish smoking tobacco from a leather case he had packed along from his wagon.

"This is fine tobacco," Kills Eagles said with a cough after inhaling his first puff. "It smells like wildflowers, but it has a good bite. I like it."

Artemis beamed. "This rare and particular type of tobacco leaf grows only on the lush high mountain plains above the Sahara Desert of Tangiers in the country of Morocco, which is near France. I once sold some lightning rods to a prince of that nation whose family I saved from certain disaster only a scant day before a particularly severe electrical storm struck his palace. To show his gratitude, the royal monarch sends me a shipment of this wonderful tobacco every year. I am proud and honored to share it with my Osage friends."

Asa Cain winced and realized the drummer was far better at storytelling and peddling than he was at geography. The man's spiel was a diversion, however, a needed one considering the rotting bodies they had found so gruesomely displayed. He kept a close eye on Going Snake and the way the medicine man's flint eyes kept scanning the darkening forest. This confirmed his earlier suspicion that the shaman knew far more about the beheadings than he had disclosed. The story he had told about having a vision and being given a spirit quest was a crock. It was only a ruse to bring the leaders of his tribe to this area and convince them to declare the land here as evil, a place to be avoided for all time. But why? The bounty hunter felt that when he knew the reason for Going Snake's odd behavior, he would have the key to a forty-thousand-dollar answer.

Asa used a stick to push the blackened coffeepot closer to the fire. He studied their surroundings with care. Counting Chief Kills Eagles, there were eight Osage Indians present. Adding in the five others, he felt almost certain that such a large number of armed men would not be attacked. However, the icy trickle of fear that played along his spine told him to keep his guard. This was a forewarning he meant to heed.

Kills Eagles took another long puff of the pungent tobacco, blinked to clear his eyes, then passed the pipe over to Many Dogs, who sat to his left.

"Last summer," the chief said to Artemis, "there was a bolt of lightning come from a cloud over our village. It struck a tepee and rubbed out Flying Dove, who was inside cooking meat. She was a good squaw. Would these lightning rods you sell keep my village safe?"

Both Cemetery John and Emil Quackenbush started to speak at the same time. Neither the undertaker or the sheriff could envision a tepee with a lightning rod attached. They were outclassed in the oration department and their protests went unnoticed over the accomplished huckster's polished spiel.

"I can understand why you have been elected to the position of chief of all of the Osage People," Artemis Wilcox boomed, drowning out the annoying attempts to squelch a potentially profitable sale. "You obviously care deeply for the security and safety of your village and the denizens under your able and most capable leadership. I commend you on your fealty."

Kills Eagles didn't understand all of the white man's words, but felt that he had been paid a great compliment. He gave a nod to Artemis Wilcox for him to continue.

"Great Chief of the Osage, I wish to inform you the never-failing, protective, and lifesaving Armbruster lightning rods that I sell — at almost no personal profit to myself, I must add — will shield any tepee or lodge on which they are installed from even the strongest, most severe of thunderbolts. This is not only guaranteed in writing by me, but also in a contract from the great Armbruster Company of New York City, which is one of the strongest, most stalwart, and best-known champions of industry the world has ever known. At the cost of a mere three dollars per tepee, we can protect the entire Osage Nation from the perils of lightning strikes."

Kills Eagles said simply, "We have many tepees. We have many lodges. We have very few dollars." This statement effectively ended Artemis Wilcox's sales pitch for the evening.

Cemetery John wiped the last trace of camphor from his upper lip, then accepted the proffered pipe from Many Dogs. He took a small polite puff of what he considered to be the most vile tobacco he had ever encountered. The undertaker forced a smile, then quickly passed the long wooden pipe on to Blue Hand, who eyed it suspiciously.

"We're going to have to do something with those bodies," Sheriff Quackenbush said, causing a pall to settle over the assemblage. "But I'm not going to venture what. They're putrid enough to gag a maggot."

Going Snake spoke for the first time since they had made camp. "They are both Osage and white-eyes, joined together for all time by the hand of a spirit. It would be an insult to put them in the ground like white men. They must be respected in the ways the Osage honor their dead."

"Those two were joined with needle and thread by the hands of man," Asa Cain said firmly. "A bit of knife work will take care of that argument."

"I wonder what became of Running Bear's and Little Badger's bodies," Blue Hand said. "If the hand of man sewed their heads on the marshals, then that man must have disposed of their bodies in some manner."

"I do not listen, you are only half Osage," Going Snake said, his dark eyes glowering. "I am a shaman, I have had a vision, a spirit quest. The scouts' bodies have been devoured by an evil entity that has made claim to this place."

"Yeah, yeah, yeah," Emil Quackenbush said with a dismissive wave. "We've already heard all of your spook balderdash and none of us here are buying any of that crap, so stow it."

Going Snake jumped to his feet. "White-eyes Sheriff, you are angering the gods. The evil spirit that infests this land of Boggy Creek will surely punish all of us for your rejection of what is."

"Sit down, Shaman," Kills Eagles said harshly. "I have spoken once again. Do not anger me further."

"When I called you a fool earlier" — Going Snake was so angry, veins on his forehead played about like writhing snakes — "I spoke the truth. Chief Kills Eagles, I am a shaman of The People. I have brought you truth from the world of the Great Spirit, yet you choose not to believe me. I call for a tribal council of elders to decide if you should continue to be our chief. And since all of the elders are here, let us call a pow-wow."

Swift Horse, as the senior member of the council of elders, turned to Buffalo Hair. "It is Going Snake's right to make this challenge. Only I do not know why he is doing it."

"His vision must have been stronger than we thought," Buffalo Hair said. "I say we listen to him and hold a council before we agree with Chief Kills Eagles."

"I count four white men in our presence," Laughing Coyote said. "Along with one Osage whose blood is only half that of The People. We have never held a tribal council of elders with them around before."

Runs Like Rabbit said, "I see no problem. They can sit among us, listen. I think we can even ask the white-eyes for their opinion. We do not have to agree with them if their thinking is bad."

"Well, I'll swan this manhunt just keeps getting better and better," Sheriff Quackenbush grumbled. "Not only have we not seen hide nor hair of a mighty valuable head-whacker, now we're stuck in the midst of a pack of quarreling Redskins. Let's get this thing worked out in as short a time as possible. I'd like to boil up some stew, have a nice relaxing meal, and enjoy a few cups of coffee, then grab a decent night's shut-eye. Tomorrow's shaping up to be as long as this day's been."

"White men have no patience," Kills Eagles said with a shrug. "This is why they suffer maladies of the stomach. We will have Going Snake's council of elders, as is his right. I also say that we keep it brief since we have our white-eyes friends as our guests. The pipe is already lit and we have wonderful tobacco to smoke. Let us sit and have the shaman speak his case against me."

"At least there's no lawyers about," Artemis Wilcox said. "Even one of the species would keep us up all night and not say anything that matters a whit."

"I buried a lawyer once down in El Paso," Cemetery John said. "I took a draft from his grieving widow as payment. It turned out to be worthless as a Confederate dollar. I should have known better than to trust even a family member. Could have planted any of 'em in a barrel, they were so crooked."

Asa Cain decided to get everyone on track. The last traces of day had given way to darkness and they had yet to begin boiling up some beef jerky along with the cattail roots and wild onions they had gathered, and have their supper. From his experience with both Indians and the likes of Cemetery John, the sun could be coming up before they were through talking about getting ready to talk.

"The question before the council," Asa

said in a commanding tone, "the only question to be considered is Going Snake's challenge against Chief Kills Eagles' decision to dismiss the shaman's vision as a false one. I call for a vote from each elder so we can get on with what matters. The facts are known to all here; nothing is to be gained by a lot of argument."

"The white-eyes speaks wisely," Buffalo Hair said, taking a seat on a rock and stretching. "I say we vote now."

Laughing Coyote agreed. "I am ready."

Runs Like Rabbit leaned back away from the flickering campfire. He started to speak, only to widen his eyes in terror and disbelief as a flash of silver came with a swish from out of the night, completely severing his head from his body.

Thirty-Six

Quick as the strike of a rattlesnake, the glistening steel blade made a return arc that severed Laughing Coyote's head from his shoulders with a shower of crimson.

Before either of the hapless Osage Indians' heads had fallen to the earth, a hail of gunfire ripped the sultry night air.

Asa Cain had caught only the most fleeting glimpse of a misshapen figure moving in the shadows, but it was enough to target his Whitney Eagle on. He sent five .36-caliber slugs of hot lead flying in the direction of their attacker as fast as he could cock and fire.

Emil Quackenbush, Blue Hand, and Artemis Wilcox both emptied their revolvers into the blackness in the hopes of hitting something, even if it was by accident.

Cemetery John jumped up and held his cocked ten-gauge shotgun at the ready, but he could see nothing to shoot at through the thick clouds of black powder smoke. The surviving Indians, holding only the knives or bows and arrows allowed them by the Army, scampered to stand alongside the better-armed white men. All stared with shocked wide eyes in the direction from which the sudden, vicious attack had come from.

A dying twitch from Laughing Coyote's body caused his leg to kick into the campfire sending up a shower of sparks. While the pistols were being reloaded, Kills Eagles bent over and dragged the still-quivering corpse from the fire.

There was no sound; even the crickets had ceased their chirping. Only the heavy breathing of men broke the stone silence that had descended upon the forest like a shroud.

"I think I hit him," Asa Cain said. "Whoever it was leapt back in the shadows before I could get a good bead."

Sheriff Quackenbush kept waving the barrel of his Colt about. "What I'd like to know is how he managed to sneak up on us like that. I thought either you or the shaman might have felt something out there." He glanced down at the two headless bodies. "That would have been helpful information."

Asa Cain remained silent. He had no answer to the sheriff's question. The attack had come without any warning at all. How anyone could sneak up on eight Osage Indian warriors along with four trained, experienced lawmen and Artemis Wilcox, who traveled with an arsenal, was beyond comprehension. The bounty hunter was dumbfounded that his sense of impeding danger had failed him for some inexplicable reason. All he had felt was a cold sense of dread.

"It was the evil spirit that I was told of in my vision. No one can sense a spirit," Going Snake said. He turned to Kills Eagles. "If my warning to leave this place had been heeded, Runs Like Rabbit and Laughing Coyote would not have been rubbed out."

"That wasn't no dad-blasted spook," Emil said sharply. "What I saw was a steel blade of some kind that was real as a bullet. I'm getting mighty tired of hearing all of that mumbo-jumbo, witchcraft, evil-spirit crap."

From a cliff high above their camp alongside Boggy Creek came a piercing scream of rage and agony.

Artemis Wilcox stared up into the darkness. "From the sounds of it, I'd say he's both hurt and *really* upset with us."

Cemetery John grabbed a long burning

stick of pitchy wood from the campfire. He held the torch high with his left hand, keeping the shotgun held at the ready with his right. "Let's go see if we can find a blood trail." He gave a fiery glance to Going Snake. "An evil spirit that leaks blood will be a new one for the books."

Asa Cain and Sheriff Quackenbush also grabbed up torches. Moving slowly, carefully, with weapons at the ready, the group entered the deep shadows from which their attacker had struck.

"There has to be at least some blood leaking off the sword or whatever it was he used to whack off those heads," Asa Cain said as he surveyed the dark red drops and rivulets of blood that lay on the forest floor, shining black as pitch in the flickering yellow light of the torches. "But not as much as we're seeing. He's definitely suffered at least one bullet wound."

"So much for it being a spook," Emil said. "Let's go after him."

Kills Eagles said, "A wounded animal or a wounded man is a very dangerous thing to pursue, even in daylight."

Asa followed the trail of blood for a few yards, accompanied by Cemetery John.

"There's sure no doubt he's shot," Cemetery John said. "And from the looks of it, you put a decent hole or two in him."

"Kills Eagles is right," Asa said. "We'll go back to camp and wait until daylight. Maybe our luck will improve and he'll bleed to death."

"At least it appears there's only one person we're dealing with," Blue Hand said as he approached them. "I can't figure a lone man attacking an armed camp like he did."

Asa Cain clucked his tongue. "Going Snake is at least partially right. There's no evil spirit we're dealing with, but whoever it is, he's crazy."

"Crazy or not," Emil Quackenbush said as he came crashing through the brush, "his carcass is worth forty thousand dollars delivered to Cyrus Warwick." The sheriff clenched his jaw and stared up at the rocky cliff where shafts of wan moonlight shooting through towering trees danced among somber shadows. "But this damn place is spooky enough in the daytime, let alone chasing after a wounded head-whacker at night. Let's go back to camp. That blood trail will still be there in the morning."

"Yeah," Cemetery John agreed. "All the money in the world ain't worth anything to you after you've lost your head."

■ ■ ■ ■

The Panther scooped up a handful of mud from the bottom of a small seep of water with a scarred hand. He packed the soothing coolness into the jagged hole where the bullet had blown out the back of his lower side. The flow of blood *had* to be stopped.

He stood in the moonlight and examined the small black hole where the slug had entered. The bullet had struck him to the left of his belly button, traveled through his gut at an angle, then torn a jagged hole where it had exited just above his hip.

This was a bad wound. It would take him a long time to heal, but heal he would. He always healed. What surprised him most was the lack of pain. It was more of a sting, like that of a hornet. Of course he had lived with the always pain for a long time, grown accustomed to pain like the company of an old friend.

When he thought of the man who shot him, he shook with rage. To enrage him further, he had managed to slay only two of his enemies. Going Snake was there among them; he should have helped him kill his foes. Yes, he had been betrayed by the one and only man he trusted. He had been shot because of his trust.

The Panther leaned back, fixed his hate-filled eyes on the moon, and screamed his fury to the heavens. The attack had gone badly. He had expected the men to be caught off guard, be hesitant, confused, which would allow him to employ his sharp, wonderful ice saw and send all of their heads falling like stalks of corn during the harvest.

But the men had been too quick. The man with hair the color of straw shot him before he could make even one more swing of his ice saw. Now he was wounded and needed to hole up and heal.

The men would come after him and try to kill him in the morning. They were surely too wise to try it at night. There might be a chance Going Snake would come to his rescue and rub them all out. This was something he should do. It would only be right. But The Panther would not depend on Going Snake to help him. Going Snake had not joined in the attack when he should have. No, The Panther had only himself to depend on, always had.

If Going Snake was foolish enough to be among the enemy when they came for him, The Panther would rub him out with impunity. When he healed, The Panther vowed to go to the village and kill him anyway. It would be a matter of honor to slay the betrayer. The one who claimed to watch over him, care for him. The liar!

Once again The Panther screamed into the night. Then, with his rage subsiding, he assured himself the flow of blood had been stifled well enough to allow him to leave no telltale droplets to be followed.

Tomorrow he would once again be the hunter. In the high cliffs of his home, his sanctuary, he had a surprise, a deadly surprise awaiting any who were foolish enough to come after him.

The Panther winced when he stood; a sharp pain stabbed at his side like a knife. There was an odd pungent taste of copper in his mouth. Yet he did not let any of this concern him. He had been hurt worse, much worse. And he had healed. He *must* heal. His collection, his mission in life, was not yet complete. No god would allow him to perish before he finished his collection. It was something he could not conceive.

Again, The Panther thought of the white-eyes with hair the color of straw and how quickly the man had shot him. With any luck the same white-eyes would come after him tomorrow. To kill him would not only be pleasurable, but the man's head was needed to fill the last few of his collection. None of his heads had beautiful straw-colored hair. Then he also remembered a fleeting glimpse of another white man, a stocky person whose hair and beard were the color of blood.

Let them come, he thought. *Let all of them come for me. I will add their heads to my collection, my gift to the gods. My final freedom is nearly complete.*

Buoyed by thoughts of beautiful hair the color of straw and red blood, The Panther strode up the narrow ledge toward his distant home, accompanied only by his pain.

THIRTY-SEVEN

Cemetery John set the blackened coffeepot on the new campfire they had built in a clearing some distance from where the attack had happened. The surroundings here were a lot less grisly. The undertaker rolled his eyes in the direction of yet another distant scream. "Yep, I'd say the lightning-rod peddler's right about him being really riled."

"He sounds more angry than dying," Asa Cain said. "That's too bad."

Emil Quackenbush poked some more dry wood into the fire; he was anxious to have a cup of coffee. "His being alive is only a temporary condition. We know now that there's only one outlaw head-whacker, and he's bleeding nice and good." The sheriff glowered at Going Snake, who had sat humped up and silent since their return. "That takes care of your spook theory."

"Do not anger the gods, white man," the

shaman said without raising his eyes from the ground. "There are many things of which you have no understanding."

Sheriff Quackenbush snorted. "What I do understand is tomorrow at first light we are going to track down and kill ourselves a screaming head-whacker that Asa was obliging enough to put a nice big hole or two in."

Blue Hand turned to Going Snake. His voice was kind. "We know it is but a man, My Shaman. Not an evil spirit. The actions of this man have brought much trouble to The People. The Army is coming to our lands. Why do you not join us in wanting to kill him?"

Chief Kills Eagles said in his deep, commanding voice, "Tell him, Shaman. Tell *all* of them the truth. You should have spoken it to me many years ago. If you had, none of the white-eyes would have died and the Army would not be coming to rub out more of The People."

Going Snake bolted upright as if he had been shot. He stared across the flickering campfire at the chief with disbelieving eyes. "You saw him."

"Yes, Shaman, I did. None of us believed he had lived, but when The Panther came and killed the two elders, I saw the hump on his back like that of a buffalo. It was then that I knew the truth and why you want all of us to leave this place and never return. I also know now that you murdered our scouts, then sewed their heads on the lawmen's bodies."

The Osage medicine man was silent for a long while, his flint eyes darting from face to face, attempting to read what each person was thinking. He knew his options were few. The shaman had lived by lies for so long, he could fathom no other course of action but to continue telling them. He only hoped and prayed to be able to buy time.

"It is he, My Chief," Going Snake said, his voice soft, his words measured. "The Panther's mind and body was terribly damaged in the fire. He constantly hurts and he hates everyone for what happened to him. It was The Panther who killed Running Bear and Little Badger, not me. In his insanity he sewed their heads onto the lawmen's bodies. I only wanted to save others from him. That was why I made up the story of having a vision. It was to keep everyone safe, which they would have been if only you had believed me and left this place alone."

Asa Cain said, "Some of this is making sense, but there are a lot of pieces to this puzzle we need to be filled in on."

Blue Hand looked into the darkness. "I was living in the village when this happened. I remember people were afraid of him, then there was the fire."

"Who in blazes is The Panther?" Sheriff Quackenbush growled. "Get to the point, for Pete's sake."

Kills Eagles said simply, "The Panther, who became very big for some reason, also grew a buffalo hump on his back. Then he turned into a mean lunatic. He is also the younger brother of Going Snake."

Asa Cain nodded to the shaman with understanding. "You were trying to protect your brother, which is laudable, but a lot of innocent people are dead because of it. I think we all deserve to hear the rest of the story."

Kills Eagles said, "I will speak. I am chief of the Osage. I bear the responsibility for letting this happen. Sit, boil the coffee, and I will tell you the sad, strange story of The Panther.

"It began nearly twenty-eight years ago when Bright Moon gave birth to her second son, Going Snake's brother, who was given the name of The Panther because when he was born a panther screamed from deep in the woods. The child grew up normally, played games, learned to hunt and fish.

Then, when he became old enough to be like a man, The Panther turned very strange. His body grew very huge. A buffalo hump formed on his back. Then, to our horror, he became mean. I was told of him torturing dogs, shooting deer with an arrow just to chase after them and watch them die, then leaving the meat to spoil.

"Then, ten years ago, The Panther stabbed his own mother to death. The Army had put us on a reservation at this time, so the tribe had to ask the white men what to do. We were told to tie him securely with ropes and lock him in a building until they could send a prison wagon to take him to what they call an insane asylum. The People did as the Army told us, but before the wagon arrived, there was a fire that burned down the wooden icehouse in which we had locked him. The Panther must have been very terribly burnt, because he could not have run off screaming with pain like he did until the fire had burned its way through the many thick ropes with which we had bound him.

"I, as did all of The People, believed The Panther had run off only to perish. But though we looked, sent out scouts, his body was never found. No one even found the big ice saw he was carrying when he fled smoking from the roaring flames. I thought this was due to someone, most likely a white-eyes, finding it and selling it. Now I know the truth of the matter, and I am sorry for all of my People because the Army is going to come and rub out many of us because The Panther still lives and he is cutting off heads with that big ice saw."

Artemis Wilcox lowered an eyebrow. "At least now I know what happened to that horse of mine. But I'd never in a million years have thought it was some hunchback with an ice saw that did it."

"Don't fret the Army," Sheriff Quackenbush said to Kills Eagles. "We'll have The Panther shot full of holes and slabbed out back in Henrietta before they get here. I'll not only send some telegraphs telling everyone who counts what the truth of the matter is, I'll also ride out personally and meet with 'em. There's no reason for any more Osage to suffer because of the actions of a single crazy one."

Chief Kills Eagles nodded. "I and my People thank you."

Asa Cain noticed the coffee had begun to boil. "Let's all have a cup. I think after the day we've had we can use it." The bounty hunter fixed Going Snake in his cold blue eyes. "Then you can tell us where your brother's holed up. Don't even think about telling me you don't know. And I'm not buying that story about you being so blasted innocent about everything. If you so much as blink wrong, I'll shoot you quicker than a heartbeat."

"You've done gone and riled him, Shaman," Cemetery John said with a shrug. "When Asa Cain gives you a warning, you'd best heed it."

Going Snake's dark eyes flitted from one stony face to another. He saw no solace, no understanding, no belief in his words. The shaman did the only thing he could think to do. He spun and bolted into the night, melting instantly into the shadowy forest.

"That went fast," Kills Eagles said. "It was a wise move, bounty hunter."

"Am I missing something here?" Emil asked eyeing the rumbling coffeepot. "Or did we simply let that medicine man run off to save sharing some of our coffee with him?"

Swift Horse took a seat on a log. "Going Snake will save his brother at any cost. It is a matter of honor for one of The People to protect their family, even a crazy one who has become a murderer."

"Asa knew that," Blue Hand said. "And none of us know if the shaman's words are true or if he speaks lies."

A glimmer of comprehension crossed the sheriff's red-bearded face. "We couldn't trust him being along with us."

"Always keep your backside covered by friends you trust," Asa Cain said, grabbing a tin cup. "There's not one thing that medicine man can do to keep us from either capturing or killing his brother. We have a blood trail and Going Snake will certainly leave us even more sign to follow when he goes charging off to find him in the middle of the night."

Sheriff Quackenbush used a piece of blanket to protect his hand when he reached down and took hold of the coffeepot from the crackling campfire. "While this stuff's cooling down enough to drink without singeing your gizzard, I'll start fixing us a pot of stew. I'm so blame hungry my belly's beginning to think my throat's been cut." Emil looked into the shadowy woods with lowered eyes. He realized that once again his choice of words could have been a lot better. "Well, I reckon we're all hungry."

Chief Kills Eagles took a seat on the log next to Swift Horse. After setting his coffee out to cool, he gave a pensive look to no one in particular. "We have a terrible task ahead of us tomorrow. I do not look forward to it."

"No, Chief," Asa Cain said, his tone one of stone resolve, "but it's a day that's been too long in coming."

"I know," were the last words the chief would speak for the rest of that night.

THIRTY-EIGHT

Asa Cain sat by the campfire sipping a steaming cup of what he thought was the worst-tasting pot of coffee Cemetery John had ever brewed. Back home in Wolf Springs, Texas, it was often joked that the undertaker got a lot of business from people who drank his brew. Asa had to believe at least some of those stories were true.

"Red sky in the morning, sailor take warning," Artemis Wilcox said cheerfully as he nodded to the newborn glow in the east. The lightning-rod salesman took a healthy drink of coffee and beamed at Cemetery John. "I'm glad we're not sailors and I must say this is the finest cup of coffee I've enjoyed for many years."

Cemetery John looked across the campfire to Asa. "See, I've been telling you forever that you simply don't know good coffee when it's offered. Fridley Newlin and I make the best cup you'll find west of the

Mississippi."

Sheriff Quackenbush dashed the dregs from his cup into the fire, sending up a few tendrils of steam. "If my horse drank any of this stuff, I'd have to walk after that head-whacker." He glanced at Artemis Wilcox. "I'm plumb sorry yours got done in like that, but today's the day we'll get even with him for chopping off all those heads, including your horse's."

"It will be light enough to take to the trail very soon," Kills Eagles said.

Many Dogs spoke up. "I am a good tracker. If the sheriff or anyone else does not object, I will take us to The Panther."

Blue Hand nodded his agreement to Emil. "Many Dogs is not only a skilled tracker, but a hunter who never comes back to the village without meat for his tepee."

"Sounds good to me," the sheriff said. "I not only wish we had some coffee to drink that don't damage your innards, but also some meat to fry up before we head out. Cattail roots and wild onions boiled up with beef jerky sure ain't filling."

Emil Quackenbush's eyes widened and he reached for the butt of his gun when Many Dogs drew back on his bow and sent an arrow whistling past his left ear. "What in the . . ." Then the sheriff spun to see a small buck deer thrashing on the ground about a hundred feet or so behind him with an arrow in its chest.

"Is that sufficient meat, Mr. Sheriff?" Many Dogs asked.

"Uh, yeah." Emil had never seen anyone quicker than the Osage. He hadn't had time to blink. "Mighty fast too."

Artemis Wilcox extracted a huge, razor-sharp bowie knife no one had any clue he possessed from the back of his belt. "A few minutes to fry up a decent meal won't be a bad idea at all. Even Napoleon Bonaparte once said that an army marches on its stomach."

Emil Quackenbush lowered an eyebrow. "There was a fat cattle rustler down near Amarillo by the name of Boneypart. Reckon there's any relation?"

"I doubt that very much," Artemis said heading for the now-still deer. "I really do."

"No matter," the sheriff said as he went to help butcher the venison. "Someone shot him years ago."

"I'll start heating the skillet," Asa Cain said. "We don't have time to lollygag; there's a manhunt we need to get on with."

"The Panther will die before this day is out," Kills Eagles said. Then the Osage chief sat silently with his arms crossed and waited for the meal.

Asa Cain started to step around a stick in the trail, then froze when he realized it was a copperhead snake. His boots were thick and high, so he kicked the annoying reptile far to the side, then led his skittish horse past it.

"Every scary story you ever heard happens in a place just like this," Artemis Wilcox said in the same hushed tone everyone was using now that they were following the blood trail. "I'm of the hopes we're not going to add to the list."

"Nah," Emil Quackenbush said. "We've got enough firepower to flatten a herd of buffalo, for Pete's sake. All we need to fret is a wounded head-whacker and possibly a spook chaser who might make the bad decision to try and help him."

"The Panther is Going Snake's brother," Blue Hand said as he tried to dig a bug from out of his ear with a small stick. "He will try to save his life. It is the honorable thing for him to do."

"As long as the medicine man doesn't get too far out of line, let's not go out of our way to kill him," Asa Cain said moving wide around a large vine of poison oak. "There has been far too much killing already."

333

"I do not know what Going Snake will do," Buffalo Hair, who was just behind Many Dogs, said. "But he has caused the Army to come. I will gladly rub him out if he causes us too much bother. I do not like the white-eyes army."

"The medicine man and The Panther's tracks are as one," Many Dogs said over his shoulder. "They are together from this point on."

"Dang, but this country's getting even more rugged and steep." Cemetery John coughed out a bug, scratched the poison ivy blisters on the back of his hand, then shook his head at the jumble of rocks, trees, and bushes that filled the canyon of Boggy Creek. "Makes West Texas look like the Garden of Eden."

"We are going to find his lair in an ice cave," Asa Cain said. He pointed a finger upward to where sheer cliffs of white limestone jutted hundreds of feet into a clear blue sky, like the stone walls of some storybook giant's fort. "And it will be up there."

Emil Quackenbush looked up at the imposing bulwarklike mountainside, then winced and began rubbing a pulled muscle in his neck. "That figures. Outlaws are just plain inconsiderate, that's what all of 'em are, dag-nab it. Why can't they choose a hideout that's easier to get at, for Pete's sake?"

"Cheer up, Sheriff." Artemis Wilcox's usual beaming smile seemed even broader. "Maybe he'll be obliging enough to show himself. Then we can shoot him from down here and let him fall to meet us. Shouldn't mess him up bad enough to make the body unrecognizable."

Cemetery John swatted a swarm of black gnats from his eyes, then looked up at the imposing cliffs that had taken everyone's attention. "I'd venture that big bounty money has just gotten a tad more dear. The Panther might be burnt to a crisp, deformed and loony as an outhouse rat, but he's wily and smart. From up there one man could hold off an army."

"And once we find the trail heading up," Asa Cain said, his voice cheerless as a preacher delivering a eulogy at a funeral, "there's where the ambush will happen. Have to keep an eye out for booby traps too. That Panther has been living here for years and has had time to prepare for visitors."

Cemetery John checked the loads in his big ten-gauge shotgun for the third time that day. He slammed the breech closed and nodded to Asa. "That's what I've always admired about you, that cheery, upbeat, balm-in-Gilead attitude of yours."

"Where's Gilead?" Sheriff Quackenbush asked. "Never heard of the place."

"It's a town in Texas," Cemetery John said, then motioned with his itchy hand to Many Dogs. "Looks like he's found something. Let's go see what it is."

THIRTY-NINE

Going Snake stood transfixed as he moved his gaze from one severed head to another. Each was lined up on shelves chiseled into a thick ledge of blue ice that was over a dozen feet high and extended into the mountain as far as the flickering light of the candles and campfire could reach. He had never been past the mouth of his brother's cave home before. He counted nineteen heads. One of them was that of a beautiful auburn-haired woman. The shaman shivered from more than the cold of the ice.

"I have a good collection," The Panther said, his voice gravelly from disuse. "It is nearly complete."

"I do not understand, my brother."

"Is it not plain to you, a shaman?"

"No. I see only the heads of many white-eyes."

"Not yet enough. I need more."

"Why, and what did you do with Little

Badger and Running Bear's bodies?"

"I will show you in a while. But I am disappointed with you, Going Snake, for not recognizing my great handiwork for what it is."

The shaman felt it prudent to proceed slowly. The Panther was nearly a foot taller than he, much more muscular, and the glistening ice saw never left his hand. "I wish you to tell me with your own lips, my brother."

"Then I shall." The hunchback grasped a candle with long, clawlike fingers. He then proceeded to move the flame in front of each of the severed heads, all of which had been frozen with their eyes propped wide open. "Do you not see the truth, Shaman?"

"I see, but I do not fully understand." He added quickly, "My brother."

"I do not yet have enough heads to call out the spirits."

"How many do you need?"

"You should know. You were there. I was bound by a rope that wrapped me twenty-four times."

"You require twenty-four heads, one for each of the coils of rope that had to burn through to allow you to escape the flames."

"Yes, my brother. Then I will be powerful enough to summon the spirits from the heads. They will come to life and be my servants, my warriors." He hesitated with the candle in front of the pretty woman's face, playing the flickering light back and forth from one of her eyes to the next. "And my lovers. I wish to have at least two women to pleasure me."

The depths of his brother's insanity struck Going Snake like a slap from a bullet. He also realized he was in much danger. The Panther was treacherous and more deadly than a rattlesnake, a wounded one at that. His brother's injury was a bad one. It was almost certainly fatal, but The Panther had lived through worse. Having to endure flames cooking his flesh until the ropes binding him had burned through must have been unbelievable agony. It would be unwise to upset him.

"You require six more heads, one of them a girl," Going Snake said. "A lovely girl."

"Ah, my brother, you do understand."

"They are coming to find you, Panther."

"Let them come. I am ready. I will slay them all."

"The white men are many. Chief Kills Eagles and the elders whose heads you did not cut off are with them."

"I care not. The Osage bound me, put me in that building."

"I will be by your side, my brother. I have brought something that might be useful."

"I have my ice saw. I have my *other* protection. What more could you bring to help me save my great collection?"

Going Snake motioned to a pair of small wooden kegs he had set near the entrance. "One of the men who is with them, the one whose horse you cut the head of off, had several of these beneath the seat of his wagon. They are full of gunpowder, enough to blow all of your pursuers from this mountain."

"Ah, my brother, you *do* honor my collection." The Panther placed his scarred face close to the head of the woman; then to Going Snake's dismay, he kissed her with his blackened lips. He turned to the shaman. "Follow me. I will show you the abyss." He added, "*Do* be careful."

Sheer walls of opalescent blue ice reflected the candle flames with dancing pinpoints of light. To the shaman it was as if a thousand staring, watching eyes were imprisoned inside those cold, glistening corridors. He followed with much trepidation. Then, The Panther stopped.

"Here," he said bending over to pick up a chunk of ice. "Step close, my brother. Are you afraid?"

Going Snake did as his brother wished. Mere inches in front of him a circular dark maw dropped straight down.

"Observe." The Panther dropped the ice. It clattered and bounced for a seeming eternity before becoming forever lost in what surely had to be the bowels of the earth.

"It is very deep, my brother. Is this where you sent the bodies of Little Badger and Running Bear?"

"Yes." The Panther spun and grabbed his wounded side.

For a brief moment Going Snake thought — hoped — that his insane kinsman might plunge into the depths, but it was not to be.

"The pain is bad," The Panther said. "They are coming. Let us go and kill them any way we can. I must heal so I can fulfill my mission."

"Yes, my brother." Going Snake's feet were leaden with dread as he followed the misshapen form of his brother past the walls of eyes to the light of day. And more killing.

FORTY

Many Dogs stood looking down to where a trickle of water ran lazily from the base of a sheer cliff, only to disappear into the dense woodlands a few feet distant.

The Osage scout pointed to what resembled claw marks in the mud. "Here is where The Panther stopped to plug up the holes he was leaking blood from. There are no more traces from this place."

Sheriff Quackenbush came stomping up. "You're saying you've lost his trail? I thought any Indian worth his feathers could follow a lizard track across a flat rock."

Many Dogs motioned with his hand. "No, he went in that direction, where the moccasins of Going Snake also traveled. I simply wanted to tell you that he used mud from here to stop his loss of blood."

Asa Cain looked in the direction the scout had indicated. "He'll likely die from an infection, but we don't have the time to wait for it to happen. Let's proceed after him. I think we'll find a trail leading upward fairly soon."

"That's when this manhunt's going to become tense," Cemetery John said.

Artemis Wilcox shrugged. "Every general knows the advantage of being on the high ground. This Panther chap is too valuable to cost us time." He smiled at Many Dogs. "Lead the way, our skilled and fearless tracker."

Many Dogs gave a slight snort, then headed off along the base of the cliff, followed close by Asa and Chief Kills Eagles. Less than ten minutes later, the Osage scout called a halt by stopping and pointing to where a narrow ledge of rock, no more than three feet wide, angled up the sheer cliff. "We must leave our horses here. The trail is a treacherous one."

Emil snorted. "Can't see where that'll be a problem. We've been having to lead them ever since we broke camp. Blasted rugged country anyway."

"It looks plenty well traveled," Asa Cain said. "That surprises me. I'd expect him to have at least attempted to cover it with brush or something."

Kills Eagles walked over to below the ledge and held up some green branches.

"The Panther did obscure his trail. I think Going Snake does not care if we follow. The shaman knows his brother will either die from his wounds or by our hands."

Asa Cain stared at the narrow ledge that wound upward into shadowy crags of rock. "There's another reason Going Snake might have left such good sign for us to follow."

"Yeah," Cemetery John said rolling the stub of a dead long nine cigar nervously in his mouth. "He wants us all nice and together on a convenient narrow ledge with a couple of hundred feet to fall."

"That does seem like a distinct possibility," Emil said. "If I'd known we'd be facing this, I'd have gone and shot that spook doc when I had the chance."

"There's a mighty valuable outlaw up there, boys," Artemis Wilcox said. "Let's not lose sight of why we're here."

"I will lead," Chief Kills Eagles said. "The Panther is one of The People."

"I will be close behind you, My Chief," Many Dogs said.

"The Panther is crazy," Asa said. "Don't forget that, and keep your eyes peeled for the unexpected."

Artemis Wilcox said firmly, "Lead the way, our Osage friends. I will do my part to make certain we are not being followed by taking the terribly dangerous position of being at the rear."

With the lightning-rod salesman's words, Kills Eagles gave a grunt and started slowly up the narrow, shadowy ledge.

"This manhunt just keeps getting better and better," Sheriff Quackenbush grumbled. "We've climbed so blame high, the fall wouldn't kill you because you'd starve to death before you hit the ground."

"Now, Emil," Cemetery John said over his shoulder, "there's cliffs in Texas bigger than this one."

"We can't go much higher," Chief Kills Eagles said from the front of the line of men strung out along the ledge. "There is very little mountain left above us."

"That's the first cheery news I've heard lately," Artemis Wilcox puffed from his position of last in line. "The climb has become a strenuous one indeed. I fear the task of hauling a dead body down this trail will also be most trying."

"When my pappy used to take me fishing," Cemetery John said, "he'd say not to worry about cleaning 'em until after you've caught 'em."

"Your pappy . . ." The lightning-rod salesman's reply was cut short by a large round rock slamming down from above into Buffalo Hair's shoulder, knocking him off the narrow ledge and sending him crashing into the rocky depths of the canyon below.

"Ambush!" Asa Cain yelled. "Keep as close to the wall as you can." Another round rock that weighed a good fifty pounds came flying past his face putting a period to his warning.

Emil Quackenbush flattened against the cliff, his revolver pointed up. He noticed a flash of movement and sent five hot slugs of lead flying to where the rocks had come from. Then there was silence.

"Did you actually see something to shoot at, or were you just letting them know you've got a gun?" Blue Hand asked, keeping his gaze focused aloft.

"I just saw something moving," the sheriff growled as he reloaded. "I've always believed in sending as many slugs toward the bad men as you can. Never can tell when you might get lucky and plug 'em."

Another huge stone flew past Cemetery John, missing him by scant inches. "I think you've gone and wasted valuable ammo," the undertaker said. "From the position we're in, it'd be a miracle if any of us can draw a bead."

There was a swishing sound from Many

Dogs' bow as he unleashed an arrow followed by a scream of pain from above. Seconds later, a large boulder came crashing harmlessly down the cliff missing everyone by several feet.

"Looks like you hit him," Asa Cain hollered to Many Dogs. "Good shooting."

The Osage merely grunted. "I put an arrow in the pit of his arm when he reached over the edge of the cliff to throw another rock. I would prefer to have hit him in the eye."

"Putting him out of commission is plenty good in my book," Artemis Wilcox said coming out as far as he could on the ledge, then staring upward. "And he might be obliging enough to bleed to death."

"You might want to remember there's two of 'em up there that we know of," Cemetery John shouted to Artemis sending the pudgy lightning-rod salesman bolting back against the shelter of the cliff.

Artemis Wilcox grew silent with contemplation for a moment, then hollered to everyone, "The English poet John Dryden once wrote, 'They can conquer who believe they can.' I think possibly we should take his good advice and charge them while they're off balance."

"Yeah," Emil said cocking his pistol.

"Let's go get that valuable head-whacker."

"Move out," Asa Cain said to Many Dogs and Kills Eagles, who were in front of him. "Let's not give them time to think."

Artemis Wilcox watched the line of nine men in front of him begin to run ahead up the narrow trail as fast as they could. He mumbled to himself, "But Shakespeare wrote that discretion is the better part of valor." He shrugged. "Oh, well." Then he joined in the charge.

To everyone's amazement, there was no sign of life when they reached the flat area in front of the imposing maw of a cave opening.

"Keep your guard up, boys," Asa Cain said sweeping the surroundings with his blue eyes. "This is too easy."

"There's quite a pile of rocks over here meant to be tossed at us," Sheriff Quackenbush said to Artemis as the lightning-rod salesman came walking over to join him.

"There is a lot of fresh blood from where my arrow pierced The Panther's armpit," Many Dogs said. Then he motioned to the dark grim maw of the cave. "He and Going Snake are in there."

"I reckon that didn't take a lot of thought." Cemetery John bit hard on his stub of cigar. "What concerns me is why they didn't make a better fight of it."

Asa Cain clucked his tongue and stared into the gloomy opening. "I wonder if this cave has got a back door. That could explain a lot."

"What the heck?" Emil Quackenbush pointed to a thin wire running from the cave opening to the big pile of round rocks.

Artemis Wilcox paled when he saw the wire ran to where two wooden kegs of what were most certainly gunpowder stolen from his wagon were buried beneath the heap of stones.

"Oh, shit!" was all the lightning-rod salesman had time to utter before the wire was jerked hard, being pulled from far inside the dark depths of the ice cave.

FORTY-ONE

Asa Cain quickly sized up the situation. He grabbed the trip wire and pulled it from the cave. There was no reason to give them another chance to trigger the bomb that, for some reason, had failed to explode.

"I can't explain it," Artemis Wilcox said shakily. "That was the keg I had rigged to blow. Whoever stole this powder recognized it for what it was and decided to use it against us. I hate it when things like this happen."

Emil Quackenbush stared at the rock pile with a jaundiced eye. "You don't reckon that stuff still might blow up, do you? We can always come back later."

Artemis Wilcox got down on his hands and knees, moved a few rocks aside, and slid out the two kegs. "Well, who would have thought that."

"What is it?" Asa asked, bending over to inspect the wooden casks.

"You just plain can't trust anybody these days." Artemis held up a small black metal device he had removed from one of the kegs. "This detonator is totally defective. The eyelet that the wire was attached to was so rusty, it pulled right through without triggering an explosion. I traded some excellent Armbruster lightning rods for a box of these. I feel totally cheated."

"If the thing had worked," Asa Cain said, "we would all be learning to play a harp. Dumb luck was all that saved our hinders. If you run across the fellow you got that detonator from, I think you owe him a drink."

"Make that *several* drinks," Cemetery John said, mopping sweat from his brow while keeping an eagle eye on the dark opening. "We came close enough to our own funeral to smell the flowers and hear the organ playing."

Asa brightened and cocked his head. "Artemis, you say all that happened was a rusty ring allowed the wire to pull loose. If we were to reattach the wire by wrapping it around the trigger, then it will explode."

"Well, of course it would. This is only the very best grade of DuPont gunpowder, which I got from another, more reliable source than the detonator. I actually paid cash money for those kegs."

"We may have need of them." Asa turned to the foreboding maw. "It's hard to say what we might need before this manhunt's over." The bounty hunter clucked his tongue. "One thing's certain. We're going to have to go in there and get them."

"I was afraid you'd say that," Emil said. "I really was."

"Think of all that reward money," Cemetery John said. "And how much fun you'll have spending it." He grinned evilly at the sheriff. "We're waiting for you to run in there and start shooting away like you're famous for doing."

A look of genuine fear and worry painted itself across Emil's red-bearded face. "Boys, I hate to admit it, but I can't stand being in a hole, never could."

"Well, here's another knockdown to endure," Cemetery John snorted. "Now we're stuck with a sheriff who's afraid of the dark."

"I'm not afraid of the dark, gol-durn it," Emil Quackenbush fumed. "I just can't stand being in tight spaces is all."

Asa Cain motioned to the cave entrance. "Forget it, Cemetery. A lot of people can't take being in a mine or cave. There's most likely only two bad men in there and one of those has been pretty well shot up. The both of us ought to be able to handle the matter."

"That sounds like a reasonable approach," Artemis Wilcox said cheerfully. "The rest of us will stand guard out here and await your return."

Blue Hand motioned to the jagged, rocky, tree-covered horizon. "Do not forget, Mr. Cain might have been correct when he wondered if this cave has other entrances. There could be another attack from any direction at any time."

The lightning-rod salesman grabbed up his shotgun and began scanning the countryside. "I'll *really* be glad when this manhunt's over. Being a mild-mannered, peaceful gentleman whose goal in life is to provide protection for families and small children is more what I'm cut out to do."

Emil Quackenbush gave a snort, then charged toward the entrance of the cave like an enraged bull. "I'd rather fight head-whackers in a dark cave than listen to any more of Artemis's crap." He looked over his shoulder without slowing. "Well, whoever's coming with me had better get to moving."

Cemetery John readied his shotgun and started after the red-bearded sheriff. "He does tend to be impetuous."

"Yep," Asa Cain said joining his friend.

"I've noticed that myself." Moments later, the three men melted into the dark maw of The Panther's ice cave.

"Your bomb did not explode, my brother." The Panther watched as Going Snake tried to stifle the flow of blood from his side and armpit. "I am very disappointed."

The Osage shaman looked along the high corridor of opalescent blue ice. It seemed to him more eyes had come to watch and stare at them from behind the icy walls. Going Snake wondered if they really were imprisoned spirits, wondered if The Panther was not insane after all. Then a rare smile crossed his usually stoic face. He would know the answer to that question soon enough.

"The gods did not will it," Going Snake said. "They often can be unpredictable."

"You must go kill the trespassers. My wounds are bad. I hurt."

"My brother, you will heal. You will complete your collection."

"Yes, this I must do. I need your help."

"I will help you. I shall do what I must, my brother."

"We have not spent much time together. I wish we had."

"Ah, my brother, we shall spend the rest

of our lives together."

"But first the white-eyes need to be killed. I hear them coming."

"Yes, they are inside the cave. There are many."

"I must rest, I need time to heal."

"Ah, my brother, you will soon have all of the time in the world. Come with me to the abyss. I have a plan."

The Panther staggered. When he turned to go deeper into the grotto, he slipped in a pool of his own blood, nearly falling. "Your plan is to lure the white-eyes to the hole. Then push them in. I think that is a good plan."

Going Snake steadied his dying brother with a strong shoulder. When they walked slowly along the wall of eyes, the shaman believed he could see some that were weeping.

FORTY-TWO

"It was unexpectedly nice of them to leave the lights on for us," Asa Cain said as the trio slowly sidled into the murky depths while keeping their backs to the cave walls. "But troubling."

"Yeah," Cemetery John agreed. "You would've thought they'd want us to have to carry one of those candles or lanterns we found at the entrance, give 'em something to shoot at."

"This cave's lit up like a Mexican funeral parlor." Emil Quackenbush's voice was tight with tension. "That means if we can see them, they can also see us. Let's not hesitate to shoot at the first thing that moves. I know I'm sure not going to lollygag any with my trigger finger."

"Somehow we didn't expect you to," Asa Cain said. "And considering the spooky circumstances, I reckon you're not going to get any objections from either of us."

"Move slow, boys." Asa Cain's breath blew white in the increasing cold. "They're expecting company."

"I'm thinking that bomb they planted not blowing up like they thought it would has upset their planning tolerable." Cemetery John poked his head out and made a cautious gaze ahead. "When did Indians take to using tactics like that anyway? Booby traps and trip wires aren't normal weapons for any tribe I've encountered."

Emil Quackenbush said, his tone hushed, "The Army's been around here for years. The Osage are mighty smart and quick to learn. That's why I hired Blue Hand for a deputy."

"Thanks, Sheriff, I appreciate the compliment." Blue Hand's unexpected words from behind him caused Emil to bump his head on a stalactite when he spun. He hadn't heard a sound from the deputy's approach.

"Dang, that hurt!" the sheriff growled. "Who the hell stuck this thing up here?" He glowered at Blue Hand. "And what are you doing sneaking up on us like that for? That's a good way to get yourself shot."

"You need one of The People to be with you," Blue Hand said, motioning with his pistol into the flickering shadows ahead.

"The Panther and Going Snake are Osage. They are natural hunters. They could be above us, or come at us from below. Possibly a passage of this cave might circle completely around allowing them to attack from behind. My eyes and senses are sharp, as you just said."

Cemetery John's eyes widened. "He's made his point as far as I'm concerned."

Asa Cain nodded. "Stay close. There's shadows everywhere. The way the flames are beginning to play around on those walls of blue ice up yonder is going to make this cave even spookier."

Emil Quackenbush said as they moved on into the depths, "As if this place wasn't bad enough already, it smells worse than a skunk den in here."

"I think The Panther eats skunks," Blue Hand said, then shrugged. "Everyone says he is crazy."

"He's worth a pile of money no matter how bad he smells or what shape we bring him back in," Cemetery John said. "There's a fact we can't lose sight of."

A few slow and cautious minutes later, the four men found themselves entering through a large opening. Here the cold was bitter; breaths came out as white fog to hang in the still air. From high overhead, drops of water fell on the cavern floor, where they echoed loudly like heartbeats, only to quickly freeze and add to the wall of opalescent ice that stretched as far as the eye could see. In the center of the grotto a campfire burned cheerfully. Its warmth was an antithesis to the stark gloominess of the immense cavern.

Sheriff Quackenbush wrinkled his nose at a frozen skunk along with other assorted animals such as raccoons, opossums, and rabbits that had been stacked like so much cordwood. "Home sweet home, if you're a head-whacking lunatic."

Asa Cain noticed that Blue Hand was staring transfixed at a section of ice. The bounty hunter came around to see what had caught the deputy's attention.

"Oh, my God!" Asa cried out.

"I reckon if I never see anything like this again, I'll consider myself lucky," Cemetery John said in a low voice. "I count over a dozen."

Emil Quackenbush shook his head in dismay. "There's more heads lined up there than I've got bodies to account for. Our boy's been busier than we knew." He reached out and grabbed up a gold watch that lay in a vacant space. "Well, looky here, this must be the dentist's watch that was stolen. He'll be glad to see this again."

Blue Hand said, "There are nineteen heads. Each one has been frozen solid with their eyes open. I cannot understand why The Panther has done this."

"Why don't you come here and ask him face-to-face, half-breed?" Going Snake's deep voice echoed throughout the grotto. "Or do you lack the courage of a warrior?"

Moving as one, the four men spun and aimed their weapons down the long opening in the blue ice from where the shaman's taunting voice had come. The flickering reflections of flames from the campfire and numerous candles danced along the tunnel like a thousand lightning bugs at midnight.

"Come on out, Going Snake," Sheriff Quackenbush shouted to the depths. "You're not wanted for anything. No one here's going to stop you from just walking away."

Blue Hand said to the sheriff, "He will stay with his brother. It is the way of The People."

"Then they'll die together," the sheriff muttered.

"I think that is their plan," Asa Cain said, his voice a whisper. "It has been for some time, especially after the bomb failed to blow us up."

"Look at all of that blood." Cemetery John pointed the twin barrels of his ten-gauge shotgun at a large puddle of crimson that was already frozen and glistening like red ice. "The arrow Many Dogs shot must have hit an artery. No one can leak that much blood and live."

"They have nothing to lose," Blue Hand said.

"Let's go take care of the matter." Emil Quackenbush cocked the hammer on his Colt and bolted down the corridor of ice before anyone could utter another word.

"Damn it," Asa Cain spit, then took off running after the sheriff, followed by Cemetery John and Blue Hand. "There he goes again."

Emil Quackenbush had made only a hundred feet of his mad dash before he skidded to a halt, face-to-face with a monster from anyone's worst nightmare. Asa Cain came to the sheriff's side. He lowered his gun when he saw that neither of their adversaries had a weapon.

The Panther snarled at them with jagged yellow teeth exposed behind open mis-shapen lips. His rippling muscles were ridged with red, ropelike lines of many old wounds. The huge hump on his back was exposed in a tear of the stitched-together animal skins he wore. The man's face was a scarred, contorted mask of black wrinkled skin that showed only hate and rage.

"You have been lucky, Sheriff Quackenbush," Going Snake said, holding his brother upright with a strong shoulder that was covered with blood. "The trap I set should have killed everyone."

"We all have our bad days," Emil said. "Now why don't you boys calm down. There's been too many killings already."

"My collection." The Panther's gravelly voice came across as a gurgling plea. "I need . . . more to live."

"What's he talking about?" Cemetery John said, pushing the barrel of his huge shotgun over Emil's shoulder.

"My brother is hurt." Going Snake looked at the dripping blood that glistened like crimson ice. "This world has been a cruel one for him. Perhaps the next one will be kinder . . . for us."

Before the last word left his lips, the shaman spun, grabbing his scarred brother in an embrace. They then plunged back and down into the abyss. For what seemed like endless minutes the sound of their bodies bouncing from stone walls could be heard until they became small enough to be lost in the rhythmic dripping of water from the roof of the grotto.

"Did I just see a forty-thousand-dollar outlaw fall clear to China?" Emil sputtered.

Blue Hand said sadly, "They have gone to the spirit world. I wish them good hunting and fair weather."

Asa Cain holstered his Whitney Eagle. "It's over. The killings have been stopped. We did what we set out to do. I'm sorry it had to end like this."

"So am I," Cemetery John said. "For more reasons than the money."

The sheriff brightened. "We can all bear witness to The Panther's demise. I think Cyrus Warwick will still pay the bounty."

"It's worth a try," Asa Cain said. He studied the twinkling lights in the blue walls of ice. "Let's get out of here, this place is evil as Hell itself."

"Evil is everywhere, Mr. Cain," Blue Hand said. "But let us leave here and seal up the entrance using the gunpowder."

"I reckon that's not a bad plan," Cemetery John said. "We can consider we're giving the remains on that shelf of ice a decent burial."

"The way The Panther had those heads all lined up like he did and was raving about his collection needing more," Emil said, "I wonder what he was thinking."

"We'll never know," Blue Hand said. "At least not until we enter the spirit world and can ask him."

"Let's go," Asa Cain said as the men turned from the abyss and headed for the bright sun of a cloudless blue sky.

FORTY-THREE

Even from a distant quarter mile away from the explosion, the earth rolled beneath their feet.

"You were sure right about that being powerful powder, Artemis," Asa Cain said looking up the mountainside to the growing gray cloud that billowed against a blue sky. "I've never seen any blow up like that went and did."

"That wasn't really gunpowder," Artemis Wilcox said sheepishly. "I didn't want to unduly alarm anyone, but it was actually dynamite I'd taken out of its wrappers and filled those kegs with it."

"*Dynamite!*" Cemetery John's eyes were wide. "That stuff's more dangerous than a pet bear. What in heaven's name caused you to go and packrat enough giant powder to blow the side of a mountain off."

The lightning-rod salesman shrugged. "Seemed like a good idea at the time. And I never had any trouble with it."

Blue Hand said, "A person seldom makes *two* mistakes with dynamite."

Sheriff Quackenbush snorted. "Can't see where it makes a whit of difference now. The cave, along with that head-whacker and most of the heads he whacked, are buried for all time." He turned to Asa. "I'm hoping you're right about bringing poor li'l Henrietta's head back to her pappy as proof we earned the reward. I think it's kinda spooky, but it should do the trick."

Cemetery John fished his last long nine cigar from his vest and lit it. "As long as we get her head back before it thaws out, there ain't no problem. Cyrus Warwick will most likely be glad to have her put back together. The rest of 'em would just cause too much paperwork, plain and simple. There were federal marshals involved. You can trust me on how much the government likes to worry things over to no end."

"I reckon," Emil said. "Let's head for town and our just rewards."

Artemis Wilcox smiled at Blue Hand. "Thank you for trading me this horse for the crossbow."

Kills Eagles, who rode next to the deputy, said, "Blue Hand has a better horse now. That one was from the Army. It is slow and better at pulling a wagon than riding."

"Just what I need," Artemis said, relieved to have gotten a horse to pull his wagon for a crossbow he had traded a pair of lightning rods for that had only cost him seventy-five cents. "I hope you'll get a lot of good use out of it." He turned to Asa. "Let's go collect our money."

Asa Cain wondered briefly just how the lightning-rod salesman figured into the bounty money, but decided that argument could be made later. "We can be there before sunset." Then he reined his horse to the south, followed by all but the Osage Indians, including Blue Hand, who had decided to return to their reservation to meet the Army. The sheriff had agreed to deposit his deputy's share of the reward money in the bank for him.

"Well, this is a fine kettle of fish," Sheriff Quackenbush said as he, along with the rest of the posse, halted on a low hill overlooking the town of Henrietta to survey the ruins with shocked disbelief. "The whole damn town's burnt down while we were gone on our manhunt."

"Your jail still looks okay," Cemetery John said optimistically with a nod to the three buildings left standing. "And the whorehouse, along with one of the saloons and the livery stable, seems not to be too scorched."

Artemis Wilcox spoke without thinking. "This turned out almost as bad as that time I installed those Armbruster lightning rods on Widow O'Leary's barn up in Chicago."

Asa Cain turned to Artemis with a look of dismay. "*You* sold the lightning rods that caused Chicago to burn! From the looks of things, you're no smarter these days. That storm we watched our first night out must have hit some of those lightning rods you sold Warwick and set the fire that destroyed darn near the whole town of Henrietta."

Artemis Wilcox turned pale. "There never was any proof! It's all hearsay, nothing admissible in court. Warwick wanted me to put them up, paid me to do it."

Sheriff Quackenbush pulled his Colt, cocked it, then aimed the pistol square at the lightning-rod salesman's anxious face. "I don't want to hear one word, you use too blasted many of 'em. What I *am* gonna do is count to three. If you ain't out of my sight by then, I'm going to blow your fire-causing town-burning ass plumb out of that saddle . . . *one!*"

Artemis Wilcox had survived as a drummer on the frontier by knowing when to cut his losses and run like hell, which the pudgy salesman did not hesitate to do this time. Before he heard the word "two" uttered by the irate sheriff, he was riding for his wagon as fast as the decrepit old Army horse would carry him.

Emil Quackenbush was so furious that he aimed to one side of the departing lightning-rod salesman and sent five slugs whistling past his ear.

"Damn peddler," he yelled after him.

"I'd venture Artemis is plenty sorry and likely won't be back this way again," Cemetery John said. "Let's forget about him and go see if Cyrus Warwick's in a forgiving mood."

"Yeah," Asa Cain said. "But I've got a really bad feeling about this."

The pungent smell of burnt wood greeted the trio when they rode into the charred remains of the town that had only days earlier been touted as the next Kansas City or Abilene. Surprisingly, not a single person could be seen rebuilding or cleaning up debris, only those poking through dead embers while wearing somber faces.

Judge Thomas Terry Rimsdale, who was driving a surrey headed out of town with his dirty-faced children and sobbing wife in the backseat, reined to a halt to talk.

"We killed the murderer of Cyrus War-wick's daughter," Emil Quackenbush said proudly to the stern-faced judge.

"I'd reckon that doesn't matter much nowadays, Sheriff." The lawyer swept an arm to the debris. "Cyrus Warwick was fried by the first lightning bolt that struck his home. Then those bolts kept striking until the whole town caught fire. I've never seen the like of that electrical storm; it seemed determined to destroy the whole place." He shook his head sadly. "We have lost our home . . . everything. We're going to Wichita, try and start over."

"How do we collect that reward money?" Emil asked.

Judge Rimsdale pointed a pudgy finger to a large patch of burnt earth and blackened rubble. "That's where the bank stood." He moved his finger to the head of the charred gulch. "You can find Warwick's grave up there. I was the man's lawyer, all he had was invested in this town. There is no money to pay even your wages as sheriff, let alone a reward." He flicked the reins. "Sorry." Then the buggy was gone.

"That fine kettle of fish I mentioned earlier just got more rotten," Emil's voice was syrupy with sarcasm. "I don't believe that man."

Asa Cain clucked his tongue. "Rimsdale's a lawyer. You need to check your watch and rings after shaking the hand of one. The majority of the crooks I've brought back to hang were more trustworthy."

"But he has the law on his side," Cemetery John said with a snort. "Hell's bells, he *is* the law."

"I reckon I'll go by the jail and see if I can find anything worth hauling off," Sheriff Quackenbush said with resignation. "There was a good pair of boots and a rain slicker I was fond of in the closet when I left to get rich."

"Hello, Emil," a woman's voice called from the shadows of one of the few remaining structures. Mattie Rose stepped out into the twilight, smiling at the sheriff. "I'm glad you came back unhurt. I've been worried."

The three men dismounted. Emil went to the tall willowy blonde and gave her an embrace.

"It looks like I'm in better shape than the town," the sheriff said, basking in the aroma of roses. "I'm happy you stayed around. There's not a lot of reason I can see for you to do that."

"I brought all of your belongings from the

jail and put them in my room," Mattie said causing the sheriff's face to flush. "You can stay there tonight."

"Obliged," was all Emil could muster before leaving with the madam.

"I reckon Quacky's not too broken up," Cemetery John said to Asa. A quick scan up and down the blackened remains showed them to be the only ones still moving about in the coming nightfall. "That's more than most of the other folks who got involved in this fine mess can say."

"We did come up empty-handed, Cemetery, but it was an interesting time and I haven't had a drink for weeks. I don't know if I ever will again." The bounty hunter nodded to the livery stable. "Let's go see if your hearse is still there. If all goes well, we ought to bury that poor little gal's head in her plot and be some ways away before it gets too dark to travel."

"Yeah, I see the wagon tongue from here." Cemetery John hesitated. "You know, Sheriff Deevers back in Wolf Springs is going to be plumb upset with me over not burying that whore before I left on this bounty hunt."

Asa Cain felt oddly happy for some reason he could not explain. He didn't want his mood tainted by asking any questions of his undertaker friend.

"Cemetery," Asa said. "Let's just go home to Texas."

EPILOGUE

Blue Hand was not at all upset to find out there would be no reward money. The former deputy felt comfortable living back on the reservation amongst The People. The Army colonel who came from Fort Smith not only treated him and all of the Osage with courtesy, but before they returned to Arkansas, Blue Hand was given a commission as an Indian policeman. The income he received from his salary along with what he had earned as a temporary hangman enabled him to take the beautiful Sunflower as his wife.

The half-breed was not entirely welcomed by all of the tribe. The section of land the council allotted the couple was a poor plot where the soil was soured by a black ooze. In spite of the handicaps of farming unproductive ground, the couple were very happy and had many healthy children.

In 1905, oil was discovered below the

Osage Nation, causing much money to come to the tribe. No plot of land was richer in oil than that of the Hand family. Their wealthy descendants are still an active factor in Oklahoma politics, championing animal rights at every opportunity.

Artemis "Lightning Rod" Wilcox decided to change his occupation for reasons of health. He converted his wagon to a traveling medicine show and began selling patent medicines guaranteed to cure any ailment. In the rich Colorado silver-mining town of Creede, one of the bottles he sold a rich widow — much to his surprise — actually cured her consumption.

The woman, while not great on looks, kept pestering him until he agreed to marry her. Hortense, his new wife, turned quickly into a shrew. But with her being a rich shrew, Artemis could afford to while away his days and evenings in saloons, drinking, playing cards, and telling stories of his many adventures as a famous frontier bounty hunter.

Artemis Wilcox kept up this routine on a daily basis until he finally passed away from the ravages of excessive alcohol consumption at the age of 103. The Volstead Act, which enforced Prohibition, came into effect only scant weeks after his death, the old lightning-rod salesman's luck having held until the very end.

Cemetery John and Bessie Coggins never married. While Asa Cain and he were on their way home from Oklahoma, the lady blacksmith was kicked in the head by a horse she was shoeing and died. The undertaker was heartbroken, but his pain was somewhat assuaged when Sheriff Deevers paid him one hundred dollars to bury both Bessie Coggins and the saloon girl he had left in the window. Cemetery John's funeral parlor began to flourish and, except for an occasional manhunt with Asa or a diverting shoot-out in Soak Malone's Rara Avis Saloon, his life became one of routine happiness.

Judge Thomas Terry Rimsdale roared onto the political arena of Kansas, spending a great deal of money from an unknown source. The lawyer paid out huge sums, both above and below the table, to garner the Republican nomination for governor, which he considered a mere stepping-stone on his way to being President of the United States.

The lawyer's campaigning was going smoothly, his election seemingly assured, when a gangly young man, who later claimed to be the illegitimate son of Cyrus Warwick, stepped up behind him during a speech he was giving at a Masonic Lodge and shot him in the back of his head, killing him instantly. Wesley Warwick insisted that Rimsdale had stolen a great deal of money from his father's estate. The young man's pleas, however, fell on deaf ears. The publicity and subsequent trial were widely followed by both Democrats and Republicans alike. Wesley Warwick's execution had the largest attendance of any ever held in the State of Kansas, the gala affair being enjoyed by all, save one.

Emil Quackenbush and Mattie Rose were married in Dodge City, Kansas, where the ex-sheriff had gone to return Doc Holliday's gold watch. The happy couple settled down there for a while, Emil working as a deputy under Wyatt Earp. Mattie was content with being a housewife who enjoyed fixing splendid dinners for her husband.

When news of a rich silver strike in the southern Arizona town of Tombstone became blasted across the headlines of every newspaper, Emil could not resist taking his beautiful wife and joining his now-good friends Doc Holliday and Wyatt Earp in a rush for riches.

What they found when they reached the booming desert mining town, however, was not at all what they had expected. But that is another story for another time.

The employees of Thorndike Press hope you have enjoyed this Large Print book. All our Thorndike and Wheeler Large Print titles are designed for easy reading, and all our books are made to last. Other Thorndike Press Large Print books are available at your library, through selected bookstores, or directly from us.

For information about titles, please call:

(800) 223-1244

or visit our Web site at:

www.gale.com/thorndike
www.gale.com/wheeler

To share your comments, please write:

Publisher
Thorndike Press
295 Kennedy Memorial Drive
Waterville, ME 04901

MG
8/11

4/07